What People Are Saying about Loree Lough and *Unbridled Hope*...

With a knack for lively writing, Loree Lough immerses readers deep into the hearts of her characters and takes them back to a time of strength of spirit and courage. In *Unbridled Hope*, readers will be drawn in by Micah and Callie in this richly conceived novel that shows the transforming power of love.

—Rita Gerlach
Author, *Surrender the Wind*

Unbridled Hope unleashes a romance of heart-stopping proportions as Micah Neville finds himself caught between a precocious baby and what seems to be a damsel in distress. Loree Lough doesn't miss a beat in this third installment of the Lone Star Legends series. Like everything else she's written, this one's a galloping success!

—Cerella Sechrist
Author, *Love Finds You in Hershey, Pennsylvania*

With *Unbridled Hope*, Loree Lough once again grips her readers with rich characters, nail-biting conflict, and heart-melting romance. You'll quickly find yourself rooting for Callie Roberts as she struggles to right her self-perceived wrong, and for Micah Neville, who will steal your heart. The trademark surprises in Lough's plots always catch readers off guard—a most wonderful experience! Another terrific read from Loree Lough.

—Trish Perry
Award-winning author, *Unforgettable* and *Tea for Two*

Like the character Jonah Roberts, I looked for the "green flash" and was blown away yet again by the action and passion of Loree's writing. This story will stick to you tighter than dust from a San Antonio storm.

—Eddie Jones
Cofounder, Christian Devotions, and author,
The Curse of Captain LaFoote

Loree Lough never fails to immediately draw you into her stories, and *Unbridled Hope* is no exception. Caught up on page one in events that will change her characters' lives forever, you'll find that Loree's characters portray real-life pain, doubts, and heartache on their rocky journeys to happiness. A genuinely inspirational story.

—Anne Ashby
Author, *Worlds Apart* and *Devon's Dream*

Unbridled Hope

Loree Lough

WHITAKER
HOUSE

Unless otherwise indicated, all Scripture quotations are taken from the King James Version of the Holy Bible. Scripture quotations in the preface "A Letter from Loree" are taken from the *Holy Bible, New International Version*®, NIV®, © 1973, 1978, 1984 by the International Bible Society. Used by permission of Zondervan. All rights reserved.

UNBRIDLED HOPE
Book Three in the Lone Star Legends Series

Loree Lough
www.loreelough.com

ISBN: 978-1-60374-227-6
Printed in the United States of America
© 2011 by Loree Lough

Whitaker House
1030 Hunt Valley Circle
New Kensington, PA 15068
www.whitakerhouse.com

Library of Congress Cataloging-in-Publication Data (Pending)

1 2 3 4 5 6 7 8 9 10 11 ᴜᴊ 18 17 16 15 14 13 12 11

Dedication

Unbridled Hope is dedicated to my faithful reader friends, whose frequent and encouraging cards, letters, and e-mails are what keep me pecking away at the keyboard; to my husband, Larry, for his caring concern and constant support; and to my daughters and grandchildren, whose love keeps me centered.

It's also dedicated to all the wonderful people at Whitaker House—the talented graphics and sales departments; the hardworking publicist, Cathy; Courtney and Lois, two of the best editors in the business; and everyone else whose talents and work ethics make Whitaker House such a delightful publishing house to work with.

And to my dear cousin Pauline, who thought it would be fun to name a not-so-nice character after her. (And it was fun!)

Most important of all, this novel—and everything else I do and am—is dedicated to my Lord and Savior, who called me to this blessed and fulfilling work and keeps me supplied with readers who find comfort in His message written on the pages of every book He guides me to write.

A Letter from Loree

Dear Readers,

If you're like me, you sometimes marvel that for every problem, there's at least one adage intended to ease the sting: "When life gives you lemons, make lemonade!" "It's always darkest before the dawn." "Don't cry over spilled milk." "All's fair in love and war."

Just between us? Those maxims don't provide any more comfort to me today than during my childhood, when it seemed as if grown-ups couldn't wait for stuff to happen just so they could spout one off. But while I was writing *Unbridled Hope*, I got a better understanding of the "grown-up" side of things and often found myself quoting yet another old saw: "There's always someone worse off than you."

As you'll soon discover in the pages of *Unbridled Hope*, Micah Neville and Callie Roberts harbor secrets, each one so dark and deep that they fear exposing it would change their lives forever—or destroy them. Despite their good intentions, guarding those secrets has distanced them from friends and family, as well as from one another.

If, like Callie and Micah, you're concealing something right now, you no doubt feel exactly as they did. The loneliness of separation is dreadfully real and painful, regardless of whether the secrets protect a loved one or yourself.

Emotional isolation is a high price to pay and a heavy weight to carry, so this, dear reader, is my heartfelt prayer for you:

O Father in heaven, I humbly ask You to lighten your servants' burdens. Remind them that, by the grace of Your Spirit, they can be free from all anxiety, simply by leaving their cares at the foot of the cross. Bless them with inner peace, Lord, that they might surrender every worry and concern unto You. And, even as they open their hearts and minds to You, help them let go of every struggle and turn loose all strife. Let them dwell instead in the knowledge that through You, they are whole and new.

Father, show them the way that You would have them go, and infuse them with the strength to know whether it is Your will for them to release the secrets hidden deep in their hearts. Let them cling to the message You relayed to Your children in James 4:8: *"Come near to God and he will come near to you,"* and in Philippians 4:6–7: *"Do not be anxious about anything, but in everything, by prayer and petition, with thanksgiving, present your requests to God. And the peace of God, which transcends all understanding, will guard your hearts and your minds in Christ Jesus."*

I'll close with a few of my favorite anonymous sayings: "May you always delight in small pleasures." "May your optimism come true." And one written by Ella Wheeler Wilcox: "Say you are well and all is well with you, and God shall hear your words and make them true."

May God shower you and those you love with joys too numerous to count, today and always, and may you never forget how much I value your friendship and treasure every letter sent to me at www.loreelough.com.

Blessings,
Loree

Chapter 1

December 1887
On the Brazos River near Sweetwater, Texas

*R*aw, unrelenting wind whistled across the deck boards, scattering newspapers and rattling the cleats as the steamboat chugged toward its next major stop, Clear Fork. Callie cupped her elbows, wishing she'd thought to grab her shawl. She didn't like this type of weather, for it reminded her too much of the bitter Baltimore winter of '85 that had nearly killed her mother and had prompted her father's decision to move the family west. Ever since, Callie had begun every day with a prayer for her mother and ended the day by asking God to ease the ache of her own homesickness.

In time, the Lord had answered her first prayer, restoring her mother to robust health. The second He'd granted in the form of a young seminary graduate who'd been hired to entertain guests with the soothing sonatas of Beethoven and Bach. And, just as the sunshine dispels the chilly mists from the river, the music of Seth's love had turned her longing for Maryland into a dim yet melodious memory.

Tonight, her beloved beau would give his final performance for the tycoons, high rollers, and politicians who gathered nightly in the grand salon. His final because, in twelve short hours, Callie's father, a chaplain and owner of the *Maybelline*, would pronounce the two of them man and wife.

Her heart throbbing with hope and excitement, she hurried toward the jackstaff, the secret meeting place where Seth had first confessed his love. Her fingers throbbed, too, from sewing fifty-two satin-covered buttons up the back of her full-skirted gown and from attaching a feathered headdress to her long, lacy veil. Callie smiled, knowing that the discomfort would vanish the instant she saw Seth smiling at her from the makeshift altar where he would become her husband.

Sadly, the gown would not fit inside her valise. What a pity she wouldn't be able to save her beautiful dress for the daughters she and Seth might have! She sighed as she imagined a bright-eyed young woman with her papa's dark eyes and her mama's diminutive stature, walking down the center aisle toward her intended in the little church in Eagle Pass, Texas, where Seth's dream of shepherding a flock of his own would soon come true, and where he would eventually unite his own daughter with her soul mate.

Still, she took comfort in knowing that her hours of hard work had not been in vain. She said a little prayer for the senator's wife who'd agreed to pay a handsome sum for the gown and veil—and for Callie's eternal silence. "Lord, help the poor woman keep secret the fact that her daughter will be married in a used—"

"Talking to yourself again?"

She stifled a tiny squeal. "Jonah Everett Roberts, you frightened me half to death!" How someone of her brother's height and weight managed to sneak up on her at least once a day, she'd never know. Raising one eyebrow, she rested a fist on her hip. "Say, what are you doing out here, anyway? Didn't I hear Papa ask you to sweep out the saloon?"

He frowned. "I'm waiting for the green flash," he said, taking a bite of an apple.

Not that again, she thought. "Well," she said on a sigh, "if that's the cause for the holdup, you'll never get the job done, because the sun went down more than an hour ago."

"Humpf. Leave it to little miss stick-in-the-mud to spoil the moment for a man."

"Man, indeed. More like a willful boy. Papa says when he was nineteen, he worked as hard as any man on the family farm, and his folks never had to remind him to do his chores."

Jonah swallowed a mouthful of fruit. "Yeah, and he also says that if I'm patient, I'll see the green flash, eventually."

Callie couldn't count the number of times she'd heard the same assurance. In fact, she'd heard so much about the elusive emerald flare, which was visible only under precise atmospheric conditions as the sun disappeared into the horizon, that she'd wished a time or two for the patience to believe in the phenomenon herself.

But wishing wouldn't get her any closer to the jackstaff and her darling Seth. "Your tactic might work on Mama and Tim," she said, giving his shoulder a playful shove, "but I see it for what it is: a 'clever' way to shirk your responsibility—"

A thunderous roar set the deck to quaking beneath their feet. *Please, Lord, not the boilers!* she
thought as a second deafening blast threw her and
Jonah to the floor. Instinct made her grab his collar
and drag him under a heavy table, where she covered their heads with a tablecloth. Shards of glass
and splinters of wood rained down as a third explosion rocked the steamer.

Choking smoke closed in around them as
flecks of glowing ash floated down like fiery snow-
flakes. With its shallow keel and inch-thin hull,
the *Maybelline*'s flimsy design assured swift river
travel—and guaranteed that it would sink swiftly,
too.

If that happened, it would be her fault.

If only she'd stoked the boilers like she was supposed to, instead of handing the job over to Tim!
She'd seen the vacant "I don't understand" stare in
her older brother's eyes enough times to recognize
it for what it was, yet she'd ignored it to gain a few
minutes more with Seth.

Callie scrambled forward with one objective: to
make sure that Tim, her parents, and her beloved
Seth had survived.

"Wait!" Jonah hollered.

"You're safer right here," she said, meeting his
frightened eyes. "I know you're scared, Jonah. I'm
scared, too." Using a corner of her apron, she dabbed
at the blood dribbling from both of his ears. "But you
need to stay here, before you're hurt even worse." She
gave him a little shake. "If the steamer starts taking
on water, I want you to make your way to the riverbank. Once you're there, find the biggest tree and
stay put. Do you understand?"

His confused expression mirrored the one that had long seemed frozen to Tim's face. But their older brother had been slow from the day he was born, unlike Jonah, who could solve arithmetic problems without the aid of slate and chalk. She blamed Jonah's expression on fear and scrambled to her feet. Why did her brothers turn to her for comfort and support, when she was younger than both of them?

On the heels of a frustrated sigh, she scooted out from under the table. "Lord, watch over him," she prayed as she raced along, darting between rivers of blue-orange fire that snaked and coiled across the deck and dodging the witch-finger flames that flared from each cabin window. When a fierce groan sounded from above, she crooked her elbow to protect her eyes and looked up. Her breath caught in her throat when she saw the tallest of the three fat smokestacks teeter as it gave way to the gluttonous fire monster gnawing at its wooden moorings.

Callie barely gathered her wits in time to side-step it. If only she'd thought to gather her skirts, too. The heel of her boot caught on a fold of muslin, slowing her escape. She was already falling when a grapefruit-sized lump of glowing coal slammed into her right temple.

"Sweet Jesus," she prayed as dizziness overwhelmed her. "Keep...them all...safe."

For the second time in minutes, her prayer was interrupted, as she slipped into the dark unconscious.

Two years later • November 2, 1889
The Lazy N Ranch • Eagle Pass, Texas

The sweet-smelling envelope was addressed to "M. Neville." At least, that's what Micah had thought at first glance. But the message inside the envelope didn't make a lick of sense. So, he studied the addressee a second time, and a third, before realizing that the fanciful *M* was, instead, a *D*. Guilt at reading his cousin's mail was quickly overshadowed by concern at the nature of the message. Dan had already lived two lifetimes' worth of misery in his twenty-eight years.

Micah shook his head and said a silent prayer for Dan, who'd shouldered a burden of self-blame ever since his twin sister had died tragically at the age of thirteen, even though nobody held him responsible. Guilt and remorse, along with the whiskey he'd used to numb the emotional pain of his loss and the physical torment of the bum leg he'd suffered in a stampede, had managed to turn the once shy, gentle boy into a man hell-bent on self-destruction and prone to angry brawls. About once a year, Dan would summon the strength to shake his addiction, but, all too soon, self-loathing would lure him back to the bottle. Fourteen months into the latest stint of sobriety, Micah had begun to notice signs that had made him fear things were about to take another ugly turn, but then, praise God, Levee O'Reilly had come to town as the new schoolteacher. She'd taught her students reading, writing, and arithmetic, all the while teaching Dan to value his own life.

The two had married, and their relationship seemed solid and strong. But now, something like this? Micah glared at the single sheet of scented ivory paper on which, with a few well-chosen words, the writer had implied a dozen sinister things, any one of which could start the dominos toppling in Dan's life yet again.

Slumping onto the edge of his bed, Micah read the letter a fourth time. Maybe he'd underestimated his cousin's ability to stand strong, even in the face of this woman's spiteful threats. He had a lot more to live for now, though. Maybe this woman wanted to destroy him, once and for all.

Micah would not take that chance. For one thing, Dan had always been his favorite cousin—a statement in itself, since there were dozens in the Neville clan. For another, Dan had protected him more times than Micah could count. As a youngster, he'd been puny and timid and had spoken with a lisp, just the sort of stuff that had invited the taunts of the bigger, older boys. But, without fail, Dan had always put a stop to it.

Eventually, when he'd lost his baby teeth, Micah's permanent teeth had grown in straight, eliminating the lisp, and his body had grown, too. At six feet three inches, and with two hundred twenty pounds of raw muscle, Micah's size alone would have discouraged any bully. But by the time the Neville men had embarked on the trail drive of '86, Dan's determination to defend Micah had become so ingrained that he hadn't thought twice about maneuvering his horse between his cousin and a bevy of gun-blasting rustlers. Dan had laughed off the bullet in his shoulder in exactly the same way he'd laughed off every swollen knuckle, bloodied lip, and black eye he'd endured to protect Micah. "You've done me a favor, cousin," he'd said, gritting his teeth as Cookie dug out the slug, "because certain ladies like a man with scars!"

Had the author of this letter been one of those ladies?

Micah harrumphed. "A female, maybe, but I'd bet my horse she's no lady." Scooting closer to the night table, he turned up the lantern and leaned into the golden light to read those ominous closing lines yet again:

> ...at two o'clock on Friday afternoon, the fifteenth of November, I will be at the train station in San Antonio, Texas. If you choose not to meet me there, I shall have no alternative but to bring this very urgent matter to the attention of the authorities.
>
> Most sincerely yours,
> Pauline Eden Devereaux

"Urgent matter"? A dozen possible scenarios flashed in Micah's brain, none of them good. Under ordinary circumstances, Dan wouldn't squash a beetle under his boot, but there was nothing ordinary about the way his personality changed once a few pints of whiskey burned in his veins. *If he was drinking when he ran into this woman....*

Micah got to his feet and started pacing. He didn't want to believe that Dan was guilty of any offense. The more likely story, he told himself, was that this Pauline character had gotten wind of how many acres made up the Lazy N Ranch and hoped to weasel a few hundred dollars in exchange for her silence about whatever matter she seemed to believe might interest the authorities. And, since the family never discussed their troubles beyond the closed door of Uncle Matthew's office, she had no way of knowing how steeply their profits had dropped due to anthrax, weevils, droughts, and storms.

There was only one way to know for sure, and that was to take a trip to San Antonio to meet this femme flimflammer face-to-face. He didn't know what excuse he'd cook up to put himself there, or how he'd squash her scam, but Micah knew this much: he intended to defend Dan for a change.

Chapter 2

November 4, 1889

Callie stood on the porch, sipping her morning tea, as she watched Jonah add a final flourish to his pencil sketch, then hold it up to look for flaws. If he found any, she'd be surprised. Perfectionism had always been one of his most salient character traits, but never more than since they'd moved to Eagle Pass nearly two years ago.

He loved sitting at the little wooden table out front, even on days like this, when angry storm clouds churned in the sky. Thunder erupted overhead, startling her so badly that her teacup rattled on its saucer. Jonah, of course, didn't react at all. And why would he? To quote the doctor back in Abilene, "This boy's deaf as a post." From time to time, she'd tried to ease her tortured conscience by telling herself that on the day the *Maybelline* had gone down, Jonah had been safer under that flimsy table than he would have been running alongside her on the flaming decks. But there was no escaping the ugly truth: the tragedy that had left her mostly unscathed had completely and permanently destroyed Jonah's hearing.

Six men riding abreast down the middle of the road distracted her from her misery. The whites of their eyes and teeth flashed through the cloud of dirt they stirred up, making it impossible to identify them, but Callie had seen this sooty parade enough times to recognize them as coal miners. They'd been gone nearly a month, and it showed in their sleepy-eyed faces. Somewhere up ahead, fresh replacements rode in the opposite direction, preparing to enter the same dark tunnels to hack with picks and axes at the rough walls of those same narrow shafts.

As the miners passed, one aimed a thumb at the menacing clouds overhead. "Looks like we're in for a big one, don't it?"

"Yessir," agreed another. "It's gonna be big, all right."

A third did a little bow, right there in his saddle. "Meb's right," he said, stirring a puff of dust when he whipped off his woolen cap. "You'd better get inside."

"Which is precisely why you gents had better get home, and soon!" she said, returning their friendly smiles.

The wind whistled up the street, taking hold of some unfortunate cowboy's Stetson. Like a tiny wagon wheel, it bounced and rolled across her yard before coming to rest in the grass near Jonah's feet. He grabbed it and turned to face her, grinning as he jammed it onto his head. "Well, looky here! It fits," he said, firing off a jaunty salute.

If she lived to the age of Abraham, Callie would never get use d to the sound of his voice. While every word was pronounced clearly and intelligibly, Jonah spoke as if something had lodged partway down his throat, making every utterance as thick as a sob. Blinking back tears of remorse, she waved him closer and mouthed, "Come in," as she pointed skyward. If the clouds above them were any indicator, nature didn't have just rain in mind. Though she did her best not to show it, Callie's nerves jangled with the memory of a day not long after they'd first arrived in town.

Jonah had been sketching out back when a sudden squall had skimmed the prairie, scattering his supplies. As Callie had zigged left to gather his pencils, he'd zagged right, laughing as he plucked his drawings from the ground. Then, a bolt of lightning had sliced the sky and left a smoking black stain on the grass near his boots, setting off an arm-flinging, leg-churning, bellowing frenzy. In the calm after the storm, Jonah had seen the terror his ranting had painted on the faces of their neighbors. It had taken weeks for his humiliation to ebb enough for him to venture outside again, and, ever since, he'd paid close attention to Callie's warnings—at least, where the weather was concerned.

"I'll start a fire," he said, his supplies pressed to his chest as he ran up the porch steps, "while you start supper."

Oh, how she loved her good-natured, gawky brother! To show it, she gave him a huge, paper-crinkling hug.

"Enough," he said, pretending to frown. "You don't want to ruin all my hard work, do you?"

Rather than wait for an answer, he busied himself starting a fire, and she began putting their meal together. In the two years since the steamboat explosion, she'd dedicated herself to her brother. It was the least she could do, since her self-centered focus had been the reason he'd lost his mother and father, his big brother, and his hearing, to boot. Whenever Callie found out about another book on the topic of coping with deafness, she bought it and memorized every page. That was how she'd taught Jonah to read lips and use sign language, and how she'd learned never to sneak up on him but always to step into his peripheral line of vision so as not to startle him. It hadn't been easy, treating him like an ordinary man, but Callie was determined that he'd live life that way, despite his deafness.

Standing on tiptoe, Callie reached for the salt. "Oh, to be two inches taller!" she complained, reaching for the stool beside the stove.

Jonah stepped up beside her and grabbed the shaker. "Half-pint," he said, smirking playfully as he handed it to her. He pointed at the worktable they'd shared for the past two years. "Finished the sketches."

She knew how much effort it took to weave together hundreds of minuscule squares until they formed a lacy hat veil. More surprising was watching him do it with a well-sharpened pencil instead of a needle. Just as much concentration went into flicking the page with thousands of individual hairs that made fur stoles and muffs look soft enough to pet. Someday, she prayed, she would save enough money so that he could focus all of his artistic talents on watercolor vistas of the hills behind their house and oil-on-canvas renditions of the bustling festivals in Eagle Pass. For now, he seemed content to have her gush over the lifelike illustrations that inspired orders for her clothing designs. She'd told him a hundred times how much she appreciated and admired his talents, how indebted she was to him for willingly becoming her partner in a business that didn't allow him much opportunity to flex his masculine muscles, and how grateful she was that God had blessed her with a brother like him.

How like Jonah to shrug off yet another round of effusive praise. But he'd earned it! "I'll send them off to New York tomorrow, when I mail those other packages to our customers."

"*Your* customers," he corrected her. "Jonah Roberts does not make ladies' hats and dresses. That, sister dear, is your job."

"And yours is creating the beautiful catalog drawings and newspaper ads that help us sell them."

"We make a good team."

"A very good team." And she meant it, too. "Would you rather have biscuits or dumplings with your stew?"

Rubbing his hands together, Jonah wiggled his eyebrows. "Dumplings? Mmm-mm."

Smiling, she went directly to the kitchen. She would have whipped up a triple-decker sweet cake—heck, she'd make five or ten of them—if he asked her to. What a wonderful, brilliant young man he'd become, no thanks to her. How much more might he have accomplished if not for the accident that had robbed him of his ears?

Head bowed and eyes closed, she whispered, "I don't expect or deserve forgiveness for the sins of my selfishness, Lord. But, for Jonah's sake, please keep these self-pitying thoughts from my mind when he's around."

The thunder must have drowned out the sound of his footsteps, for Callie had no idea that Jonah was behind her until he rested a hand on her shoulder. "Is it too early to set the table?"

If he'd felt her lurch, he showed no sign of it. She blanketed his fingers with her own and faced him. "It's sweet of you to offer," she said, "but you've put in a long day, working on those drawings. Why not relax by the fire with *Treasure Island*?"

Instantly, his dark eyebrows rose. After pressing a noisy kiss to her cheek, he said, "I can hardly wait to find out what happens to Jim Hawkins next."

After what had happened to the *Maybelline*, Callie never would have guessed that Jonah would find such enjoyment in a story about boats. Yet, from the instant he'd first seen the tome on the shelf at J. W. Riddle's grocery store, he'd spent every spare moment with his nose in its pages. After every reading session, he recounted just about every detail for her, his brown eyes alight with excitement.

Callie reached inside the cupboard for the can of Black Cow baking powder and added a spoonful to the flour and salt in her favorite mixing bowl. She'd never much cared for peppery dumplings, but, because Jonah liked his spicy, she sprinkled the seasoning onto the white mound.

The fire hissed and crackled, and the stew bubbled gently, drowning out the sound of milk splashing into the mixture. Outside, Meb Stewart's thick voice rose above the wind and rain as he attempted to slow the pace of his stubborn mules. Jonah's rocking chair creaked, and he chuckled at something he read. And Callie concentrated on committing each sound to memory on his behalf. It seemed grossly unfair that Jonah, who'd never done a wrong thing in his entire life, couldn't enjoy pleasant, everyday sounds, while she, the one who'd caused his deafness, could.

Not long after his grim diagnosis, Callie had stuffed cotton into her ears and pressed her palms over them to get a sense of what life was like for Jonah, now that he couldn't hear the ordinary noises of an ordinary day. Despite her efforts, the sounds of birdsongs and cricket chirps, wagon wheels grinding over the gritty road, and the distant toot of the morning train still snuck through, albeit muffled.

But not so for Jonah, who had not once mentioned the chilling night when they'd become orphans. He had accepted his deafness with dignity. And, while she loved him all the more for it, his quiet acceptance only added to her guilt.

Uncle Matthew, patriarch of the Neville clan, took a bite from a sugar cookie. "Nice of Kate to bake us something to gnaw on while we talk," he said to his son, Josh, who was Micah's cousin.

The rest of the men nodded. Micah wasn't sure if it was Uncle Mark or Uncle Luke who said, "You picked a winner, boy, that much is sure."

Josh was quick to concur. "You can say that again. And again!"

The quiet rumble of masculine laughter ended when Uncle Matthew stood up behind his desk and, knuckles pressed into the blotter, reminded them of every calamity that had beset the Lazy N over the past several years. First, the anthrax had destroyed nearly a thousand head of cattle. Next, a tornado had blown the tops off the silos, allowing the soaking rains to turn the feed stored inside to useless, moldy mush. As if that weren't enough, weevils had attacked the grain crops mere weeks before harvest. And, now, there was a stubborn, unforgiving drought.

Uncle Matthew's youngest brother, John—Micah's pa—balanced his elbows on his knees. "We'll need to dig new wells if we hope to irrigate what's left of the crops."

"Uncle John's right," Dan agreed. "But that's not something that'll come cheap. We'll need to hire extra hands to run the digging rig, for starters."

With his teeth, Josh moved a blade of straw from one side of his mouth to the other. "And, while that's going on, we'll need to plow and plant those grain fields again. Which means we'll need to buy seed."

Micah had been praying for an opening exactly like this, and he met Uncle Matthew's serious gaze with one of his own. "I've saved up a few dollars. I'll leave at first light, make a stop at the bank—high time you older gents let us young pups make a financial contribution to this place—then head on out to San Antone." He held up a hand to forestall any disagreement. "I can be there and back in a couple of weeks." *And, while I'm at it, I'll put a stop to the threats of one Pauline Eden Devereaux.*

The men took a moment to consider his proposition. It was Uncle Matthew who broke the uncomfortable silence. "You don't reckon to go all that way alone, do you?"

Micah shrugged. "I don't see why not. The rest of you have, couple of times apiece." He nodded at his cousin. "Why, Josh did it just—"

Paul chuckled. "Yeah, and brought a woman home with him." He grabbed a cookie. "Lucky for her, she learned to bake, or we might've had to send her packin'."

Good-natured laughter filled the room. "Only the good Lord knows what this fella will bring home," Josh said, slinging an arm around his cousin's shoulders.

Just seeds, Micah thought, smirking, *and the peace of mind that'll come from making sure that schemin' woman can't get her claws on Neville money.* "Don't waste your energy worryin' about me," he teased. "Aim your focus on what you need to do while I'm gone." He elbowed Josh. "Why, y'all should have more than enough time to get three new wells dug and pumpin' before I get back."

Uncle Matthew grunted and helped himself to another cookie. "Well, boys," he said around a mouthful, "guess we'd best head on up to bed. We've all got a hard day ahead of us come daylight."

Uncle Luke groaned. "And more of the same the day after."

"And the day after that," said Dan.

But Micah only smiled. His hardest work would begin the moment he laid eyes on Pauline.

Micah's pa cleared his throat. "So, what-say we end this discussion with a blessing?"

Uncle Matthew dusted the cookie crumbs from his fingertips. "Start prayin', brother."

Strangely, not one head bowed; no eyes closed. Instead, every man in the room turned to face the intense blue eyes of Ezra Neville, blazing down at them from the oil portrait above the massive wooden desk. His imposing expression and posture made it easy to believe that, decades earlier, he'd loaded his devoted wife, Esther, and their boys—Matthew, Mark, Luke, and John—into a covered wagon and delivered them, five months and a thousand miles later, to the Texas land that had become the Lazy N Ranch.

The secret of why he'd chosen the peculiar name for the ranch had gone with him to the grave, but no one had ever speculated it was because Ezra had been lazy! Though his sons had helped out as much as young boys could, he'd basically built it all sin-glehandedly—the house, the outbuildings, and the fences, which stretched as far as the eye could see.

In his day, he'd been larger than life, literally and figuratively. Taller than any man in Maverick County, Ezra would enter rooms sideways because his broad, hard-muscled shoulders wouldn't fit through most doors. Hands capable of taming even the wildest maverick were just as likely to pull a crying child into his lap as his powerful baritone soothed the tot with a "There, now" or a "You'll forget that skinned knee before you're wed."

Ezra had lived hard, loved fiercely, and drilled ethics, honesty, and family loyalty into everyone who carried his name. As a result, he'd earned the respect and admiration of every man who'd met him, but none more than those gathered in this room.

Micah felt his chest swell with pride whenever folks compared him to this great man, whether in size or in temperament, and he'd spent his life trying to live up to that reputation. He could almost picture his grandpa, giving his nod of approval to what his offspring were about to do to save the ranch and the family.

And Micah felt just as certain that his grandfather would endorse his plans to save Dan, too.

Chapter 3

The postmaster peered over his reading glasses. "Well, good morning, and don't you look lovely today."

If the man had ever frowned, she'd never witnessed it. Callie returned his friendly smile. "And the same to you, Zack." She looked past him. "Where's Hilda this morning?"

Zack harrumphed. "That silly wife o' mine is out back, tendin' her posies or some other foolishness."

Many husbands in the area shared Zack's attitude toward flowers; if a plant couldn't provide food for people or livestock, it wasn't worth the water to keep it alive, especially during the dry months. Callie had lived in Eagle Pass long enough to appreciate that, but she understood the wives' position, too. "I remember my mama's rose garden," she said, stacking her packages on the counter, "and few things gave her more pleasure than inhaling the scents of the pretty blossoms." When one of Zack's wiry eyebrows shot up, Callie quickly added, "Her favorite Scripture was Matthew six, verse twenty-nine: *'Even*

Solomon in all his glory was not arrayed like one of these.'"

"You make a good point, I suppose," he said, weighing the first package, then pecking its price into his adding machine. "Nothing for San Francisco today?"

"No orders from California at all, I'm afraid." She watched him weigh the next box, and then the next. "Hopefully, though, Jonah's latest set of sketches will change that."

Zack nodded, not missing a beat as he weighed the items. "Not many young'uns know how to exercise patience the way you do, Miss Roberts." He pulled the handle on his adding machine to tally her total and squinted at the numbers printed on the narrow band of paper, which was coiling from its top. "Hmm, I need to ink the spool," he said to himself. To Callie, he added, "I reckon patience explains why you always seem so at peace with your lot in life."

"At peace"? Callie usually felt just the opposite. "Yes, these things take time, even with telegraph communication to hurry things along." She forced a giggle. "Can you imagine how long it took to get things from here to there before trains and telegraphs?"

"I remember those days, all too well." Zack wrote up a bill of sale and handed it to her. "Things took longer, but they still got done." Nodding, he tacked on, "Got done right, too."

She accepted the slip of paper. "I suppose occasional errors are the price we pay for all these modern conveniences," she said, opening her purse.

"There's another thing I like about you, Miss Roberts," he said as she handed him the money she owed. "You pay your bill in full and on time."

"A lesson my papa taught me."

"I have a feeling I would've liked your papa."

And Callie agreed. Everyone had liked her papa, because.... She straightened her posture and forced the thought from her mind. "I'd better get back to the shop. Lots of bonnets and skirts to finish before the holidays."

"Hilda will be happy to hear that. She's lookin' forward to seein' how her hat turned out." Zack laughed. "Way she tells it, hers has got so many feathers on it, some poor bird is probably flyin' around in its birthday suit!"

Callie laughed as she headed for the door. "I'll move her order to the top of the list," she said over her shoulder, "so as not to keep her in suspense. Have a good day, now, and be sure to tell Hilda that—oomph! Goodness, I'm so sorry!" How she'd managed not to notice the man as big as a grizzly, she couldn't say, but everything he'd been holding had clattered to the floor when she'd plowed head-long into him.

"Oh, my! I'm so sorry!" she said again, stooping to help him retrieve his packages and envelopes. "Let me help you. It's the least I can—"

"Ouch!" he exclaimed when their foreheads collided.

"Goodness," she repeated, rubbing her temple. "Seems I'm just as clumsy as—" Her voice caught in her throat as she noticed his line of vision; he stared straight at the hideous scar that snaked from her right temple to the hinge of her right jawbone. When she'd reached up to pat the spot where her head had bumped his, she must have moved her hair aside. Quickly, she fluffed it back in place.

One of his eyebrows lifted. "There's the last of it," he said, picking up one more envelope. "No harm done."

The timid smile that slanted his mouth and glittered in his dark blue eyes didn't seem to go with his voice, which was every bit as big as his stature. He must have sensed her discomfort, for he got to his feet and held out a hand to help her up. "You pack quite a wallop for such a li'l slip of a thing."

She felt the heat of a blush color her cheeks and heard herself giggle like a schoolgirl, too. Of all the people to crash into on a crisp, autumn morning, why Micah Neville? Once a week, she'd watched him ride into town on his big, brown horse to fetch and deliver mail or to pick up a few items at J. W. Riddle's grocery store. He never said much, but it was clear by the way folks reacted to his nods and smiles that they liked and respected him. She couldn't help but admire how manly he always looked in his leather vests and pressed white shirts; couldn't help but feel guilty for thinking how handsome he was, either, because, if it hadn't been for her selfishness, she would have arrived in Eagle Pass a married woman. Besides, Micah had always been too busy conducting ranch business to notice her hovering on the porch of her shop or scurrying across the street to avoid meeting him in person.

"Well, that knocks my theory all the way to Lubbock and back," Zack said, interrupting her thoughts. "I would've bet good money that Micah was the most bashful human in these here parts, but from the look of you, Miss Roberts, all red-faced an' blinkin'...." He punctuated his opinion with a boisterous laugh that echoed all through the post office.

Callie and Micah looked at him, then at one another, and then back again as Zack added, "You're lucky the horsefly population dwindled with that last cold spell. You'd catch one for sure, with your mouth open thataway!"

Callie heard her teeth click as she clamped her lips together. Micah's did the same, and she noticed that he hadn't let go of her hand.

"Name's Micah Neville," he said, giving it a slight squeeze, then pumping her arm up and down. "I was hoping that I'd run into you someday, but not literally."

So, he had seen her! She prayed that her pounding heartbeat wouldn't travel down her arm and cause her palm to pulse noticeably. "Callie Roberts," she said, praying, too, that he hadn't heard the tremor in her voice. "Pleased to meet you."

"Oh, the pleasure's all mine."

"Hilda," Zack muttered, walking toward the back of the post office, "you'll never believe this. Micah Neville strung more than two words together in a sentence."

As Zack's voice faded, Micah's smile grew.

Callie giggled again. "Guess that's the price you pay for being a man of few words." Would he ever turn her hand loose?

As if on cue, he let go. "Well, I'd best make tracks. It's a long ride to San Antone."

She tightened the drawstring on her purse, mostly to have something to do with her now-free hands. "Oh? What sends you all that way at this time of year?"

His brows drew together slightly. "Ranch business," he said, holding the door for her.

Now, why did Callie get the feeling he could just as easily have substituted the word "unpleasant" for "ranch"?

"I'll pray that you have a safe trip there and back, and that whatever business you're conducting will be successful."

"Thank you, Miss Roberts," he said, leaving her alone on the post office steps to ponder what meaning lay behind the lopsided grin that made him look more like a schoolboy than a member of one of the most influential families in Maverick County.

Micah carried the memory of Miss Roberts's beautiful, befuddled expression all the way to San Antonio, which made the onerous and time-consuming trip—and the burden of knowing why he'd volunteered to head east—far easier to bear. He had no earthly idea why his simple "Thank you" had confused her, but the fact that it did only added to her charm.

As if she wasn't already delightful enough with her sweet smile and lilting voice!

Of all the ways he'd imagined meeting her—and he'd imagined a dozen ways since she'd come to town—knocking foreheads had never entered his mind. Micah absently rubbed the small bump that had formed above his left eyebrow and smiled, remembering how the second collision as she'd helped him retrieve his packages had been harder than the first.

Then, he pictured the raised, red scar on her lovely face. The only other time he'd seen anything like it had been at a hotel in Lubbock, when the fellow signing the guest book in front of him had caught an angry earful from the desk clerk: "I'll thank you kindly not to stare at my husband," the old woman had growled. "Ain't his fault he was burned tryin' to save his comrade at Gettysburg, is it?"

Callie had done a good job at concealing her scar under her gleaming curls, but she hadn't succeeded at hiding her discomfort once she realized he'd noticed it. Having grown up in a house with three sisters and spent countless hours with assorted female cousins, Micah knew his reaction would be the first thing she'd think of the next time they met up.

If there was a next time. For all he knew, she'd go right back to crossing the road to avoid him, same as she'd done since moving to Eagle Pass. Something told him it wasn't typical female vanity or conceit that prompted her behavior, because she'd earned a reputation for being a hard worker and for being totally dedicated to her brother, too.

Micah didn't know much about her past, and, to the best of his knowledge, neither did anyone else. But he had to give her a lot of credit for turning that sorry excuse for a building at the end of the main road into one of the best-looking houses in town. She'd put that same determination into building her business, as well as teaching Jonah how to take care of himself—not an easy task, considering his condition.

It was hard not to think highly of a woman like that. And it didn't hurt that she was just about the prettiest little thing he'd ever seen, either. "Shouldn't've let her catch you starin'," he muttered to himself.

His voice caught the attention of the draft horses, and their ears swiveled toward him, waiting, he supposed, to find out if he'd say "Whoa," or "Ease up, boys," or "Let's ride full tilt!" Grinning to himself, he made a *chuck-chuck* noise to let them know it was all right if they simply kept their steady pace, while he went right back to thinking about Miss Callie Roberts.

Micah didn't understand the thoughts spinning in his head or the feelings churning in his heart. Prior to getting married and settling down, many of his cousins' escapades had earned them the reputation of ladies' men, but Micah could count on one hand the number of girls he'd even considered courting— and he'd still have a finger or two left over. He had his self-conscious nature to blame for his lack of experience with the fairer sex, but that had never bothered him much—until meeting Callie face-to-face. If only he had a way with women, like his uncles and cousins. Then, maybe, if he had the good fortune of seeing her again, he could come up with something clever to say, something that would put her at ease and maybe even increase her likelihood of saying yes if he invited her to sit with him at the annual children's Christmas pageant at the schoolhouse.

Sighing, he shrugged. "She'll either say yes, or she won't."

The echo of every courteous "No, thank you" he'd heard in the past rang loudly in his memory, but something told him none of those refusals had stung nearly as much as Callie's rejection would. If he had the sense God gave a mule, he'd start praying that the good Lord would inspire her to accept his invitation—if he worked up the guts to ask her—or bless him with the strength to cope if she didn't.

The sign for San Antonio came into view, reminding Micah of Pauline Devereaux and her carefully veiled threats to his cousin. A sense of dread settled over him, and he turned his prayers in a different direction, asking the Almighty to infuse him with the good sense to handle her wisely, so that Dan would be rid of her, once and for all.

He gave the reins a slight flick. "Let's get a move on, boys," he said. "The sooner we get this miserable business over with, the sooner we can get home." *Home to Eagle Pass and the Rio Grande, to the Lazy N and my loving family, and to Callie Roberts and her amazing, long-lashed eyes.* He spent a moment trying to recall if they were brown or green and soon realized that it didn't matter, as long as he got a second chance to gaze into them.

That thought was all it took to double the pace of his heartbeat, and, when he caught himself grinning like a buffoon, Micah chuckled under his breath. *Better get hold of yourself, fool; a woman like Pauline Devereaux probably gobbles up cowboys like you for breakfast.*

He didn't doubt for a minute she'd be a beauty—the only thing she was likely to have in common with Callie. But, like a spider, she'd already spun a web and trapped Dan into doing who knows what.

He had some time before the meeting—not a lot, but enough for a shave and a haircut. And while he was under the hot towels and lather, he'd pray that God would guide his every action and word, because a lot more than Dan's reputation was riding on the outcome of this appointment.

Chapter 4

*T*he uncomfortable wooden bench at the train station reminded Micah of the rocky dirt where he'd spent so many nights on the trail, counting stars until he fell asleep after a long day of driving cattle. He'd plunked down on the hard seat two hours earlier, at ten o'clock, and hadn't moved a muscle since, save for turning the pages of the newspaper he held. Time on the trail had taught him the importance of choosing a good vantage point, and from his position, partially hidden behind the newspaper, he could see both the front and back doors of the depot.

A woman entered the station, and he knew in an instant that she was Pauline Eden Devereaux. She'd arrived nearly an hour early, no doubt for the same reason he had, and the knowledge inspired a self-satisfied smirk. It seemed he'd gotten the advantage over a professional swindler. Perhaps he had a chance of beating her at her own game, after all.

Don't get a swollen head, now, he cautioned himself as he watched her scan the room. Even from this distance, he could see the cold, steely glare emanating from her dark, heavily made-up eyes. The afternoon sun, spilling in through the multipaned windows, glinted from her green satin gown and dangly earrings, and he wondered how she managed to hold her head erect with that enormous, gaudy hat perched atop her elaborate coiffure. He wondered, too, what she carried in the big cloth valise. Hopefully, not a derringer!

She put her back to him, most likely to have a look at the people seated on the other side of the room, and it struck him that Callie didn't seem to go for the latest fashion trends. Yet her simple muslin dress, in his opinion, was far more beautiful and elegant than Pauline's frilly, bustled gown.

Keep your mind on your work! There'll be plenty of time to daydream about the lovely seamstress on your way back to Eagle Pass, and, hopefully, long after you get home, too....

The fact that Pauline had passed right over him during that first stealthy inspection woke a glimmer of hope in Micah's heart. Maybe she wasn't as shrewd and cunning as her letter had made her sound.

Or, maybe she was like a cougar, pretending not to see him as she prepared to pounce.

He'd learned many lessons on the trail, not the least of which was that the element of surprise usually worked in a body's favor. When he was satisfied that she was otherwise occupied, he'd walk up behind her and give her a good scare. Unkind? Probably. Yet whatever she had planned was anything but kind. So, if startling her subtracted some of the cunning from her plan, so much the better.

Earlier, Micah had spotted another cowboy, leaning against the far wall. He'd never seen the man before and assumed he was just passing through to swap a ride on the westbound Galveston–Harrisburg–San Antonio train for another train going north or south. The man alternated between glancing at the big, ornate clock that hung down from the ceiling and inspecting his fingernails. Now, as he lit a sloppily rolled cigarette, Pauline stepped up behind him and used her parasol to tap his shoulder. She grinned a bit when he lurched. Then, she launched into a flurry of words, no doubt asking if he knew where she might find Daniel Neville.

Hands up, the cowboy shook his head, which sent Pauline back to studying every face in the depot. It would be only a matter of time before she got around to him, so Micah decided he'd best make his move. He waited for her to face the opposite direction again, and then he rose from the bench and, in less than a dozen steps, found himself standing at arm's length from her. "Miss Devereaux, I presume?"

She turned around so quickly that a feather popped free from her hat and floated slowly to the floor. "My word," she said, her voice soft and husky, "you frightened me half to death."

He watched her bat those long, fake-looking lashes and tilt her head to send an enticing smile his way. She extended her free hand, and, as he shook it, he gained insight on how a trout must feel when a fisherman's net scooped it up. He released her hand and patted his pocket. "I'm here in response to your letter, Miss Devereaux, requestin' that I meet you here today." He grinned and nodded toward the clock. "You're a tad early."

Her eyes narrowed, and it was all he could do to hold his tongue as her gaze traveled the length of him.

"My," she said, branding him with those dark eyes, "it seems you've put on a few pounds since last I saw you."

He was relieved to be able to pass for Dan. And his success told him two things: one, Pauline hadn't known his cousin long, and, two, she hadn't known him very well, either. "Ranch work tends to build a man's muscles," Micah said, choosing his words carefully. "Do you want to discuss your, uh, important matter here in the station? Or, would you prefer a more private location?"

She raised her chin a notch. "I'm perfectly comfortable here, where there are plenty of witnesses," she said, almost as an afterthought.

"Well, then," he said, gesturing toward the bench he'd just vacated, "be my guest."

Pauline walked over to the bench, adjusted her bustle, and lowered herself onto the seat. She set down her valise between them as he joined her. "I've thought and thought and thought, but I simply cannot think of a better way to say this...."

Micah prayed that the Lord would keep his emotions in check. A woman like this was dangerous enough, but if she smelled his fear, he was doomed, as sure as he drew breath. He'd made a point of finishing up all his other business in town. The wagon was loaded, and the team had been harnessed, so his departure would be quick and easy once he set this bilker straight.

Despite his best efforts to appear calm and collected, his heart thundered, and his pulse pounded, as she unfastened the clasp of her bag of tricks. He could only hope his apprehension wasn't outwardly visible. Never in a million years would he have predicted what she'd say next, not even with a thousand hours of prayer to prepare himself.

"Mr. Neville, I think it's high time you met your son. His name is Reid."

Chapter 5

evee Neville stood at the big, oval mirror at the back of the dressing room in Callie's shop. "Oh, Callie," she said, turning this way and that, "it fits beautifully. You're an artist, I tell you. An artist!"

Kate Neville, Josh's wife, stepped up beside her and admired her own reflection. "It's truly lovely, dear cousin-in-law, but not nearly as lovely as mine," she teased.

Smiling, Callie opened the lids of the boxes containing the hats she'd made to go with their dresses. "I hope you'll like these just as much." She'd been sewing for the ladies of Eagle Pass for almost two years now, yet she still hadn't figured out how, exactly, to honor the request to "Keep it simple." For some, "simple" meant fashionably plain, while others were nowhere near satisfied until she'd adorned the brim with every type of feather and fancy doodad in the shop.

Seeing the hats, Levee gasped. "Beautiful!" she exclaimed, setting hers carefully on her head. "Just beautiful!"

"It's as though you can read my mind," Kate said with a sigh. "This is exactly what I envisioned when you drew the sketch."

Callie sighed, too, with relief. There had been a time or two when her customers' reactions had been anything but gleeful. "I'm happy that you're happy."

"Oh, will you look at her," Kate said, nudging Levee. "Callie's blushing."

"So she is." Levee wiggled her eyebrows. "You know what I'm thinking?"

"That she's shy and sweet, and...."

"Wouldn't she be absolutely perfect for Cousin Micah!" the women said in unison.

Callie groaned. "I met your cousin a few days ago, in the post office, but I'm afraid I didn't make a very good impression." *Unless, by "impression," one considered the egg-sized bump I made on his brow.*

Levee pulled her into a sideways hug. "What? You mean to say you met Micah, and neither of you said anything to us about it?" She gave an exasperated harrumph. "I'll admit, I'm a little hurt, but I guess I'll forgive you," she said with a giggle.

From Callie's other side, Kate joined the hug. "All right, dearie, out with it. What did you mean when you said that you didn't make a very good impression?"

Callie looked up at the ceiling, as if hoping to find divine guidance written up there. "Well, I was so busy talking with Zack, you see, that I wasn't paying a bit of attention to where I was going, and, on the way outside, I crashed headlong into Micah." Eyes closed, she envisioned his armload of envelopes and small packages scattering around their feet. "And when I bent to help him pick up the items I'd caused him to drop, our foreheads collided. I expect he'll have a greenish-yellow lump there for days."

Levee and Kate leaned forward to exchange glances, then burst into a round of merry laughter. "Can you picture that?" Kate asked.

"Yes," Levee said, wiping tears of mirth from her eyes, "I most certainly can."

"And how did you fare after the crash?" Kate asked Callie.

She shrugged. "Just a tiny bruise on my—"

"Oh, let me see," Kate interrupted her.

When she attempted to brush Callie's bangs aside to peek at the damage, Callie grabbed her wrist. "I'm fine. Really."

This time, when the women exchanged glances, confusion and concern furrowed their brows. "Well," Levee said, "we'd best change out of these stunning outfits so that you can box them up. We have half a dozen other errands to run before we drive back to the Lazy N."

As they bustled into the changing room, Levee sent Kate a look that said, "What was *that* all about?" which Kate returned with a one-shouldered shrug.

When they disappeared behind the curtain, Kate called out, "Callie, what do we owe you for these amazing hats and gowns?"

"Let me check." Callie stepped over to her desk, did some quick arithmetic, and announced the total.

"For all this detail work?" Levee called out. "Why, twice the price would be a bargain!"

Once they'd changed, the women emerged from the dressing room, and Kate linked arms with her cousin-in-law. "We'll just head over to the bank and come right back with your money," she said as they walked to the door. "That should give you plenty of time to pack everything up."

Amid a flurry of chatter and giggles, they stepped into the bright sunshine, leaving Callie to recover her wits. It hadn't been her intention to be rude or brusque, but, if she hadn't stopped Kate, her hideous scar would have been revealed to her and Levee. And, because they were compassionate, big-hearted women, they would have showered her with pity and peppered her with questions. She could live with their thinking that she could be a grouch on occasion. But, if she were to oblige them by answering their questions, it would confirm that she was far worse than a grouch. Seeing the scar may not have altered their opinion of her, but the story of how she'd gotten it might, and, for Jonah's sake more than her own, she could not afford to share that. Her brother and she had settled in Eagle Pass because that was where Seth had planned to pastor the little church in the center of town. Here, they were going to set up house, raise their children, and grow old together. If only....

Callie shuddered. She placed two boxes on her long worktable and lined each one with tissue paper. Then, she took Kate's dress from the peg in the dressing room, folded it carefully, and laid it in the box. Once she'd done the same with Levee's, she tied the boxes with twine, then prepared to package up their hats. But these tasks did not turn off her mind. If anything, the activity seemed to awaken the part of her brain where memories were stored—memories of the cold, dark night when Jonah had lost his hearing, and they'd both lost almost everyone dear to them.

Thankfully, Callie had found her father's strong-box, bobbing on the riverbank in Brazos. Inside, she'd found nearly two thousand dollars, and she'd spent the fortune wisely. If it had not been for those funds, securing a future for Jonah and herself would have been rather hopeless.

Upon arriving in Eagle Pass, she'd opened two savings accounts, one in her name and another in Jonah's, and deposited equal amounts in each. With her share, she'd bought and repaired the house, and, as their little business had grown, she'd put 75 percent of the profits in Jonah's account. If any money remained after she'd paid the bills and purchased supplies, it went into her account. The last time she'd checked, Jonah's account balance was more than three times her own, which, in her opinion, was as it should be. He'd need that money to support himself, as well as his wife, if ever he married.

She heard his footsteps upstairs. He was always considerate in making himself scarce when customers came in, knowing they would prefer privacy while they tried on their dresses. As soon as Kate and Levee had claimed their outfits and left, she'd prepare a special lunch for him, then carry it up to the little balcony off of his bedroom.

Meanwhile, she needed to figure out a way to make up for her discourteous behavior toward Kate and Levee. She considered apologizing but dismissed that idea, as she knew that it would not be sincere. So, she removed the twine from their boxes and tucked a pair of lacy gloves into each one, along with a generous length of matching satin ribbon, which they could use to fashion a belt or to tie up their hair.

Callie grinned a bit wistfully when the proverb "The shoemaker's children are often shoeless" came to mind. So many of the good women of Maverick County—and many more in New York, Chicago, Baltimore, and Boston—wore her fancy fashions, and yet Callie designed only the simplest of dresses for herself. She never adorned her head with feathered hats or silky ribbons, and, if she ever wore gloves, they were made of plain, practical fabric. It made no sense to spend her earnings on such things. Besides, she couldn't shed the notion that she didn't deserve the finer things in life.

The finer things in life....

Callie sighed, remembering how Levee and Kate had joked that she and Micah would make a perfect couple. It was just as well that she'd made a terrible first impression on him, because a fine, upstanding man like that deserved far better than the likes of her...a woman whose selfishness had brought misery and suffering upon so many.

And when he found the good woman he deserved, Callie hoped the good Lord would bless her with the grace to feel truly happy for him.

The baby's grin exposed six tiny teeth that gleamed from pink gums, and he extended his chubby arms, fingers wiggling, as he reached for Micah.

Pauline all but shoved him onto Micah's lap. "He favors you, don't you think?"

Me just as easily as Dan, I guess. He kept the thought to himself. So far, the ruse had worked. Pauline believed he was Dan. If he could keep up the pretense for a few more minutes, the Nevilles would be safe from her clutches, and she'd leave town with a few extra dollars in her purse. Hopefully, she'd spend them on the boy, because his tiny outfit had seen better days.

Micah turned the boy around and bounced him on his knee. "So," he said over Reid's head, "where were you before coming to San Antonio?"

She hadn't expected his question, as evidenced by her rapid blinking. He heard her swallow and watched her fiddle with the frizzy bangs above her eyebrows. "Reid and I have been here in San Antonio, of course. Right where you left us."

Eyes narrowed, he lowered his voice. "Us?"

"Why, Reid and me, of course."

Did she mean to imply that Dan knew that this child had come about as a result of his relationship with Pauline? Micah could never believe such a thing about his cousin. "And how do you know I'm the boy's father?" he asked.

Sitting up straight, Pauline lifted her chin and sniffed. "A woman just knows these things."

"But the boy is, what, eight months old?"

"Nine. At least, he will be next week."

Reid squealed with glee as a woman pushed a baby carriage past them. Micah held him a bit tighter. "Why did you wait all this time to...uh, introduce us?" *Here it comes*, he thought. *The demand for money.*

"At first, I thought I could handle Reid and the many expenses he entailed. There were doctor's bills, of course, and his layette, and...." With her chin buried among the ruffles of her bodice, she bit her lower lip. "But I was wrong," she said in a small, wavering voice. "The proper care of a baby costs far more than I ever would have guessed." She met Micah's gaze to add, "And, in case you think I came here to demand that you marry me, though that would be well within my rights...well, that's the very last thing on my mind."

He branded her with a sizzling glare. "Then, why did you come here?"

She leaned back, as if he were a fire-breathing dragon. "I came because I need...because I must have...."

Odd how flustered this skilled pretender seemed to be. *All part of her scheme, no doubt.* Well, if everything went according to his plan, she'd be tongue-tied for real when he was through with her. Liars and cheats were always tripped up by seemingly insignificant facts. "Refresh my memory, if you'll be so kind. When did our, uh, interlude occur?"

Her cheeks darkened with a blush, and tears filled her eyes. "I remember it like it was yesterday," she whispered. "It was the eleventh of May. A Friday."

Nice touch, adding that little hitch to her voice. He hid his cynicism behind a smirk. "Where?"

She looked at him as if he'd grown a second head. "Where?"

Micah merely stared her down.

"You mean...you mean, you don't remember?"

He chuckled quietly. "You're fairly easy to look at, Pauline, I'll give you that. But you're like a thousand other—" He stopped himself. Telling her the type of woman he thought she was might get her too riled up, and he couldn't afford to do that—not until he'd found out how much it would cost to put her on the next outbound train chugging away from Dan's life, once and for all. He wondered what his cousin might have said if he'd received Pauline's letter. "So, tell me, Pauline, exactly how much whiskey did we drink on Friday, May eleventh?"

A smile wavered at the corners of her mouth. "I had enough." She batted her lashes. "You had a lot. A whole lot."

Micah nodded. So far, things were pretty much as he'd expected them to be. If Dan had been with this woman at all, he'd been blind drunk. "Remind me again how we met?"

"We were both alone, and looking forlorn." She heaved a shaky sigh. "I suppose the barkeep thought we might be able to console one another, and so he made the introductions."

Console one another, indeed. It was all he could do to keep from mocking her out loud. Micah had never been one to hang around saloons, but he knew the kind of women who frequented such places.

The baby started to squirm and fret. When Micah made a move to hand him back to his mother, Reid grabbed hold of his shirt collar and refused to let go. Poor little guy probably didn't want to end up back inside that valise. So, he hugged the boy close and patted his back. "Let's cut to the chase, Pauline. How much will it take to put an end to this charade?"

Her eyes widened in surprise as her hands fluttered near her throat. "Charade?" she echoed. "I have no idea what you're talking about, Dan Neville. Isn't it bad enough you left me to cope with impending motherhood on my own? Or that I had no help supporting our child once he was born? Is it your intent to further humiliate me by insinuating that I arranged this meeting for the sole purpose of taking your money?"

Oh, she was good, all right. Her indignant tirade had captured the attention of those seated nearby, but Micah refused to allow raised eyebrows and disapproving glares to get him off course. "Who said I was insinuating?" he said. "I'm telling you candidly, I believe that is precisely why you arranged this meeting." He turned in the seat to face her head-on. "I can't prove one way or another if what you say is true, though logic and common sense tell me you wouldn't know the truth if it came up and bit you on the bustle." He leaned in close and said through clenched teeth, "Stop wasting my time and get to the point."

Pauline made a scoffing noise and then glanced slyly around the room. "Do you really think any of these good people will believe your story over mine?" A wily laugh punctuated her words. "I want what's coming to me."

He snorted. "Which is?"

"Five thousand dollars."

That inspired a round of hearty laughter. "You must be joking! Why, I don't have that kind of—"

"Don't insult my intelligence by pretending you can't afford that. Do you think I'd have come all this way without first investigating you and your family? My source told me what you're worth. If you want to avoid the indignity of a scandal, you'll pay up."

All this way? Hadn't she told him that she'd been here in San Antone all along? And wasn't she aware that most of her audience had left the building? Micah controlled the urge to scowl. He should have been surprised at how quickly her personality had switched from demure victim to seasoned criminal, but he wasn't. "I hate to disappoint you, Pauline, but your source is full of beans. Anyone who knows my family also knows that our ranch was hit hard these past few seasons. Between drought and weevils and tornadoes, we couldn't come up with an amount like that, even if we pooled all our resources." It hadn't been easy admitting that, especially to the likes of her, but it bought him time and gave him leverage. Not giving her a chance to rebut, he concluded, "So, if you hope to leave here today a few dollars richer than when you arrived, you'll have to come up with a far more reasonable demand than that."

She squared her shoulders. "I don't believe you."

"What you believe or don't believe is of no concern to me. I've told you the truth, which is far more than you can say, Pauline Eden Devereaux, if that's even your real name."

She got to her feet so rapidly, she caused a breeze that mussed the baby's dark hair. As she turned to face him, her skirts whirled around her ankles. "How much can you pay, then?"

His pocket watch ticked twice before he answered. "I'll give you five hundred."

Pauline's mouth dropped open. Two more ticks of the watch later, she whispered, "Dollars?"

"Take it or leave it."

"You must be joking."

Micah only shrugged.

Pauline pursed her lips till they all but disappeared as she processed the information. "When?"

"When, what?"

A frustrated sigh exited her painted lips. "When can you get me the money?"

He could let her sweat for a few minutes, but that would force him to remain in her company. "Today."

"Five hundred." She leaned closer to add, "Cash?"

Micah gave a nonchalant nod. "I have an account at the bank here in town. It'll take a few minutes, but I'm certain I can make a withdrawal."

She glanced at the big clock, then gathered up the writhing baby and stuffed him partway into the satchel. He protested, but only feebly. Obviously, even at his age, he'd learned better than to disobey this single-purposed woman.

Pauline gripped the handles and slid the valise from the bench. "Fine. I'll meet you back here in.... How long will it take you? To make a withdrawal, I mean."

He shrugged. "Fifteen, twenty minutes, I suppose."

She started to walk away, then stopped in her tracks and turned around. "All right, then. I'll meet you back here in half an hour." Pointing one gloved finger at his forehead like an uncocked pistol, she added, "And if you have a mind to sneak off without paying me, you'd better hire the best lawyer in Texas, because I'll bring every charge known to man against you." She took a step closer and smirked. "Make no mistake, Daniel Neville—I know how to dress for that part, too."

As she stomped toward the station's rear doors, Micah shook his head. A slight shiver ran up his spine. He believed her, to the last word. Still, very little about her story made sense, and even less of it sounded true. Clearly, he'd underestimated her talents and overestimated his ability to handle her. An eerie sensation set his teeth on edge as he wrestled with the facts: Pauline Eden Devereaux was a woman to be reckoned with, for she had more wit and craftiness under her hat than he had in his whole body. As difficult as it was to picture his cousin with someone like her, even with whiskey fogging his brain, Micah had no choice but to consider the possibility.

He looked up at the clock and saw that his wool-gathering had wasted a full minute. Not good, not good at all. What if he got stuck behind some gossipy hen in the line at the bank? He'd need every spare minute if he hoped to fine-tune his plan and beat her at her own game. Hands pocketed and head down, Micah crossed the street and hustled toward the bank. Hopefully, his five-hundred-dollar withdrawal would put her on the next train out of town. Why, she'd probably hunt down and snare another chump before the locomotive chugged into the next station. How long, Micah wondered, before the poor sap's pockets would be inside out and empty?

Micah stepped up to the teller's window. "Good afternoon, Mr. Neville," said the man behind the barred counter. "And what might I do for you today?"

You might say a prayer that a certain she-bandit in a bustle won't come back for more.... "I'd like to make a withdrawal," was his gruff reply. "Five hundred dollars."

He waited while the teller collected the necessary forms. Minutes later, the teller slid a withdrawal form across the counter. "Here you go, Mr. Neville," the man said, handing him a pen. "If you'll just sign there, please."

Micah dipped its nib into the ink well and scratched the dollar amount on the proper line, then scribbled his name beside it. Then, he held his breath and said another prayer, this time that the transaction he was about to make wouldn't backfire.

Chapter 6

An angry Jonah was a rare sight, indeed, and Callie didn't like being responsible for his flaring temper. "It's a waste of perfectly good money," he snarled, shoving the wooden box aside.

"Please, Jonah, be reasonable. There's no shame in trying something new, especially if it might help you hear. Why, Beethoven used an ear trumpet, and—"

"It didn't work for him, either."

Oh, but he could be stubborn! "But how do you know it won't work for you? You haven't even taken it out of the box!" She prayed he wouldn't remind her of similar instruments she'd ordered from as near as Philadelphia and as far as London, all collecting dust now on the shelf in her armoire.

His frown deepened, but at least he hadn't shot down the possibility. Callie decided to take advantage of his hesitation. "I'll make you a deal. Try it out, and, if it doesn't work, I'll stop pestering you to test new devices."

Jonah harrumphed, then met her gaze and grinned. "Now, why am I having trouble believing that?" He quickly added, "It looks like the one in the ad next to Horatio Alger's story."

"Oh?"

"The one in the April issue of *Leisure Hour Library*."

Ah, that, Callie thought. Months ago, knowing how much Jonah enjoyed reading, she'd subscribed him to the publication, which printed novels for three cents a copy, six cents for the more popular authors' work. It had been worth every penny of hard-earned money. Hopefully, the $2.75 she'd paid for the ear trumpet wouldn't be a "waste of perfectly good money," as Jonah had put it.

She picked up the device and tipped it this way and that, as if inspecting it for defects. Maybe, if he saw how well-crafted it was, he'd put it to his ear, if for no other reason than to pacify her.

He held out his hand. "I have your word that this will be your last attempt to find a funnel to pour noise into my head, correct?"

Surely, he didn't expect her to give up just like that! What if, in a week, six months, or a year from now, she came across an article about some brilliant fellow who'd invented something that actually could pour sound into his ear? But she wouldn't lie to him. "If it doesn't work," she said carefully, "I promise: no more ear trumpets." *Hopefully, whatever other instruments I may find will be called by another name*, she thought, grinning to herself.

Jonah waved his right forefinger like a metronome. "Make no mistake, Calista May Roberts," he said, eyes narrowed. "I intend to hold you to your word." With that, he tucked the narrow end of the trumpet into his ear. "Well, go ahead. Say something so we can put this ridiculous contraption to the test."

Hands clasped as if in prayer, she shouted, "I love you, Jonah Everett Roberts!" Then, she held her breath. *Oh, Lord, let it work. Please, please, let it work!*

Jonah shrugged, and she saw the anguish of disappointment in his big, golden eyes. It was proof that, despite his tough talk, he had hoped the thing would work just as much as she had. Why hadn't she realized before now that each of her attempts to help him had hurt him instead?

She couldn't help but wonder if her resolve to bring sound into his silent world was more for his benefit or for hers. Finding a solution to his problem would certainly help to lighten the never-ending burden of guilt she'd carried for so long. Shame hit her like a cold slap to the face. Fighting tears, Callie hung her head. *Your selfishness knows no bounds*, she thought. Oh, she had plenty to confess and ask forgiveness for when she got down on her knees tonight!

"Aw, don't look so sad, Callie. It isn't your fault this confounded thing doesn't work." Jonah scowled at the ear trumpet. "It's elegant, all right, with its shiny brass and fancy burled wood." He scoffed. "Seems to me that if the manufacturers put as much work into functionality as they do style, they might just have something, here." He carefully eased the contraption back into its box. "If you return it, will they reimburse you?"

"Probably," she said, though she wasn't certain. For one thing, in her excitement to open the parcel, she'd destroyed the packing slip. For another, she seemed to recall that the ad indicated all sales were final.

Jonah leaned in closer. "I know how much you'd like to give me back my ears, but you aren't a miracle worker." Patting her hand, he added, "I've told you again and again, you aren't to blame for my deafness. Why won't you believe me when I say that you're no more responsible for my condition than for anything else that happened on that night?"

How good Jonah was to try to comfort her, even though "anything else" that had happened on the steamboat that night had been no one's fault but hers. She didn't deserve her brother's loyalty or his love, but, for some peculiar reason, God had seen fit to bless her with both. Perhaps, someday, He'd bless her with a selfless spirit, as He had Jonah.

And, if He did, maybe she could begin to forgive herself for the death and destruction that had taken place aboard the *Maybelline*.

Back inside the train station, Micah stared at the huge timepiece overhead, watching as its skinny, scrolled black hands counted out the minutes.

Pauline didn't seem like the type who would arrive late for an appointment that would fill her purse with money she hadn't earned. But then, she didn't seem the motherly type, either, yet she'd orchestrated this meeting on behalf of her boy. Would she have threatened to hire a lawyer if she'd intended to stand him up?

Micah didn't think so.

Still, something about her connection with baby Reid didn't seem to add up. Most of his cousins, whether male or female, had children and had formed strong bonds with them, beginning at birth and growing more visible with each passing day. Not long ago, on his way to deliver mail to his cousin Susan, and her husband, Sam, Micah had followed the sounds of voices to the second floor and found them in the nursery. He'd stood there in awed silence, watching and listening as Susan and Sam leaned over a cradle and tucked in their infant daughter. The devotion in their eyes could have lit an entire shaft down at the coal mine. Why, even little Willie, their young son, looked upon his baby sister with bright-eyed affection.

Yet nothing even remotely close to that glimmer shone in Pauline's eyes when she looked at her son. Could that explain why the baby had seemed content in the arms of a total stranger? Hopefully, when the two of them were alone, Pauline showered the boy with affection and attention.

Seconds later, she breezed up and plopped the valise on the bench beside him. Without as much as a howdy-do, she blurted out, "Well? Do you have my money?"

Your money? he wanted to say. Instead, Micah shook his head, then met her cold, steady gaze. "I do." He patted the front of his jacket, on the other side of which was the breast pocket that held the thick envelope. "Before I hand it over, though, you'll need to assure me that the, uh, 'important matter' you referred to in your letter won't require similar meetings at some point down the road." He rarely gave in to anger, but, when he did, folks said his glare could melt a stone. Micah found it surprisingly easy to summon a glower as he added, "Believe me when I say, you do not want to find out what I'm capable of doing if you so much as attempt to contact me or anybody else in my family again."

In an instant, Pauline's eyes widened slightly, and she took a tiny step back. In the next moment, the already-familiar smug expression and conceited posture returned. "Unfortunately, very few situations in life provide any guarantees, Mr. Neville." Her eyes narrowed slightly. "I'm afraid we're just going to have to trust one another, now, aren't we, Daniel?"

Micah got to his feet and stood as close to her as decorum would permit. "I'm afraid, Miss Devereaux, that simply won't do." He gave the envelope another pat. "Five hundred dollars is a lot of money. And, unlike you, I earned every penny of it through honest work."

She blinked once, twice, as she mulled over his words. "Then, it seems my next stop will be the courthouse."

Micah had never much liked playing poker, but he'd watched enough games to know a bluff when he saw one. "It's easy enough to find," he said, pointing across the street. "Just look for the big building with a whole lot of steps." Then, he leaned over the bag and smiled down at Reid. "Good-bye, little man," he said, tickling the boy's chin. "Been a genuine pleasure meeting you."

The baby gripped Micah's finger with a strength that belied his size and age. Was he seeing things, or had the boy sent a silent plea by way of that dark-eyed gaze? Micah felt his heart clench, and, as much as he hated to do it, he pried his finger from the child's grasp. Clearing his throat, he faced Pauline and donned his Stetson. "I'm more than happy to carry your bag back to the courthouse." He nodded at her square-toed, brown suede boots, then softened his tone to say, "It's quite a hike from here to there, and those sure don't look like the most comfortable walking shoes."

Reid chose that moment to erupt into tears. He reached for Micah, causing the bag to shift, and if Micah hadn't extended a hand when he had, the baby would have toppled headfirst onto the hard, dusty floor. "It appears he wants some attention," he said to Pauline. *And maybe some freedom from the confines of that smelly suitcase.* "Think maybe he's hungry?"

"I haven't the foggiest notion what makes him behave that way," she snapped. "Some days, there's just no making him happy."

Now that he thought about it, Micah didn't recall seeing any bottles in the bag. He hadn't noticed a change of clothes or a stash of fresh diapers, either, which was strange. He'd never known a mother of an infant to leave home without a huge sack of bibs, diapers, and pap. What sort of mother went anywhere without the supplies her child might need?

"How far did you travel to get here?" he demanded.

"That, Mr. Neville, is none of your concern."

He scooped up the boy from the valise and held him close. "I'm afraid you've made it my concern, Miss Devereaux, and the concern of every other traveler in earshot." Just then, Micah noticed a warm wet sensation seeping through the fabric of his shirt. "Well, now," he said, frowning at Pauline, "here's the problem. His diaper's soaked clean through!"

"I—I have a...." She licked her lips. "I have another satchel. It's out on the platform, with a fresh dress for him. I'll get it, just as soon as you and I have put our business behind us." Her hand shook slightly as she tugged a lace-edged hanky from her sleeve. "What will you demand," she asked, patting beads of perspiration from her forehead, "as proof that I'll never darken your door again?"

"You can start by lowering your voice." When she clamped her lips together, Micah added, "And sit your bustled self down right there." He pointed at the bench. "You're attracting too much attention, standing there, waving your arms about like a broken windmill."

She did as she was told, then folded her hands in her lap.

"Now, if you'll tell me where that other satchel is, I'll happily fetch it for you, so you can give this boy the care he needs."

Her eyes darted left and right, and her shoulders stiffened. "I—I changed him while you were at the bank. Whatever's in his pants can wait until we've completed our...transaction."

Whether the lie was connected to the nonexistent bag of baby clothes or the conclusion of their business, Micah couldn't say, but it didn't matter. He'd pushed her enough to make her lose her composure. *But if you're smart,* he told himself, *you'll get back to business before she gathers it again.*

He sat on the bench and balanced Reid on the knee farther from Pauline. "Go on. Out with it. And I feel it only fair to warn you that if I suspect you're lying again, it'll be me who goes to the courthouse. Then, we'll find out together who the authorities believe, the woman swindler or the man whose family's business has been supporting politicians in these parts since long before you hoodwinked your first chump." She gasped, which made him chuckle. "Why, I'll be surprised if they don't chase you out of town, just to see if you'll trip over your fancy bootlaces." If he knew what was good for him, he wouldn't give her enough time to build up a new head of steam. He gave her a long, hard look, meanwhile hoping she wouldn't call his bluff. "Well?"

Reid popped two fingers into his mouth and snuggled close to Micah's vest, as if he, too, wanted to hear the tale this woman would tell.

"You...I...we...." She sighed and looked up, as if cues for the fable she was about to tell were printed on the ceiling. "My father used me to pay off a gambling debt, see, and the man who owned me dragged me into the saloon, and—"

What did any of this have to do with Dan and Reid and—what had she called it? This transaction? "What saloon?"

"The one here in town, down at the far end of the street."

If memory served him right, that establishment had closed more than a year ago. But Micah would check out that portion of her story later. For now, it was far better to watch her tighten the rope around her own neck. "And who was this fellow you contend won you in a game of cards?"

"I don't just contend it," she insisted, batting her eyelashes. "It's true!" Her feigned outrage bought her just enough time to conjure a name he wouldn't recognize. "Jeremiah. Jeremiah Turner."

"Never heard of him." *Because he doesn't exist.*

"Jeremiah put me to work, you see, gathering up loose coins and folding money the drunkards left behind. And when he saw that you were—"

"Jeremiah? A man like that allowed you to call him by his first name?"

She swallowed hard enough for him to hear it. "Why, yes, he did."

"I'm sorry for interrupting," Micah said, grinning. "Please, go on."

Pauline sighed, then continued. "'That's one of the Nevilles,' Jeremiah said one morning. 'Why, they've got more money than God!' He'd overheard you telling the barkeep that you were in town to buy a stud bull. 'Those don't come cheap!' he said. 'Get him off to himself and separate him from that money, and I'll set you free.'"

She exhaled a shaky sigh. "So, I did what anyone in my position would have done. I talked you into buying a bottle of cheap whiskey and pretended to share it with you. Once it was empty, it didn't take much coaxing to get you alone in one of the upstairs rooms. I had planned to wait until you passed out, so I could empty your pockets." Pauline studied her hands. "You seemed so polite and gentlemanly that I never expected.... You were the last man I ever would have thought would...."

But if she'd spent that much time alone with Dan—if he'd been guilty of the despicable act she was accusing him of—shouldn't she realize that Micah was a total stranger?

Tears filled her eyes, and she chewed her lower lip, no doubt to give him the impression she was working hard to stifle a sob.

"You're a powerful man, Dan Neville," she croaked, "and I'm just a small, weak woman. I didn't have the strength to fight you off."

Thankfully, no one else in the depot had been close enough to overhear her lies, because, as much as he hated to admit it, she almost had him convinced that Dan was guilty.

Almost.

"If I had—," he began. "If—" He couldn't bear to say the word "rape." He cleared his throat. "Why didn't you go to the authorities and have me arrested that very night?"

"I was too ashamed. And you'd torn my dress to shreds. I had to wait for the maid to come make up the room, so she could bring me some clothes."

Moments ago, she'd told him it was morning when Jeremiah had spotted Dan in the saloon. Surely, she didn't expect him to believe it had taken all day to get Dan drunk enough to go along with their plan, and that the maid hadn't reported what she'd seen.

He felt Reid's soft, steady breaths, and a glance at his innocent face was all it took to make him hold the sleeping baby closer. Why, he didn't even mind the damp spot from the boy's round bottom on the leg of his trousers.

If this tiny bundle was, indeed, Dan's son, he owed it to him—and Dan—to put everything on the line. So, Micah started with the letter that had brought him here, and he didn't stop until he'd listed every doubt her yarn had roused, right up to her claim that the maid, the only person who'd seen Pauline in those first humiliating moments after the attack, hadn't thought it necessary to report the incident.

"I know it all sounds too preposterous to be true," Pauline conceded, "but everything happened just as I said it did!"

Sure, it did.

"Look, Mr. Neville...Dan. I—I don't want any trouble. Just give me the money. Give me the money now, and I'll be out of your hair. For good. You have my word."

Her word, indeed. Well, he'd half expected things to turn out this way. And that was what had prompted him, prior to departing for San Antonio, to pen the document he then pulled out of his pocket. Even signed and dated, it wouldn't give him a legal leg to stand on, but maybe, just maybe, it would look official enough to fool Pauline. "You get your money after you sign that," he snarled quietly, not wanting to wake Reid.

Pauline nodded, her hands trembling as she took the folded paper from him. She read it, then heaved a long sigh. "Well, it seems fair." Her gaze never left the page as she said, "I don't have a pen."

Micah reached inside his pocket once more and took out the stubby pencil he always carried. When he handed it to her, their eyes met for a heartbeat. A chill coursed through him as he looked into Pauline's inky orbs. If Herman Melville was right about the eyes being the "gateway to the soul," she either had no soul at all, or he needed more time—a lot more time—to search for it.

Their gazes unlocked when she laid the paper between them on the bench, then scrawled her signature on the line. She handed back his pencil and watched him tuck it inside his pocket again, and, during her momentary hesitation before handing him the paper, the chill between them intensified.

Standing, she huffed and smoothed her skirts. "If you don't mind holding Reid for a moment longer, I'll just see about our passage west."

Reid squirmed, snuggling closer. "Where are you taking him?" Micah whispered over his head.

"Well," Pauline began, twirling a ringlet of hair that dangled down her cheek, "I'm an actress, you see...."

No surprise there.

"And there's a Shakespearean troupe forming in San Francisco. If there aren't any lengthy delays in our travels, I should arrive in plenty of time to audition for one of the leading roles in the upcoming production of *Hamlet*."

"Don't you worry," he said, handing her the envelope stuffed with money. "I'll take good care of your boy while you buy the tickets."

Perhaps her stage talents explained how she'd gone from a cringing, crying female to a proud, vivacious woman in a matter of seconds. How odd that she could blithely chat about her future in theater as if she was talking to an old friend instead of the man whom she believed had violently despoiled her. Odder still that she could so easily leave her defenseless baby in the care of that very man, even if it was for a short time. Micah shook his head.

She'd been gone all of a minute when Reid stirred, then opened his big, dark eyes. Micah braced for the wail that would surely pierce the air once the baby realized his mama had left him in the arms of a stranger.

Instead, a wide, nearly toothless grin lit the little face. The boy kicked and squealed as he pointed at the puffing smokestack of the train visible through

an open door to the platform. His movement reminded Micah yet again of the wet spot on his trousers.
"Oh, to have that satchel filled with fresh diapers and
such," he muttered with a grin. "Maybe your mama'll
change you and feed you once you're settled in your
car." *Yes*, he thought, nodding. *That makes sense.*

"Ga," Reid said, grabbing Micah's thick mus-
tache with both chubby hands. "Ga-ga."

After several minutes of "chattering" with the
baby, it dawned on Micah that there wasn't a line at
the ticket counter. Why was it taking Pauline so long
to purchase two tickets? He stood up and turned in
a slow circle, searching for her. Had she gone to the
outhouse, perhaps? As he looked around, he prayed
that the wet blotch on his trousers would not be followed by another on his jacket.

"Ga," the baby repeated, sticking a finger in Micah's ear. "Aah, ga-ga!"

He might have joined in the banter, if it weren't
for the sinking sensation in his gut. Micah hurried
toward the door. Surely, he'd find Pauline right outside, instructing the conductor on where to stow her
luggage or demanding a double compartment for the
overnight legs of their westward trip.

The baby squealed happily, pointing at the
bright-red caboose, growing smaller and smaller as
it clattered down the tracks. "Oh, little man," Micah
said softly, "let's hope and pray that your mama isn't
on that train." Because, if she was…. He didn't want
to consider the possibilities.

Back inside, he half ran from one side of the
depot to the other, asking everyone he came upon
if they'd seen a woman in a green satin dress. His
panic doubled with each negative response. He had

to find Pauline. *Had to!* What did he know about caring for a child this young? What did he know about caring for any child, no matter the age?

Desperation drove him to the ticket counter, where the man behind the bars asked, "Was she wearing a big, ugly feathered hat?"

Hope thrummed in his heart. "Why, yes! Yes, she was!"

"The li'l lady bought herself a one-way ticket." He slid a pencil from behind his ear and, using it as a pointer, indicated the window out to the platform, where the white plumes that had billowed from the smokestack were barely a memory on the wide horizon. "Yes, indeedy, she did. And that's her train there, the one that just left the station."

Micah groaned. "No," he muttered huskily. "Oh, Lord, no."

The man winked. "Lovers' spat?"

The question would have been laughable under other circumstances. He shook his head. "No, no. Nothing like that."

"Maybe you can catch up with her in Albuquerque. She'll have to change trains there. A one-day stopover. I can check the schedule, if you'd like."

Micah's draft horses were fast and strong, but, even without the load of grain and seed in the wagon, they couldn't get him to New Mexico in time to hand Reid over before she continued rolling west. "Ma," Reid said, as if on cue. "Ma-ma!"

When he shifted the boy from his left hip to his right, something crinkled beneath Micah's palm. It was a note, pinned to Reid's gown. Clearly, Pauline had been in a hurry when she'd written it, for it bore none of the fanciful curlicues and embellishments of the letter she'd sent to the ranch. The only constant was that this message, too, was addressed to D. Neville.

He barely noticed when the ticket agent threw up his hands. "Fine," the man said. "I won't check the schedule. And you're very welcome for my time and trouble."

Muttering an apology, Micah stepped woodenly back to the bench, sat down beside the brocade valise, and unfolded the note. Reid promptly grabbed a corner of the paper and tried to stuff it into his mouth. Micah pulled the note back out and read, "I'll never achieve success in my chosen career with a baby in tow. Besides, what sort of life would the boy have, traveling around with a cast of unruly performers?"

What sort of woman chose acting over parenting? Even if hers was the smallest of hearts, surely there was at least a spark of love in it for her child. Micah gently pried the note from Reid's chubby fist and read the closing lines, his heart aching for the tiny, defenseless person who looked trustingly into his eyes. "He's as much yours as anyone's, after all, and with your big family and unlimited resources, I have every confidence that you'll raise him well."

The note was signed simply, "Pauline Eden Devereaux."

Chapter 7

$\mathscr{C}$allie watched Jonah frown at the latest issue of the *Eagle Pass Times.* "Neither of those inventions is of any interest to me," he said, plopping the publication into the kindling bucket. Then, wiggling his eyebrows, he added, "Now, a motorcar? There's an invention I wouldn't mind putting to the test!"

Callie had read the article, which discussed the growing interest in such innovations as the gramophone. She smiled. "If electric lighting ever catches on enough to be affordable, you can be sure I'll invest in it." Oh, to be able to work through the night without having to inhale the sickening odors of whale oil and kerosene!

"Did I tell you," Jonah injected, "that I got me some of that chewing gum over at J. W. Riddle's?"

She'd come so close to buying him a pack of Black Jack just the other day. But, after paying for the sugar, flour, and baking powder, which she would use to bake assorted goodies for Thanksgiving and

Christmas, she'd been a few cents shy of the price. "Is it any good?"

Jonah shrugged. "It's all right, I suppose, but I've never been a big fan of licorice."

Callie, on the other hand, loved it. If it weren't for the way it blackened her teeth, she probably would have made it a regular part of her diet. "Well, maybe in a year or so, Thomas Adams and his company will come up with some other flavors."

"I gave what was left to Miss Levee. Thought maybe she could use it for one of the prizes she hands out to students when they get all the answers right on their homework assignments."

"Oh, Jonah," Callie said, hugging him. "What a marvelous idea. I'm sure Levee was thrilled."

"Thrilled about what?" asked a masculine voice.

Callie smiled over Jonah's shoulder at Josh Neville's brother-in-law, who had married Josh's sister Sarah, herself a seamstress. Recently, however, her pregnancy had slowed her productivity. "Well, if it isn't Mack Burdette. What brings you to my humble shop today?"

Mack shook Jonah's hand, then turned to Callie. "I'm hoping you can help me come up with an anniversary present for my beautiful wife. Something special that'll make her eyes pop."

She led him to her hat display at the rear of the shop, where the wall was lined with dozens of padded stands Jonah had built for Callie. "Something to wear to Sunday services, maybe?"

He scratched his chin. "I wouldn't know the first thing about choosing a woman's bonnet. What if I got the wrong size? Or a color that doesn't match anything in her wardrobe?"

"Not to worry. We'll find something completely perfect and unique." As he followed her to the counter, Callie asked, "And how is the little mother-to-be?"

"She's plumb tuckered out all the time." He shrugged. "But Doc Lane says that's normal for some women."

She'd heard that Sarah's baby was due in mid-February. If Mack trusted the doctor, then why the faint worry lines on his brow? "She's probably just not getting enough sleep," she said, opening a velvet-lined drawer, "what with thinking about getting the nursery and layette ready, and choosing names, and—"

"Two months ago, I would have agreed." Mack shook his head. "Every woman at the ranch warned her not to get the room ready too early, but that wife of mine has a mind of her own. All that's been done for weeks."

"Well, I'm sure Doc knows what he's talking about, but I'll pray for her and the baby, all the same. For your peace of mind, too." In the next breath, she added, "Now, then, what do you suppose Sarah would prefer? A pretty necklace? Earrings?"

He pointed at a gleaming pendant. "How about that one? Why, it's almost the color of her eyes."

"It's called moonstone." Callie held out the necklace, letting the silvery chain puddle into his upturned palm. "See the way it changes color ever so slightly when it catches the light? It's beautiful, isn't it?"

Mack nodded. "I suppose."

She grinned. "You suppose?"

"Well, if it's hanging around her neck, she won't be able to see it unless she steps up to the mirror.

And my Sarah has never been one to gawk in the looking glass."

His Sarah. Callie sighed softly. If the Lord ever chose to bless her with such a sweet, caring husband, she'd spend the rest of her days thanking Him. *You would have had a sweet, caring husband in Seth, yet you ruined it. Do you honestly expect the Lord to reward you again, considering all the trouble you've left in your wake?* She set her jaw, then laid the necklace back in its velvet-lined box and handed him a matching ring. "Pretty, isn't it?"

"Yes'm, it most certainly is." Just as quickly as his smile had appeared, it vanished. "But...but it's much too big." He met Callie's eyes. "She's a sentimental li'l thing, that wife of mine, and it'd break her heart if she lost it."

It didn't seem too large to Callie, but she shrugged. Who was she to argue with the man who'd spent month after month holding the delicate hand that would wear it? She opened another drawer and took out a bracelet. "How about this, instead?"

She watched him study it. "Are these moonstones?"

"No, that's aquamarine. The traveling salesman I bought it from said it was mined in South America. Brazil, to be precise." Hands clasped, she rested her chin on a fist. "You wouldn't believe all the fanciful stories about the gem." She went on to tell him the Roman legend about how the stone glittered because it had absorbed the atmosphere of young love. "When blessed and worn, it joins in love and does great things," she recited. "And, in olden days in Europe, bridegrooms often gave their brides aquamarine on the morning of their wedding day. Sailors thought it would keep them safe during storms at sea, and soldiers believed it made them invincible in battle."

"Hmm."

"A skeptic!" Callie teased. "Why, even the philosopher Pliny paid tribute to the jewel, saying, 'The lovely aquamarine, which seems to have come from some mermaid's treasure house in the depths of a summer sea, has charms not to be denied.'"

Mack chuckled. "Seems your traveling salesman sold you a whole lot more than a few jewels." He winked. "I'll take it, if you can you wrap it up for me."

"I'd be happy to." As she worked, Callie thought of other stories she'd heard, these ones about the Neville women, many of whom had trouble carrying healthy babies to term. The kinder, gentler ladies of Eagle Pass blamed some lethal element in the water at the Lazy N Ranch, while others pointed to Scripture as proof that God was punishing the sons for the sins of their father, who'd greedily bought up nearly every Texas acre before anyone else had a chance to. Callie didn't believe for an instant that the Lord had taken those innocent, unborn babes to mete out Old Testament justice. Besides, Ezra had done what any man would have, given the opportunity!

She couldn't imagine the pain the Neville women must have suffered each time a little one, a celebration of the God-given love between man and wife, had lived, grown, and died inside of them.

For reasons unknown to Callie, Micah's image hovered in her mind. How surprising that a man as big as a mountain had such a gentle touch. Since that day in the post office, she'd longed to see that warm smile aimed in her direction again. Now, really, how silly was that!

"Sarah tells me you ran into my cousin?"

Callie knew exactly which cousin Mack meant, and her heartbeat doubled as she recalled the way she and Micah had crawled around like toddlers, retrieving his mail from where the letters and packages had scattered on the ground. She pretended to be engrossed in tying the red ribbon around the package into a pretty bow. "It's a rare week when I don't run into one Neville or another."

Mack chuckled. "I'm no expert when it comes to women, and I'm not a gambling man, either." He winked. "But something tells me, if I bet on why you're blushing right now, I'd win."

She ignored his comment. "Would you like me to write up a little card?" She showed him a box filled with tiny envelopes and matching stationery.

Mack grinned and held up a hand. "Never let it be said that Mack Burdette doesn't know when to back off. What happens between you and Micah is none of my business. And, yes, I think Sarah would like one of those little cards." He selected one, turning it over and over in his big hand.

Why, it was almost laughable that Mack thought it possible for something to blossom between her and Micah.

Almost.

"Would you like to write a message on the card?"

Mack's laughter filled the shop. "I'd be lucky to get the first three letters of her name to fit on that tiny thing! Please, be my guest." He handed the card back to her.

Callie inked her pen and wrote, "I am my beloved, and my beloved is mine."

"It's perfect. Thank you, Callie." He paused, then added, "That thick-skulled cousin of mine is a fool if he doesn't snap you up before someone else does."

As she inscribed the envelope with "Sarah," Callie prayed Mack wouldn't notice that the mere mention of Micah had made her blush yet again.

Micah entered the mercantile and met the eyes of the storekeeper.

"Well, look what the cat drug in." Aggie spat a wad of tobacco into the spittoon beside the counter and held out her arms. "Hand that young'un over, 'fore I'm forced to whup you with my broom."

Micah handed the boy to her. "He takes to people quickly. Don't know any other boy his age who does that."

"That tells me he's used to bein' passed around." Aggie aimed a steely glance his way. "Didn't know you took a wife, Micah."

"Didn't." He began grabbing baby supplies from the shelves, then looked back at Aggie.

One brow rose on her wrinkled forehead. "Then, how'd you come by this stinky li'l package?"

Reid reminded him a bit of a monkey, the way he clung to her ample hip. And Aggie's honest face reminded him that, of all the people he knew, she was the only one he could count on to keep his secret without judging him.

While he told her about the letter he'd opened by mistake and the meeting that had ensued, she began to heat a tea kettle of water, then filled a wash pan with the tepid liquid. By the time he'd explained how he'd ended up being shouldered with the responsibility of caring for this baby, she'd stripped the boy bare and plunked him into the bath.

"You're gonna need a wife," she said as Reid splashed and giggled. "Man like you can't care for a baby on his own."

"I've done fair to middling so far."

Aggie harrumphed. "He needs more care than you can give him, what with all your ranchin' work." She wrapped the baby in a fat towel and carried him to the counter. "What d'you know 'bout keepin' a child fed? And what'll you do if he spikes a fever or falls and bumps his noggin?"

Micah's heart twisted into a knot. Aggie was right. He didn't know a thing about children—babies, in particular.

"Watch and learn." Aggie proceeded to show Micah how to diaper a baby, then undid the cloth and stood back. "Now, you try it."

It seemed someone had nailed his boots to the floor, for he couldn't budge from the spot.

"Well, go on," she said, giving him a gentle shove.

Somehow, he managed to get the piece of cloth wrapped around Reid, despite his kicking and wiggling. "I did it!" he finally said, lifting the baby for a congratulatory hug.

But before he had the chance to pull the boy close, the diaper plopped onto the counter. He gave Reid a sheepish smile.

"It's easy as pie," Aggie scolded, taking the baby from him.

"I've watched my ma bake enough pies to know that isn't easy." He pointed at the diaper. "And neither is that."

"You'll get the hang of it." She leveled him with one of her bold stares. "If you're keepin' him, that is."

"What else can I do? His mother is long gone."

Aggie scowled as she re-diapered Reid. "Well, he's better off without her, if you want my honest opinion. What sort of mother leaves her boy with a total stranger? Especially one she claims is a good-for-nothin' deadbeat?"

He bristled a bit at the phrase. While the circumstances seemed to indicate that Dan was a deadbeat, he knew better.

"There, now," Aggie said, planting a smooch on the baby's cheek. "He's clean and shiny as a new penny." She handed him back to Micah and grabbed a big straw basket from a shelf. "Come with me while I gather up some things you'll need for the trip home."

Into the basket, she tossed a stack of diapers, several gowns, a couple of bonnets, and a pair of bootees. As she added several glass bottles and rubber nipples, she told him that a good boiling would take away the nasty smell and taste of the rubber, then explained how to make gruel from rice paste, cow's milk, and broth, and how to feed the stuff to Reid using a porcelain pap boat. Into the basket, she also tossed a few rattles and a ring made from ox bone.

"What's that thing for?"

"He'll be cutting more teeth soon, and he'll need somethin' to gnaw on to ease the soreness."

"Oh." It made sense. And, at the same time, it made no sense at all. Micah wondered how he'd remember everything she'd told him. Wondered, too, how she'd come by all of this information. To his knowledge, Aggie had never married and had no children of her own. "Where'd you learn so much about young'uns, Aggie?"

Eyes narrowed, she said, "Let's just say I've lived a colorful life. I'll leave it at that." Her frown soon softened into a dreamy smile. "If I'd met somebody like you back in my day, well...." She harrumphed. "You'll need a crib. And a chair to set him in when you feed him. Just so happens I have one of each in the back room. You can't miss 'em. Fetch an oilcloth from the shelf above the canned peaches, too," she said, taking the baby from him. "Hard to tell what sort o' weather you'll run into between here and Eagle Pass."

Aggie carried Reid through the swinging doors that separated her living quarters from the store. "Now then, li'l fella, what-say you 'n' me rustle up somethin' to eat while your...uh, while Micah puts your things in the wagon?"

When Micah entered her private quarters half an hour later, Aggie was dozing in her big rocking chair with Reid sound asleep in her arms. After all she'd done to help him, the last thing Micah wanted to do was startle her awake. But he did want to hit the old post road before nightfall.

Just then, she opened one eye and whispered, "What're you gawkin' at, cowboy?"

"Has he been asleep this whole time?"

"No, I fed him some porridge and burped him real good," she said, tapping the baby's back. "I'd say he conked out 'bout ten minutes ago."

"Good. Maybe he'll sleep some in the wagon. I took a cradle, too, and padded it with one of those big pillows you had stowed on the shelf."

"Well, just take care that he doesn't roll onto his belly. A child could get smothered if he sleeps face-down in feathers for more 'n a few minutes."

"I'll check him often." *Please, God, remind me to check on him often.*

Aggie eased out of the chair and gave the sleeping baby to Micah. "Hold on to him, will ya, while I rustle you up some grub for the road."

"You've already done so much, Aggie. I couldn't ask—"

She was already rummaging in a cabinet when she said, "Hard to tell when I'll see you again, you big lummox. 'Specially now that you have a baby to care for. Don't worry. I won't charge you for the food."

Micah grinned. "Don't rightly know how to thank you, Ags. You're a good friend."

Aggie waved the compliment away and wiped a tear with the back of her hand. "Let this old friend give you some good advice: pay Gus Applegate a visit on your way out of town. He's got hisself a little office right beside the bank."

"Gus Applegate, the Texas Ranger?"

She shook her head. "Got hisself shot up in a gunfight a year or so ago and traded his silver star for a Pinkerton badge. But I have it on good authority that he's not workin' any cases right now, so you'd be smart to hire him to, you know, look into the background of one Pauline Devereaux."

It was a good idea, Micah conceded. "But Pauline was headed for San Francisco. It's unlikely he'd be eager to launch an investigation that could keep him away from his wife for months," he pointed out.

"Gus lost his wife a few months back. Doc said her ticker plumb gave out. Trust me, that man'll jump at any chance to get his mind off his troubles."

Nodding as Aggie bagged the food, Micah silently thanked God for the solution to yet another problem. He leaned to the side to peer behind Aggie.

"What're you doin', you fool cowboy?"

"Looking for angel's wings." He gave the top of her head an affectionate pat. "You seem to have misplaced your halo, too."

Aggie blushed and giggled like a schoolgirl, then clucked her tongue. "Now, get on your way," she said, shoving him through the back door. "You think I've got nothin' better to do than stand here yammerin' with the likes of you all day?"

She stood on the porch, her arms crossed over her ample bosom, as he laid Reid in the makeshift traveling bed and then gathered the reins. "Thanks again, Aggie. Man couldn't ask for a better friend. You've turned this awful day into something relatively pleasant."

"I have a feelin' when that young'un wakes up, you'll think of another word to describe your day."

Micah urged the horses forward. As they plodded along toward Gus Applegate's office at the edge of town, he wondered just how long he might enjoy the quiet.

He'd barely tied up the horses when the crying started. "Hush, now," he said softly, lifting the boy from his cradle. "You want to make a good impression on Mr. Applegate, don't you?"

"Well, as I live and breathe, if it ain't Micah Neville." Gravelly laughter filled the air. "How're them rowdy cousins o' yours, boy?"

Micah stepped onto the porch as Reid snuggled into the crook of his neck. "Fine, all fine."

Gus tousled the baby's thick, dark curls. "Got yourself hitched since I last saw you, eh?" Winking, he added, "Didn't waste any time gettin' yourself henpecked, either, I see." He leaned left and right to look over Micah's shoulder. "Where's the li'l one's mama? Down at that fancy dress shop, spending your hard-earned money whilst you look after the young'un, no doubt."

"I have no idea where she is."

Gus's playful smirk disappeared, and he cleared his throat.

"Aggie tells me you're a Pinkerton now," Micah said.

"True enough." Gus opened the door to his office and ushered his guests inside. "Coffee's hot. Want some?"

With a nod, Micah plopped onto the seat of a weathered wooden chair, then started talking while Gus poured the coffee.

He was still talking when Gus wrinkled his nose and waved a hand in front of his face. "Dunno what that boy ate for his last meal, but, for his sake and yours, I hope his mama saw fit to leave you with some clean diapers."

Micah winced at the odor, then grinned when he remembered the last thing Aggie had said as he'd rolled away from her store. *Dan, Dan, Dan. What have you gotten us into this time?* he thought.

Chapter 8

"I can't believe you haven't heard any of this before," Blanche Potter exclaimed with a perplexed look at Callie. "It's common knowledge 'round these parts that the Neville boys are trouble with a capital T."

Callie wanted to gasp. Or sigh. Or refuse to listen to any more gossip. But a fear of swallowing the needle between her teeth kept her quiet. Gently, she urged Blanche to turn, so that she could baste the hem of the back of her dress.

"I pity their mamas, especially Judith. That Daniel gave the woman fits almost from the day he was born. If it wasn't for Micah, why, it's hard to tell what might have become of him!"

At the mention of Micah's name, Callie pricked her thumb. Yet the woman seemed not to notice the hiccup, and she chattered on, oblivious. Hopefully, she would tell her what, exactly, Micah had done to save his cousin.

"But, to be fair," Blanche continued, "Daniel's a good man now, thanks in no small part to Micah.

And he started out such a sweet and quiet boy...before his twin sister died, that is."

"I hadn't heard that Dan had a twin sister."

"Oh, yes. Daisy was her name, and, oh, what a darling she was." Blanche drew tiny circles in the air beside her temple and whispered, "A tad slow, and nearly blind. Half deaf, too, poor little thing."

"How did she die?"

"Hydrophobia."

Hydrophobia, as in rabies? Callie knew very little about the disease, but she was aware that it caused a slow, horrible death. "That's terrible! How old was she?"

"Oh, I forget. Twelve, thirteen, maybe?" Blanche clucked her tongue. "She saw what she thought was a wounded dog. God love her, she was always trying to help every critter she could. Turned out it was a rabid coyote, and, when she went to comfort it, the mangy cur bit her." Frowning, Blanche shook her head. "Daniel was supposed to be minding her, you see, but the fool boy and those cousins of his were more interested in what was on the business end of their fishing poles than what Daisy was doing." She sighed. "Daniel blamed himself for the tragic way she died, and no matter how many folks told him it wasn't his fault, he had no esteem for his own life after that. You wouldn't believe the dangerous things he got himself into. Why, it was as though he hoped one of his escapades would kill him as punishment for what happened to Daisy."

Callie knew exactly how Dan had felt, but she couldn't very well admit that to Blanche. If only she'd had someone like Micah looking out for her. She pictured the tall, broad-shouldered cowboy with a smile as gentle as—

"Micah saved him from himself more times than I can count. Bailed him out of jail, broke up fights... stuck to Daniel like glue, he did. Tried to make the boy believe that what had happened to Daisy wasn't his fault, but Daniel wouldn't listen. Lord bless his bighearted soul, Micah kept that young fellow alive and healthy, till Levee came along and helped even more." Blanche turned to look in the mirror, then giggled. "Oh, Callie, it's just lovely! Why, you've made it look as though I still have a waist. And this shade of pink makes me look like a blushing bride again!"

Callie was so busy picturing Micah's long-lashed blue eyes that she barely had the presence of mind to say, "I'm happy you like it." *He must have been a rare boy*, she thought, *to give up so much of his own playtime to protect Dan.*

"When do you think you'll have it finished?"

Callie gathered her needles and thread, tucking them back inside her basket of notions. "Oh, in a day or two, at most." Sliding the basket onto the shelf beneath her sewing machine, she added, "Unless you need it sooner."

"No. There's really no hurry." Blanche winked. "Wouldn't want you pricking your pretty fingers again, now, would we?"

Callie immediately formed a fist, tucking the still-tender thumb out of sight. "I can deliver the dress on Sunday after services, if you'd like."

"That would be just perfect." Blanche loosened the drawstring on her purse and pulled out a wad of bills. "How much do I owe you?"

Callie held up a hand. "You can pay me Monday, after you've had a chance to try it on."

"Fair enough," Blanche said, shrugging into her shawl. She propped a fist on her hip and added, "If you want my advice, you'll spend some time at the mirror between now and Sunday."

"At the mirror?" Callie laughed. "Whatever for?"

"So you can practice not looking love struck. You know, in case Micah Neville attends services? For what it's worth, I happen to think you'd make a right handsome couple, but you don't want him to know that." She chuckled. "At least, not yet."

Love struck? Handsome couple? Callie couldn't decide if she felt hopeful or horrified.

"See you Sunday, then," Blanche said as she pushed the door open. "By the way, you'll catch more flies with a swatter, dearie."

Callie snapped her jaw closed as the door banged shut. Maybe she needed to give Blanche's advice some serious consideration. If the mere mention of his name caused gap-mouthed silence, how much more like a simpleton would she seem in the very presence of the handsome man?

At this rate, Micah wondered if he'd ever get back to Eagle Pass. He'd stopped a half dozen times to check on Reid and had taken advantage of each lull to inspect the baby's diaper or get more pap into him. All things considered, the boy wasn't a bad travel companion, once Micah figured out that he preferred riding on the wagon floor near his feet.

For the past couple of miles, Reid had snoozed peacefully. He'd make a good cowboy, because not everyone was born with the talent to sleep through long, plodding trips, especially in a wagon that bumped and bounced along the rutty, wheel-pocked road.

Micah found himself searching the baby's face for some telltale resemblance to his cousin. Strange, but he reminded Micah more of Callie Roberts than Dan, with eyelashes that were longer and darker than a heifer's. He could think of no one with a smile sweeter or lovelier than Callie's, and he wondered if her shiny, brownish-blonde curls actually felt as soft as his ma's favorite fur coat or merely looked as silky.

Chuckling, Micah shook his head. "You're losing your mind, man." He would have blamed the sun for the peculiar ramblings of his thoughts if it hadn't been obscured by dreary clouds. And he might have managed to hold the heat accountable for the way his heart thumped as he pictured her, but there was a finger-numbing chill in the air.

Reid stirred, and Micah secured his blankets around him. "Good thing Aggie thought to give us this thick, warm quilt, isn't it?" he whispered, tucking the satiny trim under the baby's chin.

He knew he ought to put the weather out of his mind and instead think about how on earth he would take care of this child. Spending time with his nephews and nieces, as well as his cousins' children, had made him keenly aware of how much time, effort, and energy went into keeping youngsters out of the flour bin and off of teetering tables. How could he hope to get his work done with Reid in tow? The boy was too big and wriggly to stuff into a papoose and take along. And then, there was the matter of explaining the boy to his family. Already, Micah could hear his ma's disappointed sigh and see his pa's confused expression. When it came to his sisters, he wondered who would be the first to say, "But he doesn't look anything like you, Micah Adam Neville!" And what about Beth? In her eyes, her big brother could do no wrong. How would her opinion of him change when he brought home a baby?

He gave a ragged sigh. And then, he had an idea. Ever since the death of her young husband a few months ago, Beth had been despondent. The family had tried a dozen different tactics to lift her spirits, but nothing had worked. She'd vacated the two-story home James had built her as a wedding gift and now spent most of her time holed up in her old bedroom at their parents' house. When she wasn't reading some maudlin tale by Dickens or Melville, she stared out her window at the grassy knoll where James had been buried. If Micah could talk her into moving into one of the spare rooms at his place to care for Reid, perhaps the chubby, giggling baby would take her mind off of losing her beloved husband.

First, though, he needed to concoct a believable story. He pictured Callie again and couldn't help but regret that her shop sat at the far end of town, miles in the opposite direction of the Lazy N, because something told him she'd know just what advice to dispense.

The thought made him chuckle again. He'd spent no more than three minutes in her company. For all he knew, the same coldhearted selfishness that had prompted Pauline to dump her son in a stranger's care was part of Callie's character, too.

Instantly, he dismissed the possibility. How could a woman with a smile so sweet and eyes so soulful be anything but good and decent?

Frustration immediately replaced hope, for what good, decent woman would link herself to a man whom she believed had fathered a child out of wedlock?

If Callie was as sweet as he believed her to be, she would probably approve of his decision to raise Reid as his own. But he'd never know for sure, because he couldn't tell her the truth about Pauline and the boy. At least, not without destroying Dan—and maybe even Levee—in the process.

In the past, he'd always taken matters such as this to the Lord—with a clean conscience, too, because he'd lived an honest, upright life, always committed to telling the truth, even when it hurt. How ironic that Micah now would need to become a skillful liar in order to protect the cousin who so often had protected him. Frustration gave way to fear as Micah realized that he was on his own. Only a fool would kneel at the foot of the cross, praying for help in living a lie, and expect God to answer him.

Chapter 9

The following week, Callie needed to make a trip to the Lazy N Ranch to deliver a dress she'd sewn for Lucinda, the housekeeper at the main residence. Callie had never been very good at handling a team, so she'd borrowed a horse and saddle from Birdie's husband, who owned the livery stable and harness shop, in addition to the hardware store and one of the three saloons in Eagle Pass. "Take care not to run her too fast," Otis had cautioned her, "'cause she's old and crotchety and might buck you right down onto the ground!"

As she hitched the mare to the iron post near the Nevilles' front porch, the horse nuzzled Callie's shoulder. "You don't seem so old and crotchety to me," she said, patting Kitty's mane. Remembering that Otis had also recommended tethering the horse near a water trough or a grassy area, she added, "Aren't you the lucky girl, because these thoughtful people have provided both!"

Kitty snorted and bobbed her head as if in agreement, then proceeded to munch the green sprouts that poked up between the flagstones along the path.

Callie moved the satchel from her right hand to her left, then rapped on the front door. "I won't be long, Kitty," she said over her shoulder. "Promise."

She barely heard the horse's second snort over the spirited welcome of Lucinda. "Please, come in!" she said. "I have coffee in the kitchen. Pie, too!"

"Sounds lovely. Maybe we can see how your dress fits before we sit down?" Yesterday, Mabel Andrews had told Callie that Lucinda had moved recently, from the home of Matthew and Eva Neville to Micah's parents' house, to help out while his mother, Hanna, recuperated from a bout of influenza.

Micah.... Callie had spent more time than usual braiding her hair that morning, in case she might run into him. She'd given her battered old boots a quick spit-shine, too, and selected her gingham dress for no other reason than it reminded her of his pale-blue eyes. Her heart fluttered a bit at the prospect of seeing him again.

Then, common sense reared its ugly head. Even if he had returned early from San Antonio, Micah wouldn't simply stroll into the room. For one thing, he lived in a ranch house of his own several miles from his folks' place. Surely, chores sent him into the fields at daybreak and kept him there until dusk.

Shaking the cobwebs from her mind, Callie opened her bag and carefully removed the neatly folded dress she'd made for Lucinda.

"Oh, *bonito!*" Lucinda exclaimed, holding it up to herself. "In thees dress, my seesters, they will be green with the envy!"

"Why don't you slip it on," Callie suggested, "so I can make sure it fits properly?"

The woman stepped into the pantry and returned moments later, wearing the new gown. "It make me feel *muy femenino*," she said, turning so that the skirt whirled around her ankles.

Callie smiled and pulled out a kitchen chair. "Would you mind standing here for a moment so that I can see if the hem is even all the way around?"

Lucinda stepped up and, bending, looked at the toes of her boots. "The heels of these new shoes, they are tall, like a flamenco dancer's." Giggling, she added, "I hope I have not forgot how to walk in them!"

Callie circled the chair a few times, fist to her chin, and inspected her handiwork. Yes, the hem was even, and it hung at the proper length.

"She is *perfecto*, no?"

"Oh, I'm sure if we looked closely enough, we'd find an imperfection somewhere." She helped Lucinda step down from the chair. "I'll pour the coffee while you get back into your other dress. Are you in the mood for a big wedge of pie, or just a tiny slice?"

"If I had the time," said a manly voice, "I'd eat the whole thing, all by myself."

Callie didn't know which startled her more, Micah's gravelly baritone or the baby he held in his arms. "Goodness, Micah, you scared me half to death!"

"Sorry," he said, grinning. "It's good to see you again, Miss Roberts."

"And both of us standing on our feet, no less!"

He chuckled as Lucinda came into the room and draped the dress over the back of a chair. "Ah, the happy wanderer," she said, hugging him, "he is home at last, I see!" She patted the baby's chubby cheek. "And who is thees fat fellow?"

Callie had never seen the child before, but that wasn't surprising. The Lazy N Ranch was miles from town, and the size of the Neville family boggled her mind. It did surprise her, however, that Lucinda didn't recognize the boy.

"Would you keep an eye on him for a few minutes?" Micah asked Lucinda. "I need to talk with Beth."

Still more surprising was the way he'd completely ignored Lucinda's question.

"Beth, she is in the parlor, staring out the window." Her brow furrowed slightly, Lucinda shook her head. "So sad, the way she still grieves for her man." Brightening a bit, she held out her arms, and the baby went willingly into them. "And what do they call you, little man?"

Frowning, Micah cleared his throat. "His name is Reid."

If she'd known the family better, Callie might have asked how the boy was related. Instead, she smiled and said, "What a good, strong name."

"*Sí. Muy bueno,*" Lucinda agreed.

Micah snorted—a peculiar reaction, Callie thought—and started for the parlor. In the hallway, he stopped and turned around and looked at Lucinda. "How's Ma?"

"She slept well last night and ate two eggs for breakfast. Good to see her sleep and eat, no?"

"Yes, all thanks to you, dear lady." He winked. "I'll have to think of a special way to thank Aunt Eva for suggesting that you move in here while Ma recovers. Just knowing you're nearby probably does her more good than any of those tonics Doc doles out."

Lucinda harrumphed, then kissed Reid's cheek. "With three healthy daughters living under the same roof, it seems a silly theeng for me to be here, but what do I know?" She shrugged. "I will stay until George and I go to Mexico."

"Ah, yes," he said, chuckling, "the great Chihuahua reunion. It's good you can both go together this year."

"*Sí*. We miss too many!"

"I won't be long," he said, then disappeared around the corner.

Once he was out of earshot, Callie asked, "What's wrong with his mother?" She thought she would confirm what she'd heard.

"The doctor, he say *la gripe*."

"Goodness. That's influenza, right? Very serious...."

"*Sí*." Lucinda stuck a spoon into her slice of pie, then held it to Reid's mouth. He slurped the apple syrup. "Me? I say she not take enough time to get recover." Another shrug. "But what do I know of such things?"

Callie nodded. As she prepared to serve herself a slice, Reid reached for her, and she gladly held him near. In one tick of time, Lucinda voiced a warning not to let the baby get hold of her dangly earrings. In the next, he wrapped a chubby fist around one of them. Laughing, Callie pried it free, then dropped it into her apron pocket. "Oh, now, don't stick out your bottom lip at me, little man. We both know it's best to remove all temptation from your reach!"

Lucinda tucked a laundry basket under one arm. "Looks like you can you handle the *niño* while I gather the wash, *sí*?"

Gurgling, Reid reached for the pastry. "I think we'll be fine," Callie said, laughing. "At least, until this pie pan is empty!"

The instant Callie sat on a well-worn kitchen chair, the baby snuggled close and leaned his head on her chest. A weirdly wonderful feeling wrapped around her, and she couldn't decide if longing or love described it better. Resting her cheek atop his head, Callie sat back and began to rock, humming quietly as she stroked his silky hair. "Is Micah your father, little one?" she whispered. "And if he isn't, how did you two become traveling companions?"

The good ladies of Eagle Pass had made a point to tell her all about every available man in town, and Micah's name had been on the list. Had he been married and widowed before she and Jonah had moved to town? No, Reid wasn't nearly old enough for that. Yet it wasn't likely the baby was the result of other circumstances, because a scandal like that would have set the gossips' tongues to wagging and telling her to stay away from Micah.

Perhaps friends or kin in another town had chosen Micah as their baby's guardian, or poor little Reid had been abandoned, only to have Micah come along just in time to save him from an orphan's life. She supposed it was even possible that, while conducting Lazy N business, Micah had taken a secret wife—a woman of whom his family wouldn't have approved. Perhaps she had died of some dread disease, like influenza or the cancer.

But what did it matter how Micah had come into possession of Reid, when every glance made it clear that he cherished the boy!

Oh, to have a man like Micah in her life, loving and caring for her and their children. Eyes closed, she pictured herself in a kitchen much like this one, where supper simmered on the stove as she folded her husband's trousers and work shirts. In her day-dream, a toddler stacked wooden blocks at her feet, while an infant slumbered in its cradle nearby. Callie heaved a soft, sad sigh. Maybe someday, the Lord would teach her how to atone for the sins of her past, but until—unless—that happened, she didn't deserve to dream such dreams.

Muffled voices filtered through the curtained glass doors separating the parlor from the kitchen. She tried reciting the Twenty-third Psalm so as not to eavesdrop. But not even that blocked her from hearing Micah say, "...so I hired a Pinkerton detective."

"Sounds to me like you've decided to keep him."

Callie guessed the pretty voice must belong to his sister Beth.

"Goodness, Micah, that's a lifetime commitment."

Silence.

Then, "Have you given any thought to what you'll do with the child while your detective conducts his investigation? I mean, a baby is a lot of work, and—"

"In the meantime," Micah interrupted, "I was hoping you'd do me an enormous favor by helping out with him."

There was a long, uncomfortable pause before she said, "You know I'd do anything for you, brother dear. But, caring for a—a baby? Especially so soon after...." She cleared her throat. "Does Ma know?"

If you feel this overwrought, hearing all this, just imagine how poor Micah must feel!

She heard him groan, then say, "No, not yet. I'd hoped to settle the matter of who'd take care of the boy before I saddled her with something else to worry about."

"Yes, yes, that makes sense, I suppose, especially considering how frail she's been these past few months. Leave it to you to think of everyone else's needs before your own."

Callie found herself smiling a bit, though she couldn't say whether it was because of Beth's last comment or the baby's sleepy breaths, puffing softly against her cheek. If Micah's sister didn't agree to help him out, she would volunteer. "I have no idea how," she whispered into Reid's hair, "but we could make it work. I just know we could!"

"This might be good for you, too, Beth. You need something to occupy your time and get you out of this house."

His sister's brittle laugh made it clear that joy was something the girl hadn't felt in quite a long time.

"You make a good point. It would certainly make it a lot harder for Emma and Astrid to try to marry off their widowed sister to every unattached cowboy who strolls into town."

Micah laughed, too. "If our baby sisters are this nosy at their tender ages, I hate to think what they'll be like once they're old married ladies!" He paused. "You'd have your own room, and, don't forget, there's indoor plumbing at my house."

"Oh, fine. Tempt me with modern conveniences, why don't you!"

"I hope that's a yes."

Expectation rang loud in Micah's voice, filling Callie with an urge to comfort him with a warm hug and reassuring words, even as she hoped that Beth would gently refuse his request. Reid seemed completely content and comfortable here in her arms, and she was more than happy to have him there.

"Where is this mysterious baby, anyway?" Beth wanted to know.

"In the kitchen with Lucinda. Would you like to meet him before you pack a bag and we head over to my house?"

Pack? Oh, no! Beth must have said yes while she'd been woolgathering.

Each footstep that brought the brother and sister nearer to the kitchen might as well have been a hammer blow to Callie's head. She stiffened and held Reid tighter, because she didn't want to let him go; she wanted to be the one to help Micah out of his predicament!

Guilt washed over her for putting her own dreams and desires ahead of what was best for them. Micah had as much as said that caring for Reid would help his widowed sister recover from her grief. *More proof that you're a self-centered little shrew, Callie Roberts!*

"I'd love to help you, brother dear, you know I would, but...."

But? Callie bit her lower lip. Dare she hope?

Beth entered the kitchen ahead of her brother. "...but I've already made plans to leave for Oklahoma City," she continued, "to spend some time with James's family." The moment she caught sight of the baby, Beth smiled. "Why, hello, Callie. I had no idea you were out here all by yourself!"

It was all Callie could do to tear her gaze from Micah's piercing blue eyes. "Lucinda is outside," she managed to squeak out, "taking the laundry down from the line, and I volunteered to mind Reid until she came back in. Or, until you came back. Or until—" *Hush, Callie. Just stop talking!*

The left side of Micah's mouth lifted in a grin. "I see," he said, nodding.

"Oh, Micah, he's beautiful, just beautiful," Beth gushed. "No wonder you were so quick to scoop him up. Why, now that I see him, I'm almost sorry for sending that telegram to my mother-in-law, promising to visit. I love him already!"

From the look on his face, Callie could tell that his disappointment that Beth couldn't help seemed to be at war with big-brotherly love for his sad-eyed sister. When affection won out and he broke into a broad smile, Callie's heart fluttered. Yet it made no sense for her to feel this way about a man she knew so little about. Why, she'd known Seth for months before anything even remotely akin to this sensation had bubbled inside of her. Maybe she could blame the sausage she'd eaten yesterday or the cider she'd sipped at lunch. Either of those reasons made more sense than admitting she was falling in love with a near stranger, or that she wanted to become full-time caretaker to—

"Ah, well. What's done is done, and the Lord will provide," Micah said. "When do you leave?"

Beth knelt beside the chair and finger-combed dark curls from Reid's forehead. "The day after tomorrow."

That didn't leave Micah much time to find someone to help him with the baby. A wave of relief coursed through Callie, and she would have made her offer right then, if Lucinda hadn't blown into the room and plopped the laundry basket onto the table. "George and I leave soon, too," she said to Beth. "But as you go east, we will go in a whole different direction."

Hanna entered the room next and set down her book beside the laundry basket. "Well, look who's home!" she said, wrapping Micah in a motherly hug. "It's good to have you back, son." She pressed a kiss to his cheek, then added, "I trust that your trip was blessedly uneventful."

Callie would have paid a high price to read his mind at that moment! Thankfully, his mother possessed no such talents, for she turned to Lucinda and her daughter and said, "Everyone at the Lazy N will miss you two while you're away."

Reid stirred, glanced around the room, and then burrowed deeper into Callie's arms.

"Why, Callie Roberts, how lovely to see you!" Hanna pulled up a chair and tickled Reid's chin. "I had no idea you'd taken a husband, yet here you sit with a baby on your lap!" Hanna mussed his dark curls. "Just look at that hair. Why, you must have had heartburn the entire time you carried him!" Giggling, she added, "How did I miss out on this glorious news? And when will I meet this beautiful boy's daddy?"

"Oh, my," Beth said, covering her face with her hands. "Oh, dear. Goodness me."

Callie glanced at Micah, hoping to read in his eyes or on his face some hint of how he wanted her to proceed.

He cleared his throat. "He belongs to...uh, he's...." Frowning, he ran a hand through his hair. "The boy is my responsibility." His frown deepened. "Temporarily." He coughed. "I...uh, I'll explain it all later."

Callie barely knew him, and yet she could see how unlikely it was that he'd fulfill that assurance. Had his mother read the truth in his expression, as well? The answer quickly became evident as the woman narrowed her eyes and pursed her lips. When she finally opened her mouth, Callie got the distinct impression that Hanna wasn't about to sing a hymn.

Beth chose that moment to come out of hiding. "So, tell us, Callie, what do you and Jonah have planned for Thanksgiving?"

Out of the corner of her eye, Callie saw Micah exhale a breath of relief. She also saw Hanna's left eyebrow rise a bit.

"Oh, the same as usual, I expect." Hopefully, they didn't hear the tremor in her voice. "We'll probably work until noon or one o'clock, share a quiet dinner, and then afterward sit by the fire with a couple of good books."

Hanna lifted her chin. "Well," she said, "we'd love for you to join us this year."

Join them? Surely, Callie had misunderstood.

The woman crossed both arms over her chest. "Dinner is at two at Matthew and Eva's. But you're welcome to come earlier." She shot a heated glance Micah's way. "And since it seems my son has involved you with this 'mystery baby,' you'll bring him, too, of course."

Callie saw Micah stiffen. She didn't need to know him well, didn't need the details of his past, either, to recognize the discomfort etched on his handsome face. If he'd fathered this child out of wedlock, well, Callie didn't feel she was in any position to judge him. She'd heard dozens of tales about men who, under similar circumstances, had simply walked away from their responsibilities. Didn't Micah deserve some credit for wanting to do right by the boy?

For two years now, thanks to her selfish decision and the destruction it had wrought, Thanksgiving had been just Jonah and she, whereas Micah had spent a lifetime in the bosom of his loving family. Maybe that's what inspired her to say, "Jonah and I will be there, and I'm sure my little man, here, would love to come, too."

As if on cue, Reid hugged Callie tighter and shouted, "Ma-*ma*!"

Micah, Beth, Lucinda, and Hanna all seemed to share one thought: *Your little man?*

A nervous grin threatened to split her face in two, and the only thing she could think to say was, "May I bring a pie to share?"

"That was a very brave—and very stupid—thing you did back there."

Callie cringed. It had all happened so fast that she couldn't remember who'd said what or in what order. After her little announcement, Micah had wasted no time offering to drive her back to her shop, and, oh, how the minutes had dragged on while she'd waited for him to tie Kitty to the back of his wagon! She'd expected a lecture of sorts during the trip, but was it too much to hope he'd deliver it with a modicum of neighborly kindness?

"It's still a long way to my place," she said, chin up and shoulders squared. "I hope you'll find it in yourself to forgive me before we roll into Eagle Pass."

"Forgive you?" Micah chuckled and slowed the team. "Is that what you think? That I'm angry with you?"

Well, if you aren't, you're certainly doing a good job of making it seem that way!

"I've been blessed with a big, loving family, but, until today, I could honestly say that only one person—my cousin Dan—has ever done anything like that for me." He turned slightly toward her in the wagon seat. "I'm grateful as can be, and extremely touched by what you tried to do back there, but...." He stared straight ahead for an uncomfortable moment. "It's just...I'm having a real hard time understanding why you'd put your reputation on the line that way." Meeting her eyes ever so briefly, Micah added, "You don't even know me."

There's where you're wrong, she thought. *I do know you, Micah Neville, and while others might call me crazy to admit it, I like what I know!*

"I grew up with sisters, so I knew by that look on your face that you were fixing to say something shocking. I should've stopped you instead of standing there like a simpleton." He gave an exasperated sigh. "Callie, what were you thinking?"

"That's just it. I wasn't thinking." Callie sighed, too. "When your mother started asking questions about the baby, well, you looked like a lost lamb, and the words just started popping out of my mouth." She shrugged. "I'm sorry if my lack of self-control forced you to tell them everything...." Callie bit her lower lip, wondering how to conclude the statement. She didn't believe for a minute that he'd told them everything, but this was neither the time nor the place for such a confrontation. "Sooner than you'd planned," she decided to tack on.

"I'm the one who should be saying I'm sorry."

To whom? she wondered. *And for what?*

"Guess your way of redirecting the truth worked pretty well."

Goodness. Was that his polite way of saying that he saw her as a masterful liar? "I never meant to mislead them. It's just...you looked so helpless, and...and I didn't know how else to stop your mother's inquisition."

He laughed—a peculiar reaction, Callie thought with a frown, because she failed to see anything humorous about the situation.

But she forgot all about her ire when he said, "I thought Lucinda's eyes would pop clean out of her head when Reid called you 'Mama.' Why, it looked to me—to everyone, I'm sure—as though that little monkey understood exactly what you were doing, and he aimed to play along."

"Oh, I know! Wasn't it just delightful? I can't tell you how it tickled me when he said it! Why, ever since I was a little girl, I've dreamed of having a sweet baby of my very own." She was rambling but felt powerless to stop. "And a house, and everything that goes with it, including—" *Good grief, Callie! Hush, before you start him running so far and fast, you'll never see or hear from him again!*

For the baby's sake more than her own, she prayed that her blathering wouldn't cause Micah to change his mind about letting her keep Reid at her place.

The brim of his Stetson cast a shadow over his face, and she couldn't read his expression. Callie tugged at her own hat, hoping to hide her flush of embarrassment. "You'll make some boy a real good mama."

Well, now, she hadn't expected him to say that!

"Someday."

Now, that was more what she would have expected.

"Not every woman is cut out to be a mother, you know. I've seen plenty who fuss and fumble and fret, and I believe it's because they don't have what it takes." He gave one nod of his head, as if to underscore his opinion, then smiled at Reid, fast asleep in the cradle between their feet. "But that young'un took to you right off. That tells me you're a natural."

Callie grinned slightly in response to the compliment, then felt the immediate need to balance it with a healthy dose of reality. "That's more because of his disposition than mine. He behaved the same way with Lucinda, your mother, and Beth. Why, if I didn't know better, I'd say he'd known them all his life."

"He's a friendly little fella, I'll give you that," Micah conceded. "But you didn't hear him calling any of them 'Mama.' Didn't see him fall asleep in their arms or snuggle close for comfort when the mood in the room turned sour, either."

As tempting as it was to bask in the glow of his admiration, Callie knew that she'd better get a grip on her tumultuous emotions, because when Beth returned from Oklahoma, of course he'd revert to his original plans for Reid's care. But she doubted living with that expectation would stop it from hurting like crazy when it happened.

"If you're worried I'll reassign Reid's care to Beth when she gets back from visiting James's family, you can rest easy."

The fact that he'd sensed her fears made her admire him all the more. If only he were a bit more like her—selfish and self-centered, and—

"I chose well, making you Reid's primary caretaker. He's already been through enough, and unless you change your mind, I have no intention of subjecting him to yet another move."

Did he know the effect his gentle, thoughtful nature was having on her? Oh, but she'd have to guard her heart very carefully, indeed. Callie sighed. "I'll care for him as if he were my own, and I won't change my mind. You have my word."

"That'll make it easier to leave him."

Reid chose that moment to cry out, and Micah stopped the wagon so that Callie could check on him. "His diaper's a little damp," she said, "but there's no sense in exposing his little bottom to the cold night air. I'm sure Jonah has a nice, warm fire going, so I'll clean him up once I get home."

"What are your plans, once we get him there?"

"I think he'll be most comfortable upstairs, in the room beside mine. It's always bright and sunny in there, with plenty of space for his things."

Micah chuckled as the lights of Eagle Pass came into view. "Speaking of which, I'll likely be here well past midnight, getting his things put away."

"We can save that till later, can't we?"

"The job has to be done, Callie."

"Yes, yes, of course. But it doesn't all have to be done tonight. Jonah will help you unload everything from the wagon and take it to the parlor. For starters, Reid needs only his crib, and I'm sure my brother and you will make short work of setting it up. Tomorrow, I'll put away the rest of his things.

That way, you'll be on the road sooner, with more hope of getting a decent night's sleep."

Why, oh why, did Micah's presence incite her to chatter like a chipmunk? She'd have to practice silence. Or, at the very least, slow the flow of her words a tad.

Micah stopped the wagon mere inches from the walk that led to her front door. Maybe someday, he'd teach her how to handle a team that way.

"See there?" he said, jumping down from the seat.

Before she had a chance to say, "See what?" he said, "Always thinking of everyone else. I was right. You're a natural-born caretaker."

You wouldn't say that if you knew about my sinful, selfish past! Now she had something else to pray about tonight: how to keep him from finding out how many people had paid the price for her self-centeredness.

Chapter 10

$\mathcal{H}$alfway home from Eagle Pass, Micah said a silent prayer of thanks that the horses knew the way from the ranch to town and back again almost as well as he did, because only the good Lord knew where his daydreaming might have put him otherwise.

He hadn't expected to get Reid's room set up so quickly. And after spending eight days with the boy as they traveled homeward, he hadn't expected he'd go so happily and willingly with Callie, either. Most of all, he hadn't thought that driving away from her place, alone, would hurt worse than having a molar extracted.

The nearest he could figure, he'd lost his mind somewhere between San Antonio and home, because no right-minded man would care this much, this soon, for a damp-bottomed baby and his pretty new nanny. But care he did, and it shamed him a little to admit that he felt at least as much affection for these two near strangers as for any kinsman he could name.

He didn't suppose it was entirely his fault that he'd lost all reason. Reid's quick smile and easy temperament made him downright irresistible. As for Callie, well, he needed only to picture the look on her face when he'd told the story of how Reid had come into his life to know why he'd fallen Stetson over boots for her.

Grinning, he remembered how she'd figured out in an instant that he hadn't told her the whole story. "I understand why you're keeping the rest of the truth to yourself," she'd said.

And it had taken all the willpower he could muster not to tuck that wayward curl behind her ear when she'd added, "The less you tell me now, the less I'll have to lie about later."

He hadn't known how to respond to that, and, as he'd sat, stammering and stuttering like a brainless idiot, Callie had smiled, setting his heart to fluttering and the blood to pounding in his veins. "Micah Neville, everybody's hero," she'd said.

Some hero, he thought, missing her so badly that he felt like a snot-nosed schoolboy whose mama had made him put his pet frog back in the pond.

Eyes closed, he inhaled the fresh, clean scent of line-dried linens. He'd worked up a sweat, hauling Reid's crib up the narrow staircase, and, after he'd put the contraption together, Callie had fetched him a bright white washcloth and towel and invited him to use the tiny lavatory upstairs. The room sparkled and shined, same as every other one in her house, and it seemed to him that she'd put a lot of thought into the placement of every knickknack and candlestick. The observation had roused a yearning like none he'd ever known. *Man could grow to like being cared for by a woman like that.*

"You're one lucky little fella, Reid," he muttered, "'cause you'll get to enjoy her woman's touch every day."

The horses' ears swiveled at the sound of his voice, listening for any new instructions from their master. "Sorry, boys," he said, chuckling softly. "Good thing you can't talk, or I'd be the laughing-stock of Maverick County."

His stomach rumbled, reminding him that Callie had offered to fry him up some eggs. "All that running up and down the stairs must have worked up your appetite," she'd said. And though he'd wanted to stay, he'd declined. "You've already saved my bacon, offering to help out with Reid," he'd said. "Wouldn't be very polite if I took your eggs, too, now, would it?"

God bless her, she'd wrapped two buttered biscuits in a blue-checkered napkin. "In case your stomach changes its mind during the drive home," she'd said.

Micah believed he'd hear her musical laughter in his dreams, maybe long into the next day and night.

As he unwrapped the snack, he saw that she'd tucked two cookies into the napkin, too, which told him she'd seen him drooling at the plate of treats on her sideboard. He bit into one, savoring the texture and flavor. If he made a list of her talents, it would likely be as long as his forearm. *Yep,* he thought, *a man sure could do worse than end up with a pretty little thing like Callie.*

Everything she'd said and done led him to believe that if he decided to pursue her, she wouldn't object. But it just wouldn't be fair to start up something until Applegate finished his investigation. Callie was beautiful, inside and out, and she deserved far better than a relationship built on half-truths and bare-faced lies. So, until he had all the facts about Reid, it was best to keep his feelings about her to himself.

Still, it was impossible to deny those feelings. In addition to her beauty, Callie had the most selfless spirit he'd ever seen. She'd refused the cash he'd offered her for caring for Reid. "If he needs anything that he doesn't already have, you can buy it when you come to visit him," she'd said. "Soon, I hope!"

She loved that baby already—that much was obvious in every word, look, and gesture. It could take weeks for Applegate to conclude his investigation, and it didn't take a genius to figure out that, as the days passed, she'd come to love the boy all the more. What would become of them all if it turned out that Reid was, in fact, Dan's child?

The image of Callie's face flashed in his brain, followed by a picture of her sitting across the table from him at Thanksgiving dinner, balancing Reid on her knee. Every year, after Uncle Matthew said the blessing, the family took turns sharing what they were thankful for. Usually, Micah mentioned the normal things—good health, a solid roof over his house, and plenty of food in the storeroom. This year, after listing those, he'd tack on a few silent words of gratitude that God had sent Callie Roberts and baby Reid into his life. And he'd pray that no matter what happened when Applegate concluded his investigation and returned from San Francisco, he could be thankful for the same things next year, too.

"Well," Beth said around a bite of her apple, "you can hardly blame Ma for reading you the riot act." She sat beside Micah on the porch swing. "It was a lot to absorb, all at once like that."

Micah chewed a stiff blade of grass, moving it from one side of his mouth to the other. "I suppose." He'd told them as much of the truth as he could afford to, not a word more.

"I think everyone would have an easier time accepting the news if they knew with certainty whether or not little Reid was your son."

He'd been feeling edgy and cranky of late, thanks to nightmares of Pauline Devereaux. That, and the fact that every time he met up with a Neville at the ranch or in town, he got "the look." It hadn't been easy, living this lie to protect his cousin Dan. Now, in response to Beth's not-so-veiled demand to divulge the details to everyone else, he said, "The truth will come out in good time. The family will just have to trust me until then."

"None of this secrecy is necessary, Micah. Don't you think our family is inclined to believe you, rather than jump to conclusions and condemn you for giving in to temptation in San Antonio?"

Micah slapped a hand to the back of his neck and prayed for patience. Beth was leaving in the morning, or he might have given in to his surly mood and shot back with a snarly retort. Yesterday, she'd admitted that if she liked it in Oklahoma, she might stay there permanently. In case that happened, he didn't want their parting words to be angry and bitter. So, he softened his tone to say, "Do me a favor, will you?"

"Of course!"

"Instead of judging me so harshly, how about praying for me, instead?"

She turned to face him. "Oh, Micah, is that how it seems? That I'm judging you? I never meant to come across that way. I love you more than life itself, and I wouldn't hurt you for all the world."

He nodded.

"I can't imagine what you must be going through, not knowing where Reid's mother is, or if she'll come back to claim him after you've formed a strong bond with him."

Whether his feelings for Reid ran deep because of the possibility of the boy being Dan's or because of Reid's endearing personality, Micah couldn't say, but the bond had formed even before Pauline left them at the station in San Antonio.

"It's best, I think, that he's with Callie most of the time," Beth said.

"Why?"

"Because it'll make the parting so much easier when—"

He ground his molars together. "Beth," he interrupted her, "do me another favor?"

Smiling, she squeezed his hand. "Name it."

"Hush, will you, please?"

Her smile faded.

"It's just that I know exactly how much I stand to lose if...if things don't go right."

She tilted her head. "Then, it must be nice to know you'll never lose Callie."

Where would she get such a notion?

"I was in the perfect position to watch the two of you yesterday, working out the plans regarding

Reid, as if you'd both raised him from the day he was born. Why, you were more like an old married couple than two people brought together by a—" She stopped talking so suddenly that Micah thought she might have a bit of apple stuck in her throat. "By this peculiar and perplexing situation."

"Ouch."

Beth crinkled her nose. "Ouch?"

"That must've been hard, keeping what you really wanted to say to yourself."

She leaned close to whisper, "I'm going to miss everyone around here, but you know what? I'll miss you most."

He slid an arm around her shoulders. "You'll write me, won't you?"

"Only if you promise to write back."

Micah grimaced. "You know I don't like making promises I can't keep."

"I don't expect you to answer every letter, silly." Standing, she said, "Will you help me bring my valise and trunk into the downstairs hall? It'll make it so much easier for Mack to load them into the wagon in the morning."

Chuckling, Micah got to his feet and slung an arm around her shoulders again. "No problem," he teased. "Everyone knows that I look for ways to make Mack's life easier."

"It isn't his fault you're twice as strong as he is."

"And twice as handsome."

"And twice as smart."

"We'd be remiss if we didn't say twice as kind." He winked. "And twice as tolerant of silly little sisters."

She stopped on the landing, threw her arms around him, and held on so tightly that his vest muffled her voice when she said, "Callie's a lucky girl to have a wonderful, brave, caring man like you in love with her, and Reid's a lucky boy, too, to have a man like you committed to his well-being after he was cast off by a strange woman." Taking a step back, she looked into his eyes. "Maybe, if their luck holds out, you'll all be a big, happy family by the time I come home."

He didn't have the heart to tell her that he didn't believe in luck. Never had. Never would. But that didn't stop him from hoping, just a little bit, that there was some truth to her words.

"You're a hard man to find."

Micah stopped brushing the horse and looked up into the eyes of the man who was more like a brother than a cousin to him. "I thought you were in Lubbock." For the first time in his life, Micah was not happy to see Dan.

"Was. Got back a day early." Dan held out a sack. "Sugar cookies. Levee baked 'em to welcome me home."

Micah waved them away. "Thanks, but I'm still stuffed from breakfast."

Dan shrugged. "Good. More for me." He grinned. "So, Beth's on her way to Oklahoma City, is she?"

Small talk. Micah hated it almost as much as the secret he'd been keeping. And so did Dan. Which told him his cousin had heard about Reid and had come searching for a polite way to introduce the subject. "Yep."

"Left today, did she?"

"Mmm-hmm."

"Well, the trip's sure to do her good."

"Yep." Maybe small talk wasn't such a bad thing if it bought him time to come up with a believable explanation for the questions brewing in Dan's brain.

"Anything new?"

"Nope."

Dan inspected a cookie, then took a bite. "That isn't how I heard it."

Micah went back to brushing the mare's rump. "Then, how 'bout telling me how you *did* hear it."

"Well," Dan said, "way the story goes, you came back from San Antone with a wagonload of seed... and a motherless baby." Dan crumbled a cookie into his palm and held the treat under the horse's nose. As she munched, he added, "You want to fill me in, or do I have to beat the story outta you?"

He did his best to mirror Dan's playful grin. "There's nothing to tell."

"You come home with a young'un and no wife and expect me to believe there's nothin' to tell?"

Micah heard none of the self-righteous judgment in Dan's voice that he'd heard in the voices of his other family members, but that didn't mean he could handle the truth. "Way I hear it, you're the one with a story to tell."

Pain glittered in Dan's eyes. "About Levee and the baby, you mean."

Micah nodded and then listened while Dan explained how this miscarriage had been harder on Levee than the others. Hearing it riled Micah. What sort of cockeyed justice was it that Dan and Levee's dreams of parenthood had been snuffed yet again, while Reid's mother viewed parenthood as a nightmare? "How's Levee holding up?"

"Clingin' to hope, same as always." Dan shook his head. "Thank God one of us has faith."

Yes, Levee was strong, all right, but strong enough to help her cope with the knowledge that Dan might have fathered a child with another woman, when she couldn't carry one to term herself? Micah didn't think so. "And you?"

Dan harrumphed. "I have good days and bad days."

Micah recognized that tone and slump-shouldered stance all too well. It was Dan's way of admitting that staying away from whiskey hadn't been easy. Micah was more certain than ever that he'd been right to keep Reid's background to himself. "So," he said cautiously, "Levee has decided to lean on God again this time."

"Yep."

"And what about you?"

"I've been prayin' for her."

"I think you know as well as I do that isn't what I meant."

Dan's halfhearted grin preceded a one-shouldered shrug. "Then, why don't you save us both a lot of time," he said wryly, "and tell me what you *did* mean."

Micah held his breath, praying Dan wouldn't confess that he'd found courage in a bottle, as he had so many times before.

"Don't worry, cousin. I haven't had a drop."

But you've wanted to, haven't you?

"It's crossed my mind. I expect it will, for the rest of my days. But I could never do that to Levee."

"Shouldn't do it to yourself, either."

"I made a promise to my ma, long before I met Levee," Dan said, his voice a grating whisper. "Swore by all that was good in my life that I was done with whiskey for good. I meant it then, and I mean it now."

Then, why did it feel as if Dan was on the verge of returning to the life that had left Reid without a mama and put Micah in the tight spot of pretending to be his daddy?

"You've got my word," Dan said. "I haven't been near the stuff, not even once in all this time."

"I believe you." Even as he said it, Micah prayed that someday, he'd mean those words.

Dan picked up another brush, and the two of them worked in companionable silence, as they'd done so many times before. Out of the corner of his eye, he peered over the mare's backside at the man who might well be little Reid's pa. Just then, a strange, unfamiliar sensation rolled over him, and Micah had no idea how to deal with it. He'd worked hard learning to separate his emotions from reality. Without that ability, he couldn't survive as a rancher. He'd relied heavily on that skill when he'd delivered Longhorns to the slaughterhouse, sold bottle-fed colts at auction, watched his pa or his uncles stuff runt barn kittens into the drowning sack, and seen hand-trained herd dogs trampled in stampedes.

Sometimes, Micah thought he'd taught himself too well to stiffen his spine and grit his teeth to get through things, for his uncles and cousins had come to expect a certain degree of toughness from him, and they looked to him for courage when theirs faltered. And Micah did not always feel courageous enough to meet that expectation.

It wouldn't be too long, now, before Gus Applegate turned in a report. The realization made him
think of Reid, big-eyed and happy, despite his unusual entrance into the Neville fold. Micah's heart
swelled with pride and love, then hammered with
fear. Immediately, he prayed for strength. Because, if
he lost that boy, he'd need it as never before.

Chapter 11

$\mathscr{F}$ortunately, Reid wasn't a fussy baby, but he'd learned to crawl within days of moving in with Callie and Jonah, and she'd had to train herself to work a different schedule. By squeezing in a few hours of work between his bedtime at seven o'clock and the midnight hour and during his afternoon naps, Callie put in nearly as many hours as she had before his arrival. And she had a lot of work to do, considering that the good ladies of Eagle Pass needed new dresses and gowns to wear to various Christmas celebrations next month. Plus, Callie had agreed to sew the costumes for the annual children's Christmas pageant.

With six teeth, and more on the way, Reid could eat the softer foods she prepared for Jonah and herself, and the more Reid ate, the faster he grew, which meant letting down the hems of his gowns every week. Just that morning, Callie had cut a longer, bigger gown from the bolt of blue cotton she'd been saving. She'd held it up in front of him and laughed. "Now, be a good boy, and let me at least get the buttons sewn on before you outgrow this one. All right?" Next, she'd tucked Reid into his high chair and given him a biscuit to teethe on.

"Buh," he'd said, grinning. "Buh!"

"Yes, you most certainly *are* a big boy." All the more reason to spend as much time as possible with him every day, despite the demands of her business. "When Micah gets here tonight, he isn't going to believe how much you've grown."

Micah.... He'd be here any time now. And, for the first time since meeting him, Callie didn't look forward to seeing him.

Earlier in the week, when she'd delivered Birdie's new blouses to the little apartment behind the livery stable, the older woman told her that Micah had been there, too, not ten minutes earlier, placing an order for a new saddle. "Said he felt like a lout," Birdie said, "not doing more to help you out with the boy."

She might as well have said "snake" or "barn rat" as "boy," and Callie had wanted to blurt out, "That boy has a name, you know!" His questionable parentage wasn't his fault, after all! But Birdie had never given her the chance.

"Said if I ran into you, I'm to let you know he'll be over to see you in a week, when he comes back to pay for his saddle."

"Well," Callie had sniffed, "when he fetches the saddle—first things first, you know—you can let *him* know that supper is at five, and Reid's bedtime is seven."

"Don't be too hard on him," Birdie had said. "The boy ain't perfect, but who of us is? Besides, he's sweet on you."

Sweet on her! Why, the phrase had hung in her memory ever since, and—

"Jo?" Reid said, jostling her out of her daze. "Jo!"

Smiling, she said, "I don't know where Jonah is, sweet boy." Callie dropped a few biscuit crumbs to his tray. "But as soon as you've finished your snack, we'll take a little walk and see where that brother of mine has been hiding."

Reid smiled, too, and bounced in his high chair. "Jo...*Jo!*"

"That's my name," Jonah said, bending to rub noses with the baby, "don't wear it out!" Reid squealed with delight. "Is he finished with his snack? I'd like to play with him for a little while."

Callie nodded. "But keep him inside, all right? I'll need to get him cleaned up and changed in a few minutes so he'll be ready when his—when Micah gets here."

At first, Micah's decision to keep the details about Reid from Callie so that she would not need to lie had made sense to her. But, with every passing day, she had come to love the baby more and more, and it had occurred to her that Micah could—God forbid!—fall ill or develop some peculiar condition that might prevent him from sharing the truth with her. Discussing Reid's parentage now seemed an urgent necessity, and, once Reid was tucked in for the night, she intended to ask Micah about it. Meanwhile, she saw no point in confusing the baby by referring to Micah as someone else, such as his father.

As if on cue, she heard the rattle of his wagon out front. Callie smoothed her skirt, then tucked a few loose curls behind her ears. As she did so, she noticed that her sleeve was starting to fray. It would have to wait until tomorrow, at the earliest. In the meantime, she rolled up the cuffs to hide the unseemly edge.

"Da!" Reid squealed when she opened the door. "Da-da!"

"Evening, Callie." Micah whipped off his hat and wiped his boots on the braided rug inside the door. Though he'd greeted her, his eyes were on Reid. With every step he took closer to the baby, Micah's smile grew, and Callie couldn't help but join him. Was it her imagination, or had he actually grown taller and broader and handsomer since the last time she'd seen him?

Finally, his gaze moved to her, sliding from her eyes to her boots and back again. A shy smile lifted the corners of his mouth. "I hope Birdie didn't get the message mixed up about supper being at five, 'cause something smells good in here."

"She was correct, and you're right on time." Fortunately, he never saw her blush, because the baby reached for his Stetson, which Micah then placed over his head. Seconds later, a muffled "Da!" penetrated the black felt. Reid peeked out from beneath the brim and aimed a gap-toothed grin at Micah. "Da!" he repeated.

"Big hat to fill," Jonah said, grinning as he took it from Reid and handed it back to Micah.

Big shoes to fill, too. "I can get supper on the table a lot faster if you three will go into the parlor, where you won't be underfoot," Callie said, grabbing her apron.

As they filed out of the room, she smiled. For the first time since the steamboat explosion, hope echoed from a long-empty space deep in her heart.

The sound of their laughter gave her reason to believe, for the moment, anyway, that the Lord had forgiven her.

Lifting the lid on the big iron kettle, she tested the dumplings and tried to come to terms with the contentment now swirling in her heart. *Give it time,* she warned, *and those old mawkish feelings will return.* But happiness hovered as she set the table and filled the tumblers with fresh-squeezed lemonade and refilled the salt shaker and pepper mill. *Enjoy it while it lasts,* she thought as Micah walked into the kitchen.

Grinning like a mischievous schoolboy, he pointed at the kettle. "Mind if I take a peek?" Before she could answer, he'd lifted the lid and waved the aromatic steam toward his nostrils. "Mmm, beef stew and dumplings." He returned the lid to the pot, then stepped up beside her at the stove. "One of my favorites." He winked. "How'd you know?"

Something told her that he'd be disappointed to know it had been a lucky guess, so, she said, "It's Jonah's favorite, too."

His gaze skipped over her face. With boots planted shoulder-width apart, Micah brought his big hands together with one noisy clap, then rubbed his palms together. "Now, tell me, what can I do to help?"

Well, for starters, you can stop standing there, looking so charming. "It's sweet of you to offer," she said, "but everything's ready. I just need to put the stew on the trivet and—"

In an eyeblink, he turned. In another, he'd carried the pot to the table after grabbing the ladle from the hook above the stove. "Your wish is my command, m'lady," he said, bowing low.

Callie had never seen him so cheerful and animated. Though, to be fair, if she totaled all the hours she'd spent in his company, they wouldn't add up to a full workday. "Thank you, Micah. I'll just call Jonah and Reid, and—"

It took only three long-legged strides to put him back in the parlor, where Jonah and Reid were playing with a wooden wagon. "Supper's ready, little man," he said, scooping the baby from the braided rug. He turned to Jonah. "Callie tells me beef stew and dumplings is one of your favorite suppers, too."

She'd told him that Jonah was deaf but hadn't elaborated on the subject of reading lips. It touched her the way Micah had figured out on his own that to include her brother in a conversation, he needed to face him head-on. *Yet another reason to admire Micah Neville*, she thought, smiling.

Her smile continued all through supper and dessert, as she tucked Reid in for the night, and then as she washed the dishes while Jonah and Micah chatted over a game of dominoes in the parlor. Her smile broadened when she remembered the way her brothers used to make silly faces at one another. "Careful," their mother would caution, "or your face might stay that way!" Was it possible, Callie wondered, for her smile to last forever?

If it was, she had Micah to thank, for sharing Reid with her. *Please, Lord, let things work out so that he can stay with me, always.* A silly giggle punctuated her prayer as she realized "he" could mean Micah just as easily as Reid.

She didn't want to spoil the mood, and so she decided that her questions about the baby's future, like her frayed cuffs, could keep.

"I've told her a thousand times that it wasn't her fault," Jonah said, "but Callie has blamed herself ever since."

"That explains a lot," Micah said. *Like that sad, faraway look in her eyes.*

"I believe those boilers would have exploded that night, no matter who stoked the fires. But I can't make her believe it." Jonah shook his head. "It's as if she wants to punish herself for surviving when so many died."

The only sound now was the ticktock of the mantel clock and the crackle of logs in the fireplace. Despite the warmth emanating from the hearth, Micah shivered.

"She blames herself for my deafness, too, and it's cost her a small fortune. If she isn't dragging me from one doctor to the next in search of a cure, she's buying some newfangled gadget that promises to help me hear."

"That's a lot for one person to bear by herself." *Let alone a woman no bigger than a minute.*

"Sometimes, I'm glad I'm deaf," Jonah put in.

Micah felt his eyebrows shoot upward.

"It means I don't have to hear her cry herself to sleep."

"But, how do you know she—"

"Her eyes are puffy and red in the morning."

Micah frowned. "You don't suppose taking care of Reid is too much for her, do you?"

Jonah shook his head. "That baby is the one bright light in her life. Well, except for you."

Chuckling, he added, "You should marry her. Then, she could take care of Reid and you, too, and put an end to folks' gossiping."

"Gossiping? What about?"

But before Jonah could answer, Callie appeared in the doorway, hands clasped in front of her. "Can I interest either of you in another helping of cobbler? I can warm it on the stove and pour some milk over it."

"I shouldn't," Micah admitted, "but I'd love some." He chose the chair facing the kitchen window and, as they chatted over the second round of dessert, watched the moon climb slowly higher until it rose clear out of sight. The cobbler was gone and the milk jug empty when he started listing reasons to leave, but neither the thought of the rooster's early call or the long ride home could prompt him out of his chair. It wasn't until he saw Callie stifle a yawn that he finally got to his feet. Even then, he took his time moving to the door. Finally, he found the gumption to step onto the porch. "So," he said, donning his hat, "I'll see you for Thanksgiving dinner, right?"

"I think your mother said dinner is at two o'clock, so—"

"She also said you're welcome to come earlier."

A shard of moonlight illuminated her uncertain smile, which he hoped was due to misgivings about making the long trip to the Lazy N with a baby and a deaf brother. After all, there had been talk of *banditos* raiding homes and robbing citizens along the road recently.

Or, perhaps she didn't have enough money to rent a horse and buggy. Had taking care of Reid cut into her work hours to the point where she was not saving enough money? The question reminded him that his main motive for stopping by tonight had been to give Callie a few dollars to help provide for the baby. *That isn't true, and you know it,* he thought. To see Callie was the reason he'd come here, and she was the reason he stood here still, spinning his Stetson in his hands so many times, it was a wonder the brim didn't separate from the dome.

Moments later, he reached for his wallet. "I declare," he said, fumbling with the snap that fixed the leather pouch to his belt, "if I ever meet the imbecile who said it's uncivilized to stow your wallet in your pocket, I might just punch him in the nose."

Jonah laughed, but Callie only smiled. Barely. Surely, she knew he would never actually do such a thing, didn't she?

Taking her hand in his, he gently pressed a few dollars into her palm, then closed her dainty fingers around them. When she blinked those enormous eyes at him, his heart thumped so hard that he worried she might hear it.

"Micah, really, I don't need—"

"What you need isn't the issue here. You shouldn't be expected to mind him day and night and pay for his expenses, to boot."

"But—"

"We had an understanding, Callie, but if you aren't going to let me hold up my end of the bargain...." He shrugged.

Evidently, Jonah had been right when he'd said Reid was the one bright spot in Callie's life, for his implied threat made her give in immediately. She stuffed the bills into her apron pocket and gave it a pat, as if to say, "Then, I guess I have no choice but to accept the payment."

My, but she was a proud little thing, with her chin up and shoulders back. Grinning, he put on his hat. "Tell you what. I'll harness the buggy and come get you on Thanksgiving morning to save you the bother of hiring a team. I'll be here at eight."

She opened her mouth and then closed it. What had she wanted to say but felt she couldn't?

"Unless you'd rather I got here earlier? Later? You name the time."

"No, no," Callie said. "Eight is fine." She pursed her lips, looking pensive, before adding, "My grandmother used to fix a big, fancy breakfast on Thanksgiving morning."

Was she about to invite him for breakfast? *A man can hope….*

"Is that a tradition with your family, too?"

"As a matter of fact, it isn't. I guess the women have enough to do, getting things ready for dinner."

"Then, why don't you join us for breakfast here? I mean, it's the least I can do, since you're going to the bother of picking us up and taking us home again."

"Believe me, it's no bother. But I'd love to have breakfast with you."

Everything Jonah had told him echoed in his head, making him want to gather her close and promise to fix everything that was wrong in her life. *All in good time*, he told himself. *All in good time.* "Well," he said, shifting his weight from one boot to the other, "guess I'll see you in two days."

When she didn't respond, Jonah elbowed her.

"Oh. Yes. See you in two days."

"You take care, now."

"And you do the same."

"Give Reid a hug for me?"

"Of course," she said, nodding. "Have a safe ride home."

"I will," he echoed. "And—"

"Why don't you just kiss her, already!" Jonah exclaimed. "You're letting all the heat out of the house."

Callie's cheeks glowed a rosy red, and she blinked. Micah might have taken Jonah up on his suggestion if she hadn't stepped back and closed the door.

Chuckling, he climbed into the saddle and urged his horse forward. It was going to be two long days until he saw her again. Two very long days.

Chapter 12

On Wednesday afternoon, Reid had been fast asleep in his cradle for nearly an hour when the tiny bell above the door jingled, announcing the arrival of a customer. Callie stopped working on the tiny suit she'd designed for him and parted the curtain that separated the shop from her workroom.

"G'mornin', Callie!"

"Why, Dan Neville, what a nice surprise! What brings you all the way to town on the day before Thanksgiving?"

"I need a gift. Levee's birthday falls on Thanksgiving this year."

"Well, then, I guess we have her birth to be thankful for, too," Callie said.

"My thoughts exactly." He glanced around the shop. "I was hoping you could recommend something special for me to give her. Levee's a tough little thing, and she's doing her best to hide it, but she could use some cheering up." He sighed heavily. "She'd have my head if she knew I told you this, but we've lost another baby."

That explained the grating edge on his usually cheerful voice. "I'm so sorry, Dan. I remember how excited Levee was to learn she was expecting."

"We both were."

"Well, your secret is safe with me. And I'll add my prayers to yours."

"Thanks," he said, nodding. Then, he clapped his hands and rubbed them together, just as Micah had when he'd come to supper. "So, what do you think might do the trick? A hat? A dress? Earrings, maybe?"

She doubted anything in her shop—or any other, for that matter—would take the sting out of losing another baby, but the pain glittering in Dan's eyes told her that he needed to give a gift even more than Levee needed to receive one.

"Let me think," Callie said, scanning the shelves and racks for something appropriate. Then, she remembered the tray of chains and pendants the salesman from Chicago had delivered only yesterday. She opened a deep drawer and revealed a row of velvet-lined boxes. "Do you have any photographs of you at home?"

"I suppose I could scrounge one up," he said, leaning over the counter to peer into the drawer. "Why...?"

Callie held up a gleaming gold chain, then found a shiny locket to match and popped it open. "See? You could slide a picture of you inside. That way, any time she wears it, she can carry you close to her heart." She held it out so he could get a better look. "You'll need a razor or a pair of good sharp scissors to cut the photograph to fit, though."

Dan palmed the locket, then inspected the tiny oval window where his photos would appear. "It's perfect," he said, smiling as he handed the locket back to Callie.

Just then, Reid sat up and peered over the edge of his cradle. "Da?"

"So, there's the little fellow I've been hearin' so much about," Dan said, stooping to lift the boy into his arms. "My, but you're a solid little tyke, aren't you?"

Reid grabbed Dan's hat, revealing a blond cowlick above the left temple, exactly where Reid had a dark one.

"If you'd do me the favor of wrappin' Levee's present," Dan mumbled around the stubby fingers Reid had shoved into his mouth, "I'll mind him for you."

Callie was more than happy to perform this little service, for it gave her time and opportunity to watch the two interact. The baby's eyes were as brown as coffee beans, and Dan's were as blue as the summer sky. Yet, if she didn't know better, Callie would have to say that Dan, not Micah, was this baby's father. But how could that be?

She wrapped the rectangular box in butcher's paper, secured with a wide, green satin ribbon left over from Martha Potter's hat. "There you go," she said, smiling. "Would you like me to make a card for you to sign?" Callie showed him a few samples, and he chose one barely bigger than a postage stamp. "I could write 'Happy Birthday' on the front, and 'To Levee' on the envelope. When you get home, you can put your own personal message inside."

"That'd be great." And as her pen's nib scratched across the heavy paper, he said, "Hard to believe that straightlaced, do-the-right-thing cousin of mine is a father but not a husband."

She'd thought the same thing—until seeing the uncanny similarity between Dan and the baby. Callie pretended to focus on the card. "So, Micah's certain, then, that Reid is his?"

He stood stock-still and looked as guilty as if she'd caught him with his hand in her cash drawer. She'd heard the rumors about Dan's former life. Surely, he wouldn't knowingly allow Micah to shoulder the burden of his past mistakes, even to protect his beloved Levee. Would he?

"How much do I owe you?"

Callie was only too happy to write up the sales ticket, for once Dan had paid her, he'd be on his way, and she would be left alone to try to make sense of things.

After handing Reid to her, he grabbed his hat from the peg near the door. "See you tomorrow," he said, then held up the package and gave it a quick shake. "And thanks again for this. You're a lifesaver."

No sooner was he out of sight than Reid's lower lip trembled, and his big, dark eyes welled with tears. "Da?" he whimpered.

Callie hugged him tight and rubbed soothing circles on his back. "Do you know something, sweet boy, that no one else knows?"

He tucked his face into the crook of her neck, and she kissed his cheek. "The better question is," she whispered, "how do you know?"

Micah's knuckles had barely connected with Callie's front door when it flew open on Thanksgiving morning. "Come in," Jonah said, grinning. "Saw you ride up," he added, stepping aside. "Callie will be down soon. She's giving Reid another bath."

"Another bath?"

"He had one last night before bed, but this morning, he was sitting on her dresser, watching her put her hair up, and he spilled a whole bottle of her toilet water on him." Jonah waved a hand in front of his face. "A little of that stuff goes a long, long way," he said, laughing.

Micah chuckled as he hung his hat on the peg with his coat. So, that explained the flowery scent that hung in the air! It reminded him of the time when, as a boy, he'd fallen from the saddle of his horse and landed nose-first in a field of flowers.

He pointed at the bowl of eggs and rasher of bacon on the counter. "From the smell of things," he said, rolling up his sleeves as he moved closer, "that could take a while. If we want breakfast today, I guess we'd better give her a hand. How 'bout I get this started while you set the table with some plates and silverware?"

Jonah nodded, opened a drawer, and began to gather forks and knives, while Micah filled the coffeepot with water and set it on the cookstove. When Jonah looked up at him, he chuckled and said, "With her nose so full of perfume, she won't know what we're up to until she gets down here."

Jonah laughed. "She'll be surprised, all right."

Micah stoked the fire, then grabbed a skillet and began filling it with a layer of bacon slices.

"You know how to cook?" Jonah asked, standing beside him to watch.

"I sure do! The only way my pa agreed to let me tag along on trail drives as a young'un was if I promised to help rustle up the grub."

But Jonah hadn't caught his explanation, because he'd started distributing plates on the table. It was hard for Micah to imagine what life must be like for Jonah. Did he have memories of specific sounds, such as the saw of a knife slicing through a loaf of fresh-baked bread, or the sizzle of bacon frying in a pan?

Suddenly, the sound of every breath seemed significant to Micah. He heard the water coming to a boil in the coffeepot, the wind whistling through the trees outside Callie's kitchen window, and the crack of each egg on the edge of the frying pan. When Callie's musical laughter floated down the stairs and into his ears, he closed his eyes for a moment, committing the sound to memory. Grinning to himself, he shook his head. *Better keep your mind on the task at hand,* he warned himself, *before you set the house on fire.*

Micah greased a second skillet and, after sliding it onto the stove top to heat up, stirred the bowl of pancake batter Callie had left on the counter. Then, he ladled three circles of batter into the skillet and left them to cook. Earlier, while snooping around for the lard, he'd noticed a tin of maple syrup in the pantry. He retrieved it now and stepped into Jonah's line of vision. "How does Callie serve this up?" he asked.

Jonah grabbed a tiny ceramic pitcher. "In this. I always say, why put yourself to the bother of washing the silly thing when it's just as easy to pour it from the tin? But she always says, 'Because we're civilized human beings, not animals, that's why.'" Laughing, he added, "I refrain from pointing out that animals don't put maple syrup on their griddle cakes."

Micah joined in his laughter. "I agree. It is a waste."

"A waste of what?" Callie asked, breezing into the room with Reid on her hip. She looked at the table, which had been set, and then focused her gaze on the stove top, where the freshly cooked bacon and eggs still sizzled. Her eyes grew wide. "And just what do the two of you think you're doing?"

Jonah grinned and began stacking slices of bread on a platter. "I don't know about Micah, but I'm chopping wood."

Her gaze slid to Micah, who began flipping the flapjacks. "And I'm fishing."

"Well, if you're fishing for compliments after making a mess of my kitchen...."

She smiled so prettily that Micah wanted to hug the stuffing out of her. "Don't worry. We'll clean it up."

Eyebrows raised, Jonah shook his head at him. "Obviously, you don't know my sister very well."

Micah looked from Jonah to Callie and back again, waiting for the explanation he knew would follow.

"We don't have a ghost of a chance of cleaning this place up to suit her." He winked at Callie. "Isn't that right, sister dear?"

"Careful, brother dear, or I might be tempted to lower my standards, just this once."

Micah waited until she'd positioned Reid in his high chair, then pulled out the chair nearest the baby's, and, with a grand sweep of his arm, said, "For you, m'lady. Cream for your coffee?"

"Just black, thanks," she said, sitting. After breaking off a bite of toast for the baby, she picked up a napkin. "My, my, but aren't we fancy today," she said, smoothing it onto her lap. "Linens and everything."

"Special day," Jonah said as he slid the platter of bacon onto the table.

As Jonah sat across from Callie, Micah delivered the flapjacks and eggs, then sat on Reid's other side. "Yes," he agreed, "a very special day."

"I'm impressed," Callie said. "And I'm touched that you two would go to all this trouble, just to keep me from having to rush."

Micah couldn't move, couldn't speak, couldn't seem to do anything but stare into her lovely face. If only he could read what was going on in that pretty head of hers!

Then, Reid squealed, snapping him back to the here and now. "Mmm!" He banged on the tray of his high chair. "Mmm!"

Callie picked up where she'd left off, as if the enchanting moment had never happened. "I...I don't know what to say."

"It's Thanksgiving," Jonah piped up. "Say..."

"Thank you!" all three adults said in unison.

Reid looked from one laughing adult face to the next, then gave his tray another slap. "Mmm!" he said, reminding them that he was ready for more. "Mmm!"

"The table looks lovely," Hanna Neville exclaimed. "Did you get any sleep at all last night, Eva?"

"Oh, a few hours," her sister-in-law said. "I had a lot of help," she added, smiling at her daughters and Lucinda.

"Lucinda," Hanna continued, "are you all packed and ready for your trip to Chihuahua?"

"*Sí, señora*. Since last week."

Her husband, George, groaned good-naturedly. "I have not been able to move in our room," he put in. "You would think we are going *para siempre*, not just a month!"

Everyone laughed, and when the merriment quieted, Matthew said, "Well, you'll both be missed, so don't get any harebrained notions about staying longer than that."

Callie took a green bean from her plate and set it on the wooden tray of Reid's high chair. He snatched it up immediately. "Mmm," he said. "Ma!"

"He has quite an appetite," Levee observed. "He'll be as tall as a tree in no time."

Callie wondered if anyone else noticed the young woman's sad smile. A quick glance around the table told her that two people, at least, shared her compassion for Levee: Dan, who gave his wife's hand a squeeze, and Micah, who nodded somberly.

His mother must have seen it, too, for she quickly changed the subject. "So, Callie," she said, "I hear you're making the costumes for the children's Christmas pageant?"

"Yes, all the usual players in the nativity, and a few angels, too."

"When will you find time, with running your shop and minding that spirited youngster and taking care of your brother?"

Thankfully, Jonah hadn't caught her remark, because he was busy sopping up gravy with a golden biscuit. "Oh, Jonah is completely self-sufficient," Callie said. "He's a big help to me. I don't know what I'd do without him."

"You mean to say he sews?"

All heads turned to the head of the table, where Matthew sat with a quizzical expression on his face. Several people stifled snickers.

Callie was tempted to giggle, herself. Instead, she said, "He can't even thread a needle! But he's right handy with a pencil. If not for his artistic talents, I wouldn't have a hope of getting my ads in the newspapers."

She'd never enjoyed being the center of attention, and today was no exception. So, she searched her mind for a topic to distract them. "Do you think President Harrison will follow through with his campaign promises on tariff reform?"

No one spoke or moved, and even Reid fell silent.

"Oh, stop looking at the girl as if she's grown a second head," Kate said. "Just because we women can't vote doesn't mean we're not aware of what's going on politically."

Callie had always liked the feisty girl Micah's cousin Josh had married, but never more than now. She sent a grateful smile down the table, then pretended that Reid needed her full attention.

"Don't get me started," Matthew said, glowering. "That fool won the election by luck and happenstance. Why, if they'd counted the people's votes, as they should have, he'd still be—"

"Now, now, Matthew," Eva said. "Why not save talk like that for after dinner, when you men retire to the parlor?"

Micah's father agreed. "Eva's right. Now then, somebody pass the mashed potatoes this way, will you?"

Conversation remained light for the next few minutes, until Micah's cousin Susan said, "So, Micah, how is Gus Applegate doing these days?"

Why, she hadn't thought it possible for a man's face to fade to white in a heartbeat. Micah's fork hovered in midair, and he frowned.

"Beth wrote to me," Susan continued, "and said that you'd hired him to do some research—"

"Susan," her mother interrupted her, "would you mind passing the gravy to your father, please?"

The young woman took the cue and ended her line of questioning. Wearing a sheepish expression, she leaned close to her husband, Sam, to whisper something to him. He merely nodded.

Callie had never witnessed a scene where the phrase "The tension was so thick, you could have sliced it with a knife" fit more perfectly than at this elegantly set table. Memories of breakfast in her humble kitchen flitted through her memory. She didn't own a single piece of porcelain, and the mismatched glass candlesticks on her mantel were as close as she'd likely ever come to having a candelabra. Yet the warmth and joy of the meal she'd shared with Micah, Jonah, and Reid stood in sharp contrast to the unease that prevailed in this well-appointed room. For the first time, she questioned her longstanding belief that life would improve if only she belonged to a big family. Even loving kin, it seemed, experienced some not-so-loving moments.

Though she and Jonah had been in Eagle Pass for two years, they hadn't had much occasion to get to know the Nevilles, except in passing. She liked them just fine, from the eldest to the youngest, but she liked Micah the most. And, because of that, she wanted to protect him from the Neville Inquisition, which was sure to start eventually, despite Eva's effort to change the subject.

As if he sensed her apprehension, Reid began to fuss, so Callie stood and gathered him up. "I hate to seem rude," she said, backing away from the table, "because it was lovely of you—all of you—to include us in your family celebration." All eyes were on her, but she focused on Micah. "I hate to impose further on your generosity, but would you mind very much taking us home? I'm afraid I don't feel very well."

A quiet murmur slid up and down the table as the men tried to make sense of what she'd said and the women pummeled her with questions: "Are you feverish?" "Is your stomach upset?" "Do you have a headache?"

Callie assured them it was probably nothing. "Reid didn't get a very good night's sleep," she said. "I hate to leave without helping with the dishes, but I promise to make it up to you."

By now, both Jonah and Micah were standing on either side of her, silent yet looking relieved.

"At least let me fix you a dessert plate to take home," Eva offered. "I'm sure you'll want something sweet once you get the little fellow tucked in bed."

Callie opened her mouth to protest, but her voice would have been drowned out by the sound of chair legs scraping the floor as every woman got to her feet. "I insist," Eva went on. "By the time you get him bundled up and into the wagon, we'll have it all ready."

"I remember only too well what it was like, trying to appease a cranky baby during big family gatherings," Hanna put in.

One by one, the women shared stories to affirm and commiserate, while the men went back to their meal, as if the commotion over Callie's early departure was not the least bit unusual.

In no time, Callie was seated up front beside Micah in the buggy, while Reid slumbered in the back, bundled in his cradle at Jonah's feet.

A mile up the road, Jonah dozed off, too. Smiling to herself, she wondered how long it would take for Micah to thank her for getting him out of that situation.

"What was all that about?" he asked moments later.

"Whatever do you mean?"

He kept his eyes on the road. "Your sudden need to escape the Lazy N, that's what."

"You can't be serious!"

When he met her eyes, Callie feared she might melt under the scrutiny of his blazing, blue stare. "You look fine. Very fine, as a matter of fact. So, I can't help but wonder why you felt it necessary to leave so abruptly."

"Well, I am fine—physically, that is. But I must admit, this conversation is taking a sickening turn." Was he so thickheaded that he didn't understand that, by leaving, she'd saved him from a barrage of questions from his family?

He chuckled, which confused her almost as much as the fact that she felt the need to defend herself, though what she'd done had been in defense of him. "I saw the way they stared at Reid, as if they'd never seen a baby before. And the way they were looking at you, why, if I ever saw more self-righteous, judgmental faces in my life, I'm very thankful that the good Lord chose to erase the memory from my mind!"

"Ah, so that's it!" And then he laughed.

Laughed!

Callie crossed her arms over her chest. "I'm waiting...."

"For what?"

"For you to explain what's so all-fired funny."

He looked left and right, as if trying to decide whether or not to share the reasons for his merriment. Thumbing his Stetson to the back of his head, he turned on the wagon seat. "Well, it's like this, Miss Callie Roberts. I grew up surrounded by females—a mother, sisters, aunts, and girl cousins—and I can't recall a single occasion when any of 'em came to my defense the way you did back there, just as you did that day in my ma's kitchen."

Callie studied the face so near her own. Micah's eyes were twinkling, one of his eyebrows was arched higher than the other, and he had a slanted grin on his lips. What in the world was he trying to tell her?

"I'm not laughing because what you did was funny. It's just...." He shrugged one shoulder. "I don't know how else to react."

Perhaps, as she'd insinuated in his aunt Eva's dining room, Reid's restlessness and her lack of sleep really could explain her peculiar, oversensitive mood. She was glad for the gloves she'd worn to fend off the chilly late-November air, for, without them, she'd probably have clammy palms to contend with. Thank goodness she'd thought to wear a scarf around her neck, too, because it helped hide the blush that had no doubt colored her cheeks. "How appropriate that today is Thanksgiving Day," she muttered to herself.

"It was as if you could read my mind," he said. "One minute, I was sitting there, racking my brain for a reasonable excuse to leave, and the next minute, you stand up and ask me to take you home." He laid a leather-gloved hand on her sleeve. "Thanks, Callie. I owe you one." He winked. "More like, I owe you another one."

The disappointment and hurt she'd been feeling disappeared, just as surely as the fog of her breath vanished in the frosty breeze. She folded her hands in her lap and smiled. "So, remind me, who's this Gus Applegate your cousin asked about earlier?"

He sighed heavily, and for a minute, perhaps two, Callie heard only the horses' hooves, clip-clopping along the hard-packed road in rhythm with every beat of her heart.

"I already owe you so much, Callie," Micah finally said. "If I live to be two hundred and ten, I couldn't begin to repay you for all you're doing for Reid and me."

"You don't owe me a thing," she countered, meaning it. "I love Reid." And she meant that, too.

"Yes, I know you do."

Why did he sound so sad about it? "And I love taking care of him. Every minute with him is pure joy, even when he's spilling the contents of an entire bottle of cologne."

"I'll replace it, if you tell me what kind you like."

"Goodness, I didn't mean to imply that I'm bothered by not having the toilet water to dab behind my ears." She waved the notion away. "Most of the time, I forget that it's there, anyway."

"I don't doubt that for a minute, and I never even considered that might be the reason you brought it up." He pulled back on the reins a tad, slowing the horses' pace. "Remember when I told you I'd share information about Reid just as soon as I could?"

Callie nodded.

"And that I'd only burden you with the necessary facts, so that if anybody asked you about his history, you wouldn't be put in the position of lying to protect him—or me?"

Another nod.

"Well, for now, I've shared as much as I can."

Which was a whole lot of nothing! "But Susan seems to know all sorts of details. Shouldn't I be privy to the same facts, if for no other reason than to ensure Reid is properly taken care of, in case—"

"Susan only thinks she knows something." Micah slowed the horses even more. "I trust you with my life. And with Reid's." He paused. "Do you trust me, too?"

Looking into those long-lashed, piercing blue eyes of his, how could she say anything but yes? She nodded.

"I know I don't deserve it, and I haven't earned it, either, but I'm grateful all the same."

The rooftops of Eagle Pass came into view. In minutes, he'd park the rig at the end of her walk, then turn it around and head back toward the Lazy N. Regret thrummed in her heart, because she didn't want him to go. Not tonight. Not ever. "Since I interrupted your dinner, the least I can do is make you something to eat when we get to my house."

"And some coffee to wash it down?"

Now, her heart thumped with happiness and hope. "And some coffee to wash it down."

"And some of that pie my aunt wrapped up?"

"Seems only fair."

He stopped the buggy so that when she stepped down from the seat, her feet would touch only the dry flagstone path, not the muddy grass on either side of it. "Someday," she said, changing the subject, "maybe you could teach me to handle a team of horses the way you do, so—"

"I'll tell you what would be fair," he said, pulling back on the brake stick, then wrapping the reins around it.

Callie waited for him to complete his thought. Instead, Micah jumped down from the seat and walked around in front of the team, patting each horse on the forehead as he passed. Jonah climbed down, then reached into the wagon and lifted the cradle. "I'll get him inside out of the wind, then start a fire," he said to Micah. "You're not in a big hurry to get back, are you?"

When Micah looked over at her, Callie thought her heart might leap clean out of her chest. "No. Not in a hurry." Realizing Jonah hadn't seen his lips, he turned toward him and repeated it. Then, he glanced skyward. "Looks like rain. Think Otis will mind if I tie up the horses at the stable till it's time to go?"

"He'll probably help you, if you rap on his door."

"Nah. No sense pestering him on a holiday." He climbed back onto the wagon seat and, without looking at her, added, "Go on in and get out of this cold wind. I'll be only a few minutes."

Thank goodness, she thought. She didn't know how she could stand to be without him longer than that.

Chapter 13

*M*icah was soaked to the skin by the time he made it back to Callie's, and, for a blink in time, he stood on the porch, wondering how to get in out of the rain without dragging along the mud, grit, and wet that clung to him. Whether she'd seen him out there shivering in the rain or had read his mind, again, Micah couldn't say. He knew only that his heart throbbed with joy and gratitude when the door swung open.

"You'll catch your death out there!" she said, grabbing him by the elbow to pull him inside.

"I don't want to make a mess o' your clean floors."

She waved off his protest. "Never mind that. It's only water, and it'll dry in no time."

On his way to the livery, he'd noticed sheets and towels flapping on the clothesline behind her house. From the looks of things, she'd taken them down in the nick of time, and the laundry now sat in a rumpled heap in the middle of the kitchen table. Callie dug through the pile and pulled out a blanket. "Just look at you!" she exclaimed, draping it around his shoulders. "Shivering like the last leaf of autumn." Grabbing his hand, she led him into the parlor, then slid a wooden bench close to the hearth and patted the seat. "Sit here while I fetch you some dry clothes from Jonah's bureau. Once you're changed, I'll get some hot food into you."

He was about to apologize for his growling stomach, but she was gone before he could formulate the words. Grinning, he tugged the blanket tighter around himself and huddled close to the fire.

Jonah walked into the room with an armload of wood. "You're learning," he said, then began adding logs to the fire.

"Learning what?"

"That it's a waste of time and energy to argue with her once she sets her mind on something." He glanced at the arched doorway that separated the front hall from the parlor and counted down on his fingers—three, two, one.

"These will probably be a tad short for you," Callie said as she burst into the room. She handed Micah a set of neatly folded long underwear, a shirt and a pair of trousers, and a towel. "But they'll do until we get your clothes dry," she added. From her pocket, she pulled out a pair of thick, woolen socks, which she added to the pile. Then, she signaled for Jonah to follow her out of the room.

When they reached the front hall, Jonah turned around and shrugged. "Waste of time," he mouthed behind Callie. "Big waste of time."

"When you're finished changing," Callie said, taking hold of the drapery to the left of the doorway, "just whistle." She gave the fabric a snap and drew it across the opening. "I'll have something hot and hearty ready for you by then," she said from the other side. "And, if Jonah is finished teasing me, I might let him join us."

Chuckling as her footsteps grew fainter, Micah got right to work, peeling off his waterlogged duds and dropping them onto the brick hearth. It was hard to believe a body could get this soaked from running a quarter of a mile.

He tugged at the too-short sleeves of the shirt Callie had given him, but it was no use; a full two inches of arm gleamed beneath each cuff. At least the socks would hide his milk-white skin, poking out from the legs of his pants. After finger-combing his damp hair out of his face, he held his thumb and forefinger between his teeth and cut loose an ear-piercing blast, then slid the parlor drapery open and padded into the tiny kitchen.

Just as she'd promised, a steaming bowl of stew waited for him on the table, and beside it was a piping-hot mug of coffee. Reid sat in his high chair, happily beating the tray with a big wooden spoon, while Jonah pretended to try to grab it from him. And Callie, wearing a blue calico apron, stood with her back to him, slicing crusty bread at the counter. If he had a lick of artistic talent, this would be just the type of scene he'd paint. Everything, from the golden glow of the lantern reflected in the forks and butter knives to the faded blue checks of the window curtains, spelled out the word *Welcome*. How strange that he felt more at home here than in the house he'd designed and built for himself on the ranch.

"Well, don't just stand there, Micah," she said over her shoulder. "Sit down and eat before your supper gets cold."

Jonah shrugged, with a grin that reminded him it was a waste of time to try changing her mind once she'd had it set on something. What her brother didn't know was that Micah had no problem coping with a mind that always seemed focused on caring for those she held dear.

He thanked God above for making him one of those people and prayed that, someday, she'd love him, too.

All through supper, lightning split the sky, thunder roared overhead, and the wind rattled the windows in their panes. The storm showed no signs of letting up, and Micah made sure to keep coals glowing in the cookstove and the parlor fire blazing. Reid, unfazed by the storm's ferocity, slept soundly in his room at the top of the stairs, while Jonah snored softly in his bed across the hall.

Finally, Micah started for home, only to return a moment later. "The road's washed out," he said. "The horses would only get bogged down in the mud if I tried to head out now. Just wanted to let you know I'll rent a room at the hotel, so that come morning—"

"You'll do no such thing!" she said, gently pulling him into the kitchen.

"But Callie, what will folks say?"

"They'll say you have the good sense to come in out of the rain." She bolted the door, then hung his hat behind it. "It doesn't make a lick of sense for you to trudge all the way to the other end of the street in this downpour when I have a perfectly good sofa in my workroom."

Half an hour later, Callie leaned against the doorframe, hugging a quilt to her chest, watching Micah sleep. A slight furrow appeared between his eyebrows, but was it any wonder, the way his neck bent at that awkward angle on one arm of the sofa, while his feet dangled over the other!

She tiptoed closer and eased the quilt over him. Because he was so tall, she needed a second blanket to cover his feet. She'd slept in that same spot enough times to know that on nights like this, a cold draft could blow through the house with enough force to ruffle her bangs. Callie clutched her shawl more tightly around her and crept silently from the room.

Minutes later, she returned with a mug of tea and sat down on the hearth. How like an innocent boy Micah looked with the firelight flickering across his sleeping face. In the bright light of day, one might not notice the faint smattering of freckles that peppered the bridge of his nose or the long, lush lashes that curved up from his eyelids or his angular cheeks. A corner of his mouth twitched, as did one eyebrow. He was close enough to touch, and, oh, how tempting it was to reach out and brush aside that golden lock of hair that had fallen across his forehead.

The big hand resting on his chest rose and fell with each breath, and, every now and then, his forefinger rapped a button, as if he was drumming out a message. *Who are you signaling?* she wanted to know. *Reid's mother?*

Overwhelming sadness engulfed her at the thought. She set down her mug, hugged her knees to her chest, and tucked her chin between them. What had become of the woman who'd given birth to the precious youngster? A hundred times—more like a thousand—Callie had tried to imagine what might motivate a woman to abandon her baby. Surely Micah, with his heart as big as Texas, could never have loved a woman who'd been cold and heartless enough to blithely walk away from her own flesh and blood!

"What's going on in that beautiful head of yours?" he whispered, propping himself up on one elbow.

Callie knew it had been a mistake to come in here and risk that he'd wake and see her weeping. She didn't understand the emotions roiling inside her, or what prompted the flurry of words that began pouring from her lips: "I said I'd trust you, Micah, and I do. I will. But the questions...." Pressing her fingertips into her temples, she shook her head. "Has Reid's mother tried to contact you?" She blotted her tears with the hem of her apron. "I can't imagine how she must be suffering. Surely, he looked at her the way he looks at me, and she could never forget that."

Micah sat up and reached across the space that separated them. "Believe me," he said, giving her hand a gentle squeeze, "she isn't capable of feelings like that."

Micah sounded angry, maybe even a bit hateful. "How could she know Reid and not feel like that?"

"Because, sweet Callie, she's nothing like you. If she were, even a little, this whole thing...."

Had the unrelenting fury of the storm silenced him, or was he trying to swallow a sob? And was that a tear she detected in his eye, or a reflection of the firelight?

Micah raked both hands through his hair, then got to his feet and pointed to her mug. "Any chance I could have a cup of that?" He sent her a sad, lopsided grin. "Not my favorite beverage, but at this hour, coffee doesn't seem like a wise choice."

The clock had already chimed midnight. Reid would be up in a few hours. What difference did it make if coffee kept them awake until then?

But Callie didn't say that. Instead, she led him to the kitchen, where she sat, spellbound, for the next half hour, listening as he told her everything.

When at last he fell silent, she blanketed his hands with her own. Words didn't seem necessary now, and that was fortunate, because she might just have been tempted to voice a confession of her own.

During the final few minutes of their conversation over tea in her cozy little kitchen, Callie had shivered, and Micah wondered if it was because of the cold wind pummeling the house or the chilling details of his story. He'd suggested they return to the parlor, where she could sit in her rocking chair near the heat of the fire.

She'd agreed, then had briefly left him alone to make sure Reid and Jonah had plenty of blankets to keep them warm. How like her to put her own comfort on hold to ensure the well-being of others.

By the time she'd returned, he'd stirred the coals and added four fat logs to the grate. He'd also brewed her a fresh cup of tea. "What took you so long?"

"Reid's diaper was wet, so I changed him...and his gown, and the bedding on his crib." She'd giggled quietly. "Wouldn't want him to catch a chill, especially on a night like this!"

As she'd settled into her upholstered rocking chair, he had formed a mental picture of her up in Reid's room, smiling sweetly and whispering tenderly as she saw to his every need. How much of this would Reid remember in a year, in five, or twenty? If life took him into dangerous territory, would his memories of happily-ever-after bedtime stories or the melodies of lullabies take him back to a time when he felt safe, treasured, and loved? Micah hoped so. He also hoped he'd have a chance to know the man Reid would become, and to see how the foundation Callie was building for him would affect his life in the long run.

Now, she slept. Her tea sat, untouched, on the three-legged table to her right. When he covered her with the quilt she'd given him earlier, she stirred— not much, but enough to expose the scar that twisted down the right side of her face. Jonah had told him she'd been hit by flying debris on the night of the steamboat explosion, and that she always made sure that her hair covered it. Micah mustered all of his self-control, because he wanted to trace it with his finger and tell her that she was beautiful, with or without it. He stood stock-still, for if she awoke and caught him gawking, what would he say? Thankfully, she only snuggled deeper beneath the blanket.

In spite of the restless storm that raged outside, she looked at peace, and Micah hoped his presence had a little something to do with that. If he could have moved heaven and earth to assure that she'd never have a care in the world, he'd have done it in a heartbeat. How else could he hope to repay her for the joy and serenity she'd brought into his life?

The swaying brass pendulum of the mantel clock caught the lantern light, tossing it left and right. Each steady ticktock served as a quiet reminder that day would dawn all too soon. Micah hated to leave, but he needed to get to the livery stable and hitch the horses before all of Eagle Pass found out where he'd spent the night. She might be willing to put her reputation on the line for him—again—but Micah had no intention of aiding and abetting her!

She'd hung his damp clothes over the backs of three kitchen chairs, which she'd moved close to the cookstove to dry. The fire-warmed material felt soothing against his chilled skin. *Better enjoy it*, he told himself as a blast of wind rattled the windows.

Once dressed, he filled the coffeepot with water and tossed in some grounds, then set it halfway on the warming plate so that it wouldn't boil over. After stoking both fires, Micah lowered all the lantern flames to a dim glow, donned his Stetson and oilskin duster, and sneaked out the back door.

Treading through the darkness, he almost wished he'd borrowed a lamp. Almost. The windows lit by lantern light in the houses he passed felt like hot, unblinking eyes, watching his every move. He and the good Lord knew how completely innocent his activities at Callie's had been, and that he'd stayed there only out of necessity, but common sense and wagging tongues rarely went together. For weeks now, the town biddies had been buzzing like bees in a hive, trying to figure out why Callie had agreed to care for the boy they believed to be his illegitimate son. If one of them saw him skulking away from her house in the dead of night....

The thunder and lightning had subsided, thankfully, but a thick rain continued to fall. The earth beneath his feet was more of a shallow river than a road, and he knew from experience that it would be days before everything dried out—himself included! With shoulders hunched, Micah ducked deeper into the collar of his slicker and pocketed both fists. When he finally reached the livery, he marveled at how the distance from Callie's house hadn't seemed nearly as long on the way there.

He'd been this uncomfortable—more uncomfortable, even—out on the prairie, where nature threw everything it had at him and his fellow drovers. Unrelenting rain and wicked wind often snuffed out campfires, making it impossible for a body to stay dry or get warm. Micah hadn't liked it then, and he didn't like it now. And, unless he was mistaken, the storm had no intention of releasing its grip on Eagle Pass anytime soon, meaning he was in for a long, wretched ride back to the Lazy N.

Just when he thought things couldn't get any more miserable, the brim of his hat, designed to protect his neck from blazing sun and driving rain, began acting like the spout of a pitcher, guiding the rain under his coat collar and straight down his back. No amount of tugging and pulling stopped the steady flow. His fidgeting seemed to agitate the horses even more than the rain did, so Micah tried focusing on the road, the reins, the buggy's wobbly wheels—anything but the biting wind and icy water that had him gritting his teeth and shivering from his hat to his boots. Oh, what he wouldn't give to be back in Callie's parlor right now, warming his cold feet by the light of the fire.

What was stopping him from doing exactly that? He knew that Callie would take one look at his drenched, trembling self and wrap him in a blanket, then sit him near the hearth with a bowl of soup and a cup of hot tea. And, despite his distaste for the watery stuff, he'd gratefully gulp down every last drop, just because she had made it for him.

All of a sudden, his drowsiness seemed to outweigh his discomfort, and he shook himself awake. "Better pay attention," he muttered, muffling a cough in the crook of his arm, "or you'll end up in a ditch."

Chapter 14

*C*allie had seen Otis Sullivan coated in grime, and she'd seen him all dressed up for Sunday services. She'd seen him jump for joy when the fire brigade found Birdie under a smoking pile of debris after a fire had nearly destroyed their barn. And she'd seen him hopping mad when a bunch of rowdy boys messed up his tidy display of stirrups and crops.

But she'd never seen him like this.

Standing on her porch and twisting a woolen cap in his hands, he reminded her more of the frightened young man Jonah had been the night the *Maybelline* had exploded than the man who'd single-handedly transformed three languishing businesses into one thriving enterprise.

"Otis," she said, ushering him inside, "what in the world...?" She led him into the kitchen and poured him a cup of coffee. "Birdie's all right, isn't she?"

Nodding, he took a swig of the coffee. "She's fine. 'Fraid the same ain't true for your fella, though."

The only men in her life were Jonah and Reid, and they were upstairs, fast asleep. She might have laughed out loud, if not for Otis's worried expression. And then, the image of Micah's handsome face materialized, and a shudder of fear rippled through her.

"Birdie an' me, we hitched up the wagon soon as the rain let up, thinkin' to head down to El Indio for a visit with Birdie's sister. Didn't get a mile outside o' town before we saw 'im on the side o' the road."

Micah had slipped out long before dawn, but not before feeding both woodstoves and dimming the lanterns. *And tucking you in so gently that you didn't even wake up.* The shudder traveled to her knees, and she gripped the back of a chair for support. "What happened? Where is he? He's all right, isn't he?"

"He's alive," Otis said, "over at our house. We carried 'im in there to get 'im out o' the wind, and—"

"Carried him?" If she sounded shrill and panicky to herself, how must she sound to Otis? Callie took a breath and prayed for the strength to remain calm. She hoped he hadn't been robbed, or worse.

"Looked to me like his buggy veered off the road and got mired in the mud. Don't know why." He jerked a thumb over his shoulder. "I'm on my way back to where we found 'im, so's I can fetch the rig and the horses 'fore some thievin' fool takes a mind to help hisself to it."

"But...but Micah handles a team better than any man I know," she said, more to herself than to Otis. "How could something like this happen?"

"Fell asleep, near as I can tell." Otis shook his head, then heaved a ragged sigh. "Don't rightly know how long he lay out there in the rain, but that boy's soaked clean through, I tell you. Long enough to work hisself into a fever, that much is sure."

Callie cupped her elbows and gasped. "Oh, my."

"Birdie got him cleaned up best she could. Doc came to see 'im a while ago, but he had to get back to 'is office to tend to a half dozen others."

"A half dozen others?"

Frowning, Otis nodded. "All burnin' up with the fever, and delirious, too, same as Micah." His frown intensified. "Couple o' years back, influenza come barrelin' into town. Doc says it ain't that, but I dunno. This sure does put me in mind of it."

"Oh, my," she said again.

"He's been askin' for you," Otis said. "Birdie sent me to fetch you. Said she'd be down here as soon as she gets into clean, dry clothes, so's she can mind that baby while you see to Micah."

As if on cue, Birdie burst in the front door. "I reckon those boys are still upstairs, fast asleep, right where anybody in their right mind would be at this hour." She hung her coat and hat on a peg, then placed one boot on the bottom step of the staircase. "Well, don't just stand there like a human fly catcher, girl! Fetch your coat and hat and hurry up across the street." She took another step up, then paused to add, "I do declare, never seen anything quite like it in all my born days."

Callie pressed her lips together and grabbed her shawl. "How bad is his fever?"

"Oh, it's high, all right. But his fever's not what I was talkin' about." She winked at her husband. "He's so moony-eyed over you that I'm thinkin' love is more to blame for his condition than—"

"Birdie Sullivan," Otis interrupted her, "get on up there and see to them young'uns, and let Callie see to her man."

Her man? Callie swallowed hard. "I should wake Jonah and tell him what's going on before I go, so that—"

"Nonsense," Birdie said, holding up a hand. "That brother o' yours 'n' me have had plenty o' heart-to-heart talks. And don't even give a thought to carin' for that baby. I might not've been blessed with a passel o' my own, but I know which end is up!"

Callie hurried down the street to Doc Lane's office, praying with every step that Micah would be all right. Because, if he wasn't, what would become of Reid?

And what would become of her?

"Never saw anything like it," Doc Lane said minutes later, running a broad forefinger across the page of a medical text. "Similar to influenza, and yet...." He scratched his head. "It's a puzzle."

As his voice trailed off, Callie gazed around at the cots lined up in the doctor's back room, where eight Eagle Pass residents lay shivering under thick blankets and colorful quilts.

Looking up from his book, the doctor added, "As you can see, there's no room for Micah here. I'd bet my stethoscope that Birdie will volunteer to nurse him back to health, but I'm going to advise against it." He closed the book and slid it back onto the shelf above his cluttered desk.

"Oh?"

"She's too stubborn and bighearted to admit it, but she hasn't fully recovered from everything that happened to her in that fire. Tending him would be too much at her age and in her condition."

Callie nodded. "Maybe Otis can take him home, where his mother and sisters can—"

"Absolutely not! That long ride would kill him, for sure."

Callie's heart beat double-time. "I don't suppose there's been time yet to notify his family."

"We'll worry about that once we find a place to put him."

"Then, bring him to my place."

The doctor's bushy white eyebrows rose, then fell. "Did you hear me say just now that he could be contagious?"

"Yes, and when I was a girl, I helped out during an outbreak of cholera." She stopped short of telling him that her pa had volunteered the *Maybelline* as a floating hospital when the town officials in Austin had quarantined the infected citizens, because the story had made headlines all over the world, and so had news of the explosion that sank the steamer three years later. She'd seen those stacks of old newspapers in the doctor's office. What if he'd read both articles and, by some strange stroke of bad luck, connected her to the latter tragedy? A long shot, she knew, but if the truth about her got out.... Callie would not gamble with her brother's happiness and well-being here, in a town where folks didn't treat him differently just because he was deaf.

"Once we separated the sickest patients from those with minor symptoms," she continued, "it was a lot easier to control the spread. I'll put Micah in the back room of my shop and keep the door closed. Jonah won't have any reason to go in there, and I'll keep Reid far from him."

"Won't work."

"What do you mean, it won't work? Of course it'll work." *It has to work, for Micah's sake!*

"You'll carry the infection on your skin and clothes straight to Jonah and that innocent little boy."

"Not if I wear a mask and a gown, like I did during the cholera outbreak. I'll wear gloves, too. Why, I must have fifty pair in the shop."

He rummaged in his medicine cabinet, muttering as bottles and vials clinked together. "You weren't here when we turned Matilda Montgomery's house into a hospital during the influenza epidemic."

"No, but I've heard so much about that great lady."

Doc Lane handed her half a dozen tiny vials, which she slid into her apron pocket.

"This is a temporary arrangement, mind you," the doctor said. "I'll send some men to fetch him once a bed opens up." He started for the door, then turned to add, "You realize, of course, that when we do, you'll have to burn his linens and scour your house from top to bottom."

"Yes. I don't mind."

"Well, it's against my better judgment, but I don't see as we have a choice. We can't let him stay with the Sullivans, for obvious reasons."

"I understand."

The doctor rattled off a short list of instructions and made Callie promise to send for him if she ran into trouble. "Uh-oh. Looks like Earl Potter needs help." He started toward Earl's bed, then stopped and turned around. "I'll give you half an hour or so to go home and get things set up, and then I'll help Otis bring Micah over." He paused and looked her in the eye. "If you change your mind between now and then—"

"I won't." Callie pulled her shawl more snugly around her shoulders and hurried to Otis and Birdie's, berating herself for wasting five minutes with the doctor that could have been spent getting a room ready for Micah. She'd wanted to gather every available scrap of information about whatever illness was toppling the men, women, and children of Eagle Pass, but, unfortunately, Doc Lane hadn't known much more than she had. When she reached the Sullivans' porch, she inhaled deeply and exhaled slowly, trying to catch her breath, then pushed the front door open.

"Callie?" Birdie appeared at the top of the stairs. "I thought you'd never get here!"

"And I thought you were staying with Jonah and Reid," Callie replied, shutting the door behind her.

"I was going to, but your brother shooed me away. Said he'd take care of the boy, and you might need help takin' care o' Micah."

"I stopped by to see Doc Lane," Callie explained, "to find out what I needed to know before taking Micah home with me."

"Home? With you? Nonsense! He's fine right where he is."

Callie remembered what the doctor had said about Birdie's big heart and her stubborn streak. "That isn't what Doc Lane said, but he'll be here in no time, so I'll just let the two of you hash it out." She glanced past Birdie. "Where's Micah?"

"Hash it out, indeed," the woman grumbled. She led Callie down the hall and into a small bedroom behind the kitchen of the Sullivans' tiny apartment. "He's been talkin' out of his head, mostly about you and some woman named Pauline. Fever must've addled his brain, 'cause I've never heard-tell of any such body."

Micah hadn't mentioned any names when he'd told her about Reid's mother, but Callie had a feeling that's exactly who Pauline was. Not that it mattered. Getting Micah healthy again was the only important thing right now.

"Otis is fetching his horses and the buggy," Birdie said, opening the door. "And, in case Micah asks, he'll get word to the Nevilles, too."

"Oh, yes. They're bound to worry when he doesn't come home."

"More important than that, they need to be warned to stay away from town."

Callie nodded and stepped into the dark, quiet room. "I'll stay only a moment. I need to get back to the boys." *And fix up a proper room for Micah.*

"Callie?" Micah's voice sounded weak.

"Go to him," Birdie said, giving her a gentle shove. "Knowing you're here will ease his mind."

"I know you work hard, but surely you could have come up with an easier way to get some time off," Callie told Micah softly.

A feeble smile lifted one corner of his mouth. "Man's gotta do what a man's gotta do...."

"See?" Birdie whispered. "That's how it's been since we found him. Sane and rational one minute, talking crazy the next." She shook her head. "I'm glad Hanna isn't here to see this. Poor woman would worry herself sick."

Callie remembered that Micah's mother, like Birdie, hadn't fully recovered from her bout of influenza. "He's young and strong," she said. "I'm sure he'll be himself again in no time."

*Who are you trying to convince, Callie Roberts?
Birdie Sullivan or yourself?*

Gus Applegate sat with his back to the wall, glowering at the door. What had made him think the woman would be on time? "'Specially a woman like that," he muttered.

Just then, a waiter breezed by and paused. "I'm sorry, sir?"

"Nothin'," he said. "Just speculatin' 'bout womenfolk."

The waiter adjusted the big plate-laden tray balanced on his shoulder. "Oh, they do like to keep a man waiting, don't they?" With a shake of his head, he added, "Just let me get rid of these dishes, and I'll be back with some coffee."

Gus nodded, though he didn't really want any coffee. He felt old and out of place, tired and crabby. He hadn't wanted to come to this part of town, or any other part of San Francisco, for that matter. But he had to earn a living, and that gunshot to his gut had ended his career with the Texas Rangers. Working as a Pinkerton, he'd visited dozens of bustling cities on both sides of the Mississippi, and, while the weather and the way people talked made each one distinct, none of them had managed to hide their gritty, sordid sides, no matter how many fancy topiary gardens or gilded buildings they boasted.

At another table across the room, a gaggle of middle-aged ladies had gathered for lunch. Their girlish tittering and dainty ways did nothing but increase Gus's annoyance. He'd be hard-pressed to choose what bothered him more, their wagging tongues or their grotesque hats.

True to his word, the waiter returned, this time carrying an ornate silver pot. He'd earn a little more than the standard tip for recognizing that Gus was in no mood for idle chitchat. As the man moved on to other tables nearby, the Ranger-turned-Pinkerton wondered how a pot that small could possibly hold enough brew to fill a dozen teacups. The answer dawned when he lifted his own tiny cup to his lips and drained the contents in one swallow.

If Pauline Devereaux thought she'd gain the upper hand by keeping him waiting, she had another think coming. He'd already wasted enough time on this broad, scouring every city west of San Antone for scraps of information about her. She'd told Micah Neville that San Francisco was her destination, but Gus would have bet his paycheck that she'd been lying as part of her scheme. He would have lost the bet, however, and now, more than ever, he hated California.

He'd never been to France, but he didn't need to travel the world to understand why San Francisco had earned the nickname "Paris of the West." Gaudy and filthy, populated by rude people and even ruder tourists, it echoed night and day with the clang of cable cars. *What a bunch of harebrained fools,* Gus thought, *squandering their gold rush wealth on silly gadgets and ridiculous outfits.*

Well, to be fair, they hadn't all frittered away the fruits of the mines. The "nabobs," as they were called, had invested prudently and now flaunted the profits of their wisdom in their stately mansions. No doubt the big-hat ladies on the other side of the restaurant ran with that crowd. Otherwise, they'd be home, cooking and scrubbing and serving the nabobs.

Exhaling a groan of displeasure, Gus pulled his gold watch out of his pocket and popped open the cover. The trusty timepiece told him that Pauline was half an hour late. He'd mete out a reprimand by not treating her to lunch, and, unless she showed up in the next five minutes, she wouldn't get coffee or tea, either. If not for that generous cash advance Micah Neville had paid him, this town and everyone in it would be history, and Gus would be back in Texas.

But that wasn't true, and Gus knew it. Not once had he gone back on his word, and he hoped to say the same on his dying day. Besides, he was genuinely curious to learn more about the woman who'd left her defenseless baby in the arms of a stranger.

Not that he was surprised. The promise of high-class theater performances might have lured her West, but vaudeville was where she'd ended up, and he'd seen enough gaudy leaflets tacked to trees and walls all over town to believe they'd deliver "a dazzling display of heterogeneous splendor, designed to educate, edify, amaze, and uplift!" A picture of Pauline, with her name printed underneath, on one of the flyers had led him straight to a tacky little warehouse near the bay, where he'd realized as he'd watched her perform that the wily grin captured by the photographer pretty much summed up Pauline Devereaux.

And then, as if choreographed by a skillful stage manager, the woman suddenly appeared at the head-waiter's station. The black-suited gent bowed low, then led her to the corner table where Gus had been waiting for more than half an hour. As she swaggered down the marble steps and across the Persian rug, he couldn't help but wonder if the headwaiter smirked because of a memory of Pauline in her scanty costume or because of her reputation alone.

Gus stood up and pulled out the chair across the table. "Miss Devereaux," he drawled, "I'm so pleased you could finally make it."

Pauline made no apology for her tardiness. Instead, she signaled the waiter. "I'll have some tea," she said, settling onto the chair's brocade seat. "And croissants with jam."

Stiff-backed and thin-lipped, he said, "Of course, ma'am. And will there be anything else for you, sir?"

"More coffee," Gus barked, "strong and black."

Leaning back in her chair, Pauline crossed her legs and tidied her skirts. Next, she proceeded, slowly and deliberately, to take off her black gloves, one finger at a time. "Now, then," she finally said. "What is it you want to know?"

He slid an envelope out of his breast pocket and tucked it under the lip of his saucer. "I'm sure you recall, Miss Devereaux, corresponding with Mr. Neville recently."

Aside from a quick glance at the name and address inked across the envelope, she didn't react. She was a good actress, but, lucky for him, not as talented as she believed herself to be. He'd have no trouble keeping up the pretense, because, without his own acting skills, Gus never would have managed to apprehend so many outlaws. He smiled slyly. "And I'm equally sure that you recall meeting with him at the train station in San Antonio, to discuss"—he patted the letter—"an important matter, if my memory serves me."

Her thick, dark lashes fluttered, but only for an instant. "Yes," she said softly, "I do recall that meeting." She took a moment, no doubt to summon a particular mood, and then met his gaze and demurely folded her hands on the table.

He wasn't fooled. He'd seen it all before, too many times to count. After the waiter had delivered her tea and refilled his coffee, Gus gave her pricy hat and elegant gown a quick glance. "It appears you spent the money he gave you wisely."

He'd expected her to take it as a compliment.

He'd been wrong. Eyes flashing, Pauline said, "How boring would this old world be, Mr. Applegate, if we all shared the same tastes in people and clothing?" She paused to sip her tea.

He'd gain nothing by spoiling her moment of victory. Instead, he'd use the time to decide whether or not to tell her that he knew she was the only child born to Paul and Eden Turner of Lubbock, Texas, and that she'd spent the last three years flitting from one obscure theater to the next, each one specializing in a brand of burlesque more tawdry than the previous. *You can dress up a pig and give it a phony, highfalutin name,* he thought, *but it's still a pig.*

Evidently, his grin unnerved her, for a trace of a shaky laugh sneaked out when she said, "Perhaps, sir, you'll be so kind as to tell me exactly why you've summoned me here."

Gus had dealt with murderers, rapists, and rustlers, yet something told him none of those experiences would help him here today. He would have to draw more on his dealings with cardsharps and the game of poker. He sat back and sipped his coffee, choosing his words. "I'm sure it will come as no surprise to you that Mr. Neville is concerned about the future well-being of young Reid."

Her eyes narrowed slightly. "As his father, that is as it should be, wouldn't you say?"

He put the letter back into his pocket. "As his mother, shouldn't you be concerned about—"

"I never claimed to be that baby's mother!" she snapped. The outburst appeared to surprise her even more than Gus, for she took a deep breath and let it out slowly. "It's hardly my fault if he misunderstood my relationship to the boy!"

Gus tried to recall, word for word, what Micah had told him about his meeting with Pauline. Unfortunately, nothing in his memory could disprove her statement. "Perhaps you'd be so kind as to help me understand the true nature of your relationship to the child." He didn't expect her to divulge anything new. At least, not without getting something in return. So, he slid a second envelope from his pocket. "A thousand dollars," he said, tapping it against the table, "for information about the boy."

When she reached for the envelope, he snatched it back. "Not so fast, missy." He leaned forward until their noses were practically touching. "Start talkin'. If you can convince me that every word you say is true, then maybe you'll get the money."

Her gaze darted from the envelope to his face and back again. Then, she sat back, lifted the delicate china cup, and took a dainty sip. "It's a long story," she said. "I think I'll order a pot to share, for you'll find that tea with plenty of sugar will make it go down a bit more easily."

Why does every part of me ache this way? Micah wondered. He'd just left the San Antonio jail, where the sheriff had refused to turn his cousin loose, even though he knew it had been grief that his wife had lost another baby that had driven Dan to drink until he'd all but destroyed the corner saloon. Maybe he'd joined Dan on this binge. That sure would explain his fuzzy thinking. Had he and Dan gone east to buy seed, or to deliver a stud bull?

One thing was certain: he couldn't tell Dan about Reid, at least not until the poor man got a grip on himself. If losing another child had messed him up this badly, what would finding out that he'd fathered an illegitimate son do to him?

A familiar male voice broke into his thoughts. "You're doing all you can," it said, "making him rest, getting plenty of soup and water into him."

Ah, that's right—Doc Lane. The flu had returned with a vengeance to Eagle Pass and laid many low. But when had he and Dan returned from San Antonio?

Next, a woman spoke. He recognized her voice, too, though she didn't sound nearly as calm as the doctor. "Rest? You must be joking. How's he supposed to get any rest, tossing and turning as he does day and night?"

"Nightmares are one of the symptoms, I'm afraid. When his fever breaks, those should stop."

Should? Micah clutched his pillow and turned to face the wall, hoping the woman who'd sounded so much like Callie would just go away. He couldn't bear to think about her, out behind the church, alone in a wooden box in the cold, hard ground. It didn't matter one whit to him that so many others had succumbed to the flu, and the pastor's reassurance that she'd joined her family in heaven hadn't soothed him, either. All he wanted was another chance to tell her how much he loved her, to thank her for stepping up to help him with Reid when even his blood kin didn't seem to want to.

The thought of the boy he'd brought home from San Antonio deepened his sorrow. It hadn't taken long for him to love that baby as his own, and he would trade places with him in a heartbeat, if the good Lord would only let him!

"Micah."

There it was, again—the angelic voice that sounded so much like Callie's.

"Open your mouth, Micah, so I can get some broth into you."

Why he so quickly obeyed, Micah didn't know. But, since the sickness had claimed the lives of everyone he cared about, what could it hurt to cooperate? Soon, it would take him, too, he hoped, and he'd never have to walk through the cemetery, reading the tombstones etched with the names of his parents, sisters, uncles, aunts, cousins, nephews, and nieces. Most heartbreaking of all would be the small, white stone engraved with a lamb, along with the name "Reid Neville."

"Lean on me," the sweet voice said. "I need to get you to the chair, so I can change your linens. You've sweat clean through another set of sheets and blankets."

Guilt surged through him when he heard her tiny grunt. If he could have helped her more, he would have, because he was worried that the sickness would attack her, too, if she kept up this pace.

At least she had the good sense to cover her face and to wear a long robe and gloves.

The next thing he knew, Micah was on his back again, inhaling the scent of line-dried sheets and feeling the weight of a thick, warm quilt being tucked around him. "There," said Callie's twin. "That should help put a stop to those shivers."

He heard another man's voice. It sounded familiar, too, but he couldn't connect it to a face or a name. The guy ranted on and on about the unfairness of this terrible illness, which had sickened old and young, male and female. If God was omnipotent and all-loving, he raged, why had He allowed the flu to take everyone he loved from him?

Micah found himself wishing someone would offer some sort of solace to the poor fellow, especially when he let out that strange, haunting sob. His voice grew louder and more insistent. "Why?" he demanded. "Why were they all taken? And why was I spared?"

"Oh, poor, sweet Micah," said the gentle voice. Wait. Did that mean he was the ranting man? But that didn't make a lick of sense!

"If only I knew how to comfort you."

Apparently, the Almighty had taken pity on him and chosen to reunite him with his loved ones. "So," he said, looking around the room, "this must be heaven, then."

"Hardly!" she said, a smile in her voice.

"No?"

She pointed at a mound of sheets and towels on the floor. "I doubt they have dirty linens in heaven, but it sure is heavenly to know you aren't delirious anymore."

Delirious?

"You've had some horrifying nightmares, I'm afraid."

Nightmares?

He didn't realize he'd repeated those words aloud until Callie said, "I never noticed before, but there's a terrible echo in this room."

Micah looked around the small room. "Where am I, and how long have I been here?"

"You're in the back room of my shop, and you've been here for eight days."

"But why am I here, instead of Doc's office?"

"You started out at the Sullivans'," she said. "They're the ones who found you alongside the road. And, don't worry, Otis is taking care of your horses and wagon. Anyway, Doc Lane said he'd send someone for you as soon as a bed opened up." She shrugged. "Either that never happened, or he was just so busy helping people that he forgot."

"So, you put your reputation on the line for me yet again." Micah shook his head. "Why are you so determined to give fodder to the gossips?"

"I'm not! Besides, I think the good citizens of Eagle Pass have had more important things to concern themselves with than—"

"I stand corrected. I'm sure a scandal was the furthest thing from their minds. So, tell me, how many...how many died this time?"

"None, praise the Lord." She pulled off a white glove and pressed her palm to his forehead. "Well, praise Him twice, because it seems your fever has broken, finally," she said, finger-combing the hair from his forehead. "Are you thirsty?"

When he nodded, she held a tumbler to his lips, and he sipped eagerly until it was empty. He waited until she'd set the glass aside to ask, "If no one died, then what about the graves and the eulogies?"

"As I said, you were delirious. And the nightmares are normal with fevers that high, too. Your poor mother was beside herself with worry when she came to visit five days ago. I sent Otis to tell your family, and he urged them to stay away, lest they catch the same illness."

Flopping back onto the pillow, Micah draped an arm over his eyes. "So, what's the diagnosis?"

"The doctor isn't quite sure what you had."

"Had?" He uncovered his face. "So, it's really over, then?"

"Mostly."

The word unnerved him slightly.

"At first, Doc thought it was influenza, but he changed his mind when it spread faster and came with different side symptoms, and more of them." She tucked the covers under his chin. "Now then, that's enough conversation from you for a while. Why don't you take a nap while I get this laundry washed and hung out to dry?"

"All right. But what about Reid? Is he fine, too?"

"Yes, he's fine."

"Is Jonah with him now?"

Callie nodded, causing a curl to pop free from her bun. When she brushed it back into place, he saw the angry, ropelike scar that twisted down the side of her face. He looked away quickly so that she wouldn't see him staring and feel the need to hide it.

"Last time I checked, they were in the parlor, looking through the Sears and Roebuck catalog." She giggled. "My, how that boy loves to sit and point at all the pictures. Reid loves to look at them, too."

A hearty laugh punctuated her little joke, and Micah thanked God his fever hadn't altered his hearing so that he'd miss the sound of it.

"And now, it's nap time, Micah Neville."

"You look like you could use one, yourself. When was the last time you got any sleep?"

One side of her mask lifted in a silly grin as she picked up the laundry basket. "Once you're hale and hearty, I'll be more than happy to take a nice, long nap."

It looked as though he'd have to be content with her word on it.

For now.

Chapter 15

"Well," Pauline said, "it all started in San Antonio, when one of the girls I worked with found herself in a family way, without a husband to round out the picture, if you know what I mean. Poor thing couldn't perform with a baby in her belly. I mean, what man would pay to see a pregnant woman prancing back and forth across the stage? So, our troupe all chipped in and took care of her. When the baby was born, we took turns caring for him, as well." She paused to pour herself another cup of tea, then continued. "Harriet never really got better after Reid was born, and we figured that was because she'd always been rather frail."

Gus nearly choked on his coffee when she added, "Turned out she had the cancer." Tears filled her eyes, and her lower lip trembled. "We were there with her, all of us, standing around her bed on her final night...."

If it had been any other woman sitting across from him, Gus might have felt guilty, wondering if her tears were the real thing or mere proof of her acting skills. But this wasn't any other woman. It was the talented Pauline Eden Devereaux.

"One by one, she forced all of us to promise we'd take care of Reid."

"Forced you?" A dying woman wielded that much power over her friends? Gus didn't understand, and he said so.

"None of us would claim to be a saint, Mr. Applegate. We know what we are, and we know what folks say about what we do." She narrowed her eyes. "But it might interest you to know that not one of us *chose* that line of work." She hesitated, then lifted her chin and focused on something over his shoulder. "None of us had any kin when we met, so, naturally, we became family to one another."

He supposed that was believable enough. He'd worked with a few men who'd joined up with the Texas Rangers for similar reasons.

"We couldn't very well send our sister into the great beyond without granting her her final wish, now, could we?"

"No, I don't suppose you could have." Pauline's story reminded him of the time, not long after he'd pinned a silver star to his vest for the very first time, when he'd made a similar pledge to a lieutenant who'd been shot in the stomach and was writhing in pain. Gus had promised to collect the man's pay and get it into his wife's hands. It had taken nearly a month to make good on his oath, and, some nights, the widow's grateful yet grief-stricken face still haunted his dreams.

"So, of course, we gave our word to take care of Reid. Once Harriet was dead and buried, we drew straws to see who'd mind the boy while the rest of us toasted her memory." He might have summoned a morsel of admiration for Pauline if she hadn't added that tidbit.

She went on to tell him that a gal by the name of Viola had drawn the shortest straw, and that, while they'd been in the bar after the funeral, singing, drinking, and swapping stories about Harriet, a cowboy had sauntered up to offer his condolences. "The minute he was out of earshot," Pauline continued, "we asked the barkeep who he was. Turned out he was Dan Neville from Eagle Pass, whose family owned half the land in West Texas."

Gus didn't need to hear the rest of the story to know what had happened next, but he sat quietly and listened, mostly to see if she'd stretch the truth or invent a new story altogether.

"He was blind drunk, see, so we carried him upstairs and put him to bed. Told him that, although he'd been to our place lots of times, he'd been that drunk only once before." Did a guilty conscience inspire her frown, or had Pauline talked herself into believing it wasn't their fault that the whiskey had numbed Dan's brain too much to count backwards, much less absolve himself of any part in Reid's parentage?

"We waited a spell to give him time to drag his drunken self home, and then we sat down to write that letter in your pocket. The only thing left to do after that was decide who'd sign it." Pauline groaned. "Lucky, lucky me. That time, I drew the shortest straw."

What would she say, Gus wondered, if he told her the letter never made it into the right hands, and that it had been Micah Neville, not Dan, who'd met her at the train station?

Pauline seemed to be finished with her story. While it sounded credible enough, Gus aimed to confirm the facts, just the same.

She glanced at the pocket where he'd stashed the envelope of cash, then met his eyes. "Do you have any more questions, Mr. Applegate?"

Gus didn't understand the overpowering desire he felt to make her squirm. She had no right to look so comfortable, spewing her well-rehearsed lines. He stared at her for a full thirty seconds, maybe more, hoping the tactic that had worked so well when he'd grilled criminals would be equally effective with her. To get right down to it, was she really all that different from a bank robber or a cattle rustler?

"Matter of fact," he finally said, "I do have a question." He rested both his arms on the table. "How'd you know Neville wouldn't abuse the boy, or worse?"

Eyes wide, she blinked. Surely, she'd considered that possibility before now.

"Well," she finally said, as if she'd given the matter all the thought in the world, "it made sense that if he and his kin owned that big a slice of Texas, he couldn't afford to bring any shame to the family name, because who'd want to do business with people like that?"

"Not too bad, Pauline, for an answer you made up on the spot. But you can do better." He leaned back and crossed his arms over his chest. "Take as long as you need. I have all the time in the world."

For an instant, she let him witness her frustration, but she quickly regained her composure. "Even falling-down drunk, he said things like 'Please' and 'Thank you' and 'Pardon me.'" She shrugged. "That told me he'd been raised right, because I'd learned the hard way how—" She clamped her mouth shut and glared into her cup for an instant. "Little Reid must have sensed it, too, because he took to him right away."

Gus only nodded. She was no different from every other swindler who'd crossed his path. With time and patience—and enough rope—she'd hang herself with the truth.

"Anything was better than the life he was living in the saloon. I mean, what kind of upbringing is that for a boy, listening to the brawling and bawling and caterwauling day in, day out? Why, I'll bet the poor little fellow has nightmares about some of the things he saw, even though he was too young to understand it all. Shootings and fistfights, and"—she buried her face in her hands—"and things even this hardened hussy is too much of a lady to repeat."

"Well, that sure is some tale, Miss Devereaux."

"It isn't a tale. It's the truth!" she snapped. "Every last word."

"Then, you'll have no trouble giving me a few days to check things out."

She smirked. "And just how do you hope to accomplish that?"

Evidently, Pauline didn't believe he had the resources or the brains to verify her story. "A few questions here, a telegram there," he said, getting to his feet. "A visit with a judge, the sheriff, and a barkeep or two, and I should have some good, solid answers by this time next week."

Her face paled, despite the rosy rouge she'd slathered on her cheeks.

Gus smiled. "Meet me right here, one week from now." He tossed enough money on the table to pay for their beverages, then patted the pocket holding the envelope stuffed with cash. "And please, don't be late. If you are, I'm afraid I'll give in to the temptation to spend every penny of this on myself."

He left her sitting there, wide-eyed and slack-jawed, and chuckled as he hustled toward the door. Finally, he'd found the magic words to melt her glacial resolve and penetrate that thick veneer of self-confidence.

Gus had never been a Sunday-go-to-meeting kind of man, but he believed in the mighty power of God. As he climbed the stairs to his room, he remembered why Micah Neville had hired him in the first place and prayed with all that was in him that his investigation would prove every word of Pauline's story.

Because, if it didn't, only the good Lord knew what would become of little Reid.

"You really put your whole self into every job, don't you?"

Callie cut loose a tiny squeal, followed by a nervous giggle. "Gracious me, Birdie, you startled me!" Grabbing a towel from the clothesline, she blotted the soapy water that had splashed everywhere, soaking her apron, shirtsleeves, and hair, being careful not to expose the ugly scar that marred her cheek.

"Sorry. Didn't mean to frighten you." The woman chuckled. "But, really, it's as much your fault as mine. I've never known anybody to focus so intently on scrubbin' pillow slips!"

Callie giggled again. "I'm just afraid that if I don't focus, I might fall asleep and drown in the washtub."

"Not getting much slumber these days, eh?"

"Oh, I expect I'm getting about as much as you." She straightened to meet the older woman's eyes. "How's Otis doing? I haven't seen him since he came to alert me about Micah last week."

"He's holdin' his own, but, I declare, he can try my patience like no other bein' on God's green earth. If it isn't 'Fetch my paper,' or 'What time's supper?' it's 'I'm powerful thirsty.' And, if I'm upstairs, you can bet the thing he needs is downstairs." Birdie sighed and looked to the heavens. "But I oughtn't be complainin'. The old buzzard annoys me to distraction, but, just between you and me, I wouldn't have it any other way."

Callie smiled. "You've experienced no symptoms of the illness yourself?"

"No, thank the good Lord! What about Jonah and the baby?"

"Both blessedly healthy."

"Praise Jesus. But that's no surprise, really. Doc told me how you hid under a gown, mask, and gloves and boiled the beans out of every blessed thing in the place. Maybe now you can catch up on your sleep."

"I'm fine, really. It was only a few days." Callie stifled a yawn.

Birdie's robust harrumph echoed across the yard. "If you ask me, it oughtta be permanent. Why, it's clear as the ribs on your washboard that he's in love with you. And you're doin' a far better job hidin' that scar o' yours than hidin' your feelings for him."

Callie didn't know which to cover first, her hard-beating heart or her scar. Instinct drew her hand to her temple. Yes, the curls still covered it, so—

"Heavens to Betsy!" Birdie exclaimed. "You don't really believe that you've been foolin' anybody, do you? Why, I spotted the silly thing the minute we met, and

I'd be surprised if that isn't true of everybody else in town." She slid an arm around Callie's shoulders and gave her a sideways hug. "Honey, even if that scar covered half your face—no, *all* of it—you'd still be the prettiest li'l thing we've seen in a long, long time."

Callie didn't know what to say, and so she went back to scrubbing the linens.

"You keep rubbing that way, you'll wear a hole clean through your sheet." Birdie grabbed Callie's wrists and pulled her hands out of the washtub. "Here," she said, handing her a dry towel. "Come inside and sit with me for a spell. You could use the rest, and I could use a slice of the pie I brought for you." She laughed, then stooped to pick up a basket. "I forgot that Otis can't hold down much more'n broth yet, and I baked three pies this mornin'. Gave one to D.W. over at the hotel and thought maybe you and Jonah might like one, too." She linked her other arm with Callie's and led her toward the back porch.

As much as she enjoyed Birdie's company, Callie couldn't invite her inside, because the woman didn't know the meaning of the word "Quiet"!

"The boys are napping," she said, her own voice barely above a whisper. "Would you mind very much if we had our pie and coffee out here on the porch?"

"Nappin'? What boys?"

"Why, Jonah, Reid, and Micah, of course."

Birdie raised one graying eyebrow and studied Callie's face. "He's not still here!"

Callie grinned. "He's about ready to go home, I think, but he's still extremely fatigued. Jonah's been helping more with Reid, so he's tired, too. I stepped inside to check on Micah a few minutes ago, and they were all snoring!"

"Well, at least we'll get a little peace an' quiet." Birdie winked, then sat down on the top porch step. "This'll do just fine. It's a mild day, and I'm more in the mood for conversation than I am for pie and coffee, anyway."

For the next few minutes, Callie listened as Birdie told her how Otis had reacted to the illness. He'd had nightmares, too, and they'd frightened Birdie every bit as much as Micah's had frightened Callie.

"I do wish that Doc Lane could identify this illness," Callie admitted. "I don't know when I've been more afraid." But, even as she said it, Callie knew that wasn't true. That night on the Brazos, when she'd dodged fiery debris while searching for.... She shook her head to clear it of the ugly memories.

"So, has Micah given you any hint as to when he might propose?"

The sudden shift in the conversation rendered Callie speechless, and Birdie was more than happy to fill the silence. "If I'd been blessed with a son, I'd want him to be just like Micah. Why, that boy is as honest as the day is long, with a heart the size o' Texas."

Callie might have voiced her agreement if Birdie hadn't launched into a story about Micah as a boy. "I hate to speak ill of the dead," Birdie said, "but that old biddy Betsy Webster loved few things more than she loved gossip. Otis and I had just made our decision to pack up and spare ourselves the humiliation of having the banker come in and kick us out when she burst into our room behind the shop, breathing like she'd just run a country mile. 'Micah Neville was just in here,' she wheezed, 'hanging around your cash register, looking all sneaky-eyed and guilty!'

"I didn't bother to remind her that the Nevilles had money to burn, and I wasn't much in the mood to point out that even if he'd been the type to rob us—which I knew for certain he wasn't—there wasn't so much as a plugged nickel in that cash drawer.

"So, after Otis thanked her and showed her to the door, curiosity made us check that cash register. We found it stuffed full o' bills and coins."

Callie shook her head in amazement. "Micah had put money into the drawer to save you from losing the stable?"

"Yep, though you'll never get him to admit it," Birdie said with a chuckle. "We asked him about it next time he came to town, and he got all red-faced and tongue-tied. Said Betsy Webster must need new spectacles, or her head examined, 'cause why would he do such a thing? But Otis an' me, we knew better."

Smiling, Callie nodded, because she knew better, too.

Birdie went on to tell Callie about the magnificent Arabian that Micah had bought to replace Abel Miller's lame horse, and how he'd ordered a new pipe organ all the way from Paris when the church's old one quit working. In addition, Micah had somehow gotten wind of the fact that a lack of funds was all that stood between Penny Franklin and the English tea service her husband had ordered before his death, and the exact amount was found beside the order blank left at the store, along with a note that said, "Happy anniversary, after all. Love, Geoffrey."

Birdie recounted more than a dozen similar stories, each of them ending with a red-faced Micah denying any involvement in delivering joy and peace of mind to those who needed them.

By the time Birdie left, Callie was more certain than ever that she loved Micah Neville.

Now, if only she could convince herself that she deserved a man like him.

Chapter 16

*W*hen Gus returned to the hotel dining room, it didn't surprise him to see Pauline seated at the same corner table they'd shared the previous week. What did surprise him, however, was how youthful and innocent she looked with her face scrubbed clean of all theater paint.

"I trust you had a productive week," she said when he sat down across from her.

He took a sip of coffee, which she'd evidently ordered for him, then bit into a dry scone. "Humpf," he said. "I reckon a fancy name and a high price tag still don't guarantee that a thing's very good."

"I reckon the same could be said of actors"—she raised an eyebrow—"and Pinkerton detectives."

She seemed so calm and patient, so much more confident in her plain blue dress than she'd been in her elegant gown, and he couldn't help but smile. "Touché," Gus said.

"I presume my story checked out?"

"It did." If she asked for details about his research, he'd provide them. But something told him that, despite her wholesome appearance, Pauline wasn't interested in anything but the wad of money in his jacket pocket.

"I took the liberty of having this document drawn up," he said, sliding a sheet of paper across the table, "to protect everyone involved from having to revisit this issue in the future."

He watched as she read aloud the words he'd so carefully written with the fancy new fountain pen he'd bought at the jewelry store across from the hotel: "I, Pauline Eden Devereaux, do solemnly swear on this second day of December, in the year of our Lord eighteen hundred and eighty-nine, that I was of sound mind and body when I agreed at the deathbed of my friend, Harriet S. Nolan...." She stopped and looked up at him. "How did you know her last name was—oh, never mind." After a quiet groan, she kept reading. "...to find a safe and secure home for her infant son, Reid. I further solemnly swear under punishment of perjury"— she quirked an eyebrow and shook her head—"that I placed him in the care of one Micah Adam Neville...."

Now, she put the paper down. "Do you think I'm a complete imbecile, Mr. Applegate? I realize you're no attorney, so I can overlook the clumsiness of your so-called document, but to deliberately replace Dan's name with—"

"Do you still contend that you carried Dan Neville up two flights of stairs that night in San Antonio and lovingly tucked him into bed?"

"Yes, of course I do."

"And would you still insist that he was heavily intoxicated on the night in question?"

Pauline bristled and sat up straighter. "Now, see here. I don't know what you're trying to pull, but—"

"You spent that much time with the man, yet you never noticed that he was a full six inches shorter and thirty pounds lighter than the one you met at the train station a few months later? The one you left an innocent baby with?"

Now he had her attention! Her smug expression vanished, replaced by a look of stunned uncertainty. If Gus could have summoned a photographer to capture the moment, he would have, because he had no doubt that he was witnessing a rare occurrence, indeed. "I reckon it's time I told you a story, Pauline."

Gus proceeded to explain how, in her attempt at fancy penmanship, she'd crafted a *D* that looked like an *M*, resulting in the letter being opened by someone other than her intended recipient. He went on to say that since Dan had recently given up whiskey and taken a wife, Micah had decided to intercept her at the train station in order to preserve his cousin's new life.

"Odd, don't you think, that you and your colleagues felt better about leaving Harriet's helpless little boy in the care of a known drunkard than caring for him yourselves." He tapped the document. "That is why this paperwork is necessary."

Pauline silently read the rest of what he'd written, and she didn't look up again until she had signed her name on the line next to which two more lines remained: one for Judge Jones, the other for Sheriff Garth.

When she handed the paper back to him, Gus folded it and slid it into his pocket. "It's all been arranged," he said, standing. "Now, if you'll come with me, we can get these nasty legalities out of the way."

He could tell that she was chomping at the bit to ask, "But what about the money?" Chuckling to himself as he led the way out of the restaurant, he decided to let her sweat it out during the few minutes it would take them to reach the judge's chambers. The proceedings weren't likely to discourage her from repeating a similar performance at some point in the future, but at least the Nevilles—most important, little Reid—would never have to worry that she'd darken their doorstep.

It took less than five minutes for everyone assembled to scribble their signatures on the lines provided. When Gus produced a second identical document—one to register here at the courthouse, so that he could take the other for the Nevilles' files—Pauline's silence made it clear that she understood it was over. She had been bested. There would be no dipping into this pot the next time her funds ran low.

"Let me buy you supper," he said as they left the courthouse, "to celebrate our respective freedom."

"I'd just as soon be on my way," she said, drawing her arms tightly across her middle.

Her stance told him she was waiting for him to pay her; meanwhile, he was waiting for some show of humility. In a test of wills, she'd win, hands down. That's how it was, he'd learned, when charlatans were separated from their beloved money.

He might have drawn it out a bit longer, just for fun, but she'd wrung every drop of patience from him. Gus pulled out the envelope, opened it, and took out a hundred dollars. "My fee for the paperwork required to make sure the Nevilles never hear from you again," he said before handing her the rest.

She looked up at him and, for an instant, appeared small and fragile. It wasn't entirely her fault she'd turned out as she had. What could it hurt to give her the benefit of some hard-earned wisdom? "That's a lot of money," he said as she tucked it into her purse. "More than enough to get you out of this town and out of this life, permanently."

In just one blink, her wistful, vulnerable expression was replaced with a sly, scheming smile. "I like it here," she said, wrapping the purse strings twice around her wrist. "I like what I do and the people I work with, too." She took a few steps in the opposite direction, then stopped and faced him again. "But I appreciate the well-intended advice, all the same."

Whether her appreciation was genuine was between her and God now, Gus realized, watching her half run in the direction of the bank. He'd already decided not to send his report in the form of a letter or a telegram. This was something better delivered in person. Besides, he'd always liked Eagle Pass. There was nothing for him in San Antonio or Lubbock or Austin, for that matter. Micah had paid him well for his services. Why not settle in Eagle Pass for a while?

Head down and hands pocketed, he walked purposefully toward his hotel. With a little luck and a whole lot of God's blessing, he'd unpack in a week or so in that quaint little town on the banks of the Rio Grande.

He'd spent decade after decade making things right for other folks, most recently, Dan and Micah Neville, little Reid, even the devious schemer, Pauline Devereaux. Perhaps, in Eagle Pass, he could begin to heal from his own heartache of loss and make things right for himself for a change.

Chapter 17

$\mathscr{M}$icah smiled into the sunshine and gave his horse's neck a pat. It felt good to be back on his feet, bathed, shaved, and dressed in his regular clothes for the first time in well over a week. It felt good holding the letter from Oklahoma City, too, which had been waiting for him at the post office when he'd gone to pick up his mail and Callie's.

Whenever she traveled, his sister Beth had always made a point of writing long, newsy letters, and this one was no exception. He wasn't sure he'd have a chance to write back, considering how much work he needed to catch up on at the ranch, but he'd refuse to wallow in guilt over it, even if Beth would give him a sound scolding once she got home. Plus, he didn't want to burden Beth with the news of his troubles, which was sure to reach her, anyway, through the correspondence of their sisters, Emma and Astrid. She needed to recover from the loss of her husband, not worry about her brother's health.

In front of Simpson National Bank, a wagon carrying a replacement crew of miners slowed to allow old Millie McKenzie to shuffle across the road. "Why do her young'uns let her out without supervision?" one of them asked.

"Don't rightly know," his seatmate answered.

"It's a minor miracle she hasn't been run over."

"Minor," another echoed, laughing. "I get it." He elbowed the first fellow. "Funny. Very funny."

A second wagon traveling in the opposite direction braked, too, giving the gritty-faced passengers time to wave and hurl good-natured barbs across the way. "Skunk got into the mine," said one, "so you're in for a real foul night!"

"No fouler than usual," said another as the wagon crunched its way north.

A dog ran across the road, startling Micah's horse enough to require a hard tug on the reins. "Easy now," he said, patting its shoulder. "Easy."

It was hard deciding whether he'd prefer to read Beth's letter here, amid the hustle and bustle of the main street, or to wait until he'd reached the old post road, where he'd need to strain his ears to hear anything other than the steady thump of the horse's hooves.

Impatience got the better of him. He held the envelope in the same hand that held the reins and, with the other hand, tore it open and pulled out the letter. The instant he saw his sister's tidy penmanship, his back straightened, and his mood brightened. "It's lovely here," she'd written, "but, oh, how I miss everyone, you in particular, dear brother! I simply cannot wait to tell you in person everything about Oklahoma City. (Who would have thought one place could be so vastly different from another?) This visit has served its purpose, and I'm finally able to believe what you told me the morning that James joined Jesus in heaven."

Micah remembered James's funeral, and how Beth had stood stone-still and silent as the men of the church lowered his coffin into the ground. He remembered, too, how she'd drooped like a flower left too long in the sun when that first shovelful of dirt clattered onto its lid. He'd gathered her up in a brotherly embrace, and she'd collapsed against him, making him wonder, as huge sobs had wracked her slender frame, if a body could break apart from grief.

"I will always miss him, of course," the letter continued, "but it doesn't hurt so much now, and I can smile when I think of him, just as you promised I would. I can hardly wait to pass beneath the big Lazy N arch, and you are the only person in the entire world who knows why it will do my heart good to see it again."

Beth couldn't have been more than nine or ten when she'd told him that the wrought-iron gateway put her in mind of long, lean arms that had the power to welcome friends—and the strength to ban enemies.

"So much has happened, Micah, that it seems it'll be forever until I'm home again!" According to her postscript, Beth would arrive on the morning train in less than a week. If Micah had anything to say about it, he'd be the one to meet her at the station and drive her home.

When Micah looked up from the page, he grinned and brought Goldie to a stop. He now knew the exact distance from the post office to Callie's place: one page of a letter from Beth.

He dismounted and absentmindedly wound Goldie's reins around the hitching post, meanwhile drinking in the now familiar porch and the faded rocking chair where he'd spent the final hours of his convalescence, dozing peacefully, inhaling the scent of the freshly laundered blanket draped around his shoulders, or rocking as he listened to Callie chatting with customers or baby-talking to Reid. It still amazed him that her tiny house felt like more like home than the one he'd built on the Lazy N.

Callie appeared at the screen door, and his heartbeat quickened at the sight of her.

"I found your list of chores..." she said with a smile.

Only Callie could say something like that and make it sound like the warmest greeting he'd ever heard. He waited, as he'd learned that her pause was a signal of more to come.

"I know you'd planned to fetch the mail for me before heading home, but I hoped you'd agree to join us for lunch first."

Though his memories of those first hours spent here, recuperating, were hazy, Micah remembered how Callie had patiently spoon-fed him soup and weak tea and watered-down milk, celebrating every swallow that reached his stomach. "Where's Reid?" he asked, climbing the porch steps.

"Napping, thank the good Lord. We both needed the rest!"

When he stepped up beside her, she smiled even more broadly, and it was all he could do to keep from taking her in his arms and confessing that a cad lived inside him, and that cad was trying to tempt him into pretending a relapse so that she'd go right on pampering and caring for him. Instead, he said, "Wasn't a scrap o' mail for you today."

She raised one shoulder in a slight shrug. "Oh, well. No news is good news, I suppose."

He opened the screen door and followed her inside. "I got a letter from Beth."

"Did you! How's she doing?"

"I'm guessing she's finally adjusted to widowhood." How long would it take him to adjust if he lost Callie forever? Frowning at the gloomy thought, he tacked on, "As much as a person can get used to losing a loved one, that is."

She turned away so quickly that a lock of hair escaped her bun. Just as clouds block the sunlight, a shadow of sadness dimmed her smile. If anyone understood the pain of loss, it was Callie, who'd buried her mother, father, brother, and fiancé, all within hours of one another. He remembered the stories Jonah had told about their life on the *Maybelline*, and about the explosion. If the fiery images her brother had described remained so clear in Micah's mind, how much more vividly did they live in Callie's? If only he could think of a way to free her from that burden.

As usual, serving others won out over her grief, and he watched her set out four bowls, then place a soup spoon beside each. He wanted to tell her how much he admired her courage and strength, but he knew that such a statement would only embarrass her. As much as he'd enjoy seeing her pretty cheeks go pink with a blush, he decided to keep the compliment to himself.

"Did Beth say how much longer she'll be in Oklahoma City?" Callie asked.

"As a matter of fact, she's on her way home." His response caused an idea to begin forming in his brain. With God's grace and Gus's help, maybe he could give Callie the gift of freedom from guilt forever.

She clasped her hands under her chin. "Oh, Micah, you must be so relieved!"

"Relieved" wasn't the word he would have chosen. "It'll be good to see her," he conceded.

"Now, now," she said, her forefinger wagging like a metronome, "you don't need to pretend with me. I remember how much fretting you did while the fever had its hold on you."

Micah harrumphed. His recollection of that time was hazy, at best. "One of these days," he said, grinning, "I hope you'll fill me in."

She began pumping water into four tumblers. "Fill you in?"

"Yeah, on all the nonsense that spewed from my mouth while, as you so astutely put it, the fever had its hold on me."

Giggling, she set a glass of water near each bowl, then grunted as she lifted the big soup pot. After setting it in the middle of the table, she pulled out the chair nearest her. At his father's house, and at every other house on the Lazy N, this was the place reserved for the head of the family. Micah didn't know which touched him more: the fact that she'd set it aside for him, or the loving expression on her face when she said, "Sit and relax while I round up the boys. I'm sure Reid is awake by now, and Jonah is out back, working on some new sketches."

He took the liberty of filling all four bowls and then sat down in the chair beside Callie's. It wasn't that he took the honor she'd bestowed lightly, but he couldn't help wondering how her brother would feel if some neighbor sauntered into his house and assumed the head-of-the-table position. By all rights, that place was Jonah's.

The minute she entered the room with Reid on one hip, Callie glanced at the empty chair, then looked at Micah. With Jonah standing right there, he couldn't very well explain why he'd ignored her offer, so he merely shrugged and sent her a sheepish smile.

A slow grin lit her face, and she nodded.

Reid flapped his arms, looking more like a baby bird eager to leave its nest than a boy who was about to be strapped into a wooden high chair. Every one of his eight teeth showed when he squealed, "Da! Da-da!"

Micah chuckled and scooted his chair closer to Reid's. "It's good to see you, too, li'l buddy." He looked at Callie. "How long since we were all together like this?"

From the head of the table, Jonah said, "Too long. It's good to have you back."

"It's good to be back."

"You had us worried," the younger man said with a wink. "I spent hours trying to think of a polite way to ask for your saddle if...well, you know."

Micah joined in his merry laughter as Callie feigned shock. "Listen to the two of you, making light of such a dreadful subject!" Then, she threw back her head and laughed, exposing the ragged, red scar. Oh, to see her this way—oblivious to it and enjoying life to its fullest, all of the time!

"Pass the biscuits, please?" she said, patting her curls back into place.

Micah held the basket just out of reach. "Trade you for the salt shaker."

"My soup is perfect, just as it is." She grinned, setting off the all-too-familiar chain of events: hammering heart, pounding pulse, sweating palms, and dry mouth. To mask it, he asked her to pass the butter, too.

It felt so normal and natural sitting here, sharing this simple meal and joyous laughter with some of the people he cared most deeply about. This was the life he wanted to live, day and night, until he drew his last breath, and he aimed to spend a lot of time on his knees, asking the Lord for guidance to make it happen.

In a strange way, putting things in motion to deliver Callie's special gift would be a blessing to Micah, too, for it would distract him from the miles and hours that would separate him from her once he returned to the Lazy N.

"I'm so sorry I had to cancel at the last minute," Callie said one week later, as Micah stepped into her parlor. "He's just been so fussy these past few days that I thought it best to stay home."

Micah hung his Stetson on a peg behind the door, then put his coat beside it. "All the women at the ranch are convinced he's cutting teeth, and that you'll be less protective as more babies come along." He winked. "I told them I'm in full agreement, if only because nobody would enjoy the visit if he's feeling poorly, least of all Reid."

"Whew," Callie said. "You don't know how relieved I am to hear that you understand, because I would have loved to share another meal with your family."

"Fibber."

If he hadn't been grinning when he said it, she might have questioned the sincerity of his previous comment. "Fibber? I'm afraid I don't—"

He helped himself to one of the mugs hanging from the hooks above the cookstove, then filled it with coffee. "You don't really expect me to believe you enjoyed Thanksgiving dinner. Remember how you couldn't wait to get out of there?"

Well, he had her there. Things had been a tad edgy that day. "But, to be fair, the idea of you and Reid was still fairly new. You can hardly blame your family for needing a little time to adjust!"

He stood in the middle of her kitchen and stared at her, both blond brows drawn together, as if she'd grown a third eye.

"You know how I feel about the situation, but they're older and more set in their ways," she said.

Now, one of his eyebrows lifted slightly.

"And besides, they don't know the whole story."

He brought the mug to his lips and sipped, then nodded. "I suppose. Still, you can hardly blame me for being surprised at the intensity of their reaction. It isn't as though I've committed a whole host of sinful offenses."

A whimper wafted downstairs from Reid's bedroom, and Micah moved his gaze from her to the ceiling. "That isn't like him," he said, then glanced at the clock. "He's usually out for the night by now."

"He felt a little warm to me when I tucked him in." She untied her apron and draped it over the back of a kitchen chair. "I'd better check on him." Halfway up the stairs, she leaned over the banister. "There's stew on the stove and a pie on the counter. If I'm not back in five minutes, help yourself."

He nodded, but something told her that if she wasn't back in five minutes, he'd join her in Reid's room.

Fortunately, nothing more than a chill had disturbed Reid's sleep. "Kicked off your blankets again, did you, my little man?" Callie eased one end of the quilt she'd designed just for him over his shoulders, then gently tucked the other end under his feet. "May God's angels watch over you as you sleep."

When she returned to the kitchen, Callie spotted Micah in the parlor, his long, muscular legs propped up on the ottoman. The latest issue of the *Eagle Pass Times* hid his face, but not his robust reactions to the articles inside. Phrases like "Well, of all the..." and "For the luvva Pete!" sounded from behind the pages, and Callie leaned against the doorframe, watching and listening as she thanked God for bringing this incredible man into her life.

When he peered over the top of the paper at her, she crossed the room and sat on the corner of the ottoman, carrying his Christmas gift.

"What's that in your lap?" he asked, tossing the paper aside.

"A sweater." She held it up for him to see.

"Very nice," he said, taking hold of one sleeve. "Let me guess. You made it?"

"Made the pattern, too."

"Excellent work." He met her gaze to add, "It should be quite a hit with your catalog customers. Especially the ones who live up north, where it's cold more than half the year."

"I didn't make it to sell."

"It's...for me?" One foot hit the floor with a quiet thud.

"It's a little early for Christmas, I know. I worked on it while your fever was raging, all the while keeping an eye on you, in case...." Callie couldn't bring herself to admit that, for at least a few days, she'd expected to attend a funeral in the near future. Grinning, she said, "Don't you remember all those times you scolded me?"

His other foot hit the floor. "Scolded you? Whatever for?"

"You didn't like the click-clack of the knitting needles. Said the sound reminded you of bones cracking. And when I teased you and asked where you had ever heard bones cracking, you sat up and said, 'I drove my ma mad for years, cracking my knuckles.'" Callie laughed, remembering the moment. "Then, you flopped back down onto your pillow and went straight back to sleep." Callie stood and held up the sweater again. "I know it's too warm in here to leave it on, with the fire blazing away and all, but I'd love to see if it fits."

On his feet now, Micah obliged her. "Amazing," he said. "The first one I've ever had that fit on the first try." He rested both hands on her shoulders, giving her little choice but to press her palms against his chest or topple backward. "Thanks, Callie. But now I feel like a heel."

"Why?"

"Because I don't have a gift for you."

You are my gift! she wanted to shout. "It isn't a gift; it's more like a...a reward. For fighting so hard to get better quickly." She grinned up at him, mostly to hide her trembling lower lip.

"Thank you. I have a question, though."

Was it her imagination, or had he taken half a step closer?

"Is there anything you don't do well, Callie Roberts?"

Well, she couldn't seem to forget that she'd caused Jonah's deafness. Couldn't forgive herself for everything else that had happened that night on the *Maybelline*. And, if he kept looking at her like he believed she'd hung the moon, Callie wouldn't be responsible if she started blubbering like a baby, either. When he raised her chin with his fingers, she noticed how cold her shoulder instantly felt without his big hand there to keep it warm—just a hint of how her whole world would feel when he figured out who and what she was. "I'm glad you like the sweater," she managed.

He slid his arms around her and pulled her close, so close that she could hear his heart, beating hard against her ear.

"I like it just fine," he said, his voice a husky whisper.

Why did it sound as if there should have been a "but..." at the end of that sentence? Callie leaned back to search his face and immediately sensed that he was about to say something along the lines of, "I like the sweater, but not as much as I like you," or "The sweater is fine, but you're finer." Then, she recognized a familiar glow in his dazzling, blue eyes. Seth used to look at her in almost the same way before saying, "I love you." And just look where loving her had gotten him!

Callie was torn between exhilaration that a man like Micah could feel that way about her and outright dread to consider the anguish a woman such as herself was likely to bring into his world. As much as she longed to hear him utter those words, she could not, in good conscience, let him. Not until she'd confessed every gory detail about the devastation she'd been responsible for, anyway. When he knew the truth, he'd have half a chance to save himself. And he deserved at least that much for the good, noble life he'd lived.

He took a breath that, while quiet and shallow, gave him more than enough air to propel the words past his lips. If only she'd been smarter, or kinder, she could have thought faster and come up with a way to keep him from uttering the beautiful phrase. For, once those three words had been spoken, a man like him would feel duty-bound to live them out for the rest of his days. In that instant, caught between confusion and urgency to protect him, Callie did the only thing she could think to do. She silenced him with a kiss.

Chapter 18

*T*he grizzled man slid his wide-brimmed hat onto the counter, then leaned a meaty hand on either side of it. He smelled faintly of soap and spiced oil, telling her this giant of a man had stopped at Gabe's barbershop or, perhaps, the hotel for a bath and a shave before stepping into her store. It was rare for a man to come here alone, without a female companion, and rarer still for one to seek someone other than Callie. "I was told you'd know how I might find Micah Neville."

The man had a voice to match his mighty stature, prompting Callie to search for a polite excuse to take a step back. She looked down and found her answer in a piece of binding twine, coiled around the heel of her boot. "Who told you that?" she asked, bending to retrieve it.

"Fella down at the barbershop said you nursed Neville through a bout of that peculiar flu that blew through town."

Apprehension swirled inside her, because it wasn't like Gabe, or anyone else in Eagle Pass, to volunteer personal information about any citizen to a total stranger. The sheriff and his deputies kept the town clean of unsavory characters, but not even the mayor expected them to round up every drifter or renegade.

Arms crossed over his barrel chest, he raised one graying eyebrow. "Well...?"

"I'm afraid you just missed him."

"Didn't happen to say where he was headed, did he?"

Micah had told her that he needed to stop at the livery and the bank before returning to the Lazy N, but she had no intention of sharing his plans with this imposing outsider. "He did."

"Smart girl," the big man said, winking. "Never divulge more information than necessary." Then, he reached into the inside pocket of his tidy leather vest. "Name's Applegate. Gus Applegate." He flashed a shield-shaped silver badge.

Pinkerton National Detective Agency? So, this was the man Micah had hired. Her heart thudding with fear and regret, Callie faced the ugly fact: Applegate's report would spell out, once and for all, whether Reid would remain with her or be reunited with his real mother.

"If you'll be so kind as to tell me where I might find him, young lady, I'll be on my way."

Callie's mouth went dry as she considered her alternatives. She could give him a straight answer or send him on a wild-goose chase, buying the time she'd need to concoct a viable plan of escape. Because she wouldn't—couldn't—return that sweet, helpless child to the woman who'd handed him off as if he were a sack of dirty laundry. She'd need money, enough to pay for train tickets and hotel rooms. There were Reid's clothes and toys to pack, and food, too, enough to last only God knew how long. And if Jonah didn't want to leave with her, well, the bank had no claim to the house, so he'd always have a roof over his head. But, had she taught him enough about finances and cooking so that he could survive on his own?

"I know Neville—his whole family, in fact," Applegate said. "He's a big man, so he won't be hard to find. And I know where he lives" He shrugged. "Even if I find him later rather than sooner, you won't have near enough time to make a clean getaway."

How had he known exactly what she was thinking? Callie ran a hand through her hair and only then realized that her palms were damp. She tucked her hands inside her apron pockets and faced the inevitable. As difficult as it was to admit, Applegate was right. "He said he had a few errands to run before going back to his family's ranch. You might find him at the post office or the bank. Failing that, it's a long ride to the Lazy N. Maybe you'll catch up with him on the road."

"I'm surprised he told you about me."

The simple statement somehow managed to stir up a lot of unease. How had Applegate known that Micah had told her about the investigation? Suddenly, the Pinkerton seemed bigger, broader, and even more daunting than at first glance, and Callie found herself wishing the little bell above her door would tinkle, announcing the entrance of a customer, or that Jonah would come downstairs. Anything to fill the shop with a friendlier, more familiar presence.

"I could count on one hand the number o' women who can be trusted with a secret, and I'd still have some fingers left over. But I guess you've already proven you're one who knows how to keep her mouth shut."

Happy hollers came from upstairs, signaling that Reid's nap had ended. The Pinkerton looked at the ceiling. Callie had no clue what he had found out about Reid and his mother, but there wasn't a doubt in her mind that he wouldn't be standing here, as big as a mountain, if he didn't know that he'd found what he'd been looking for.

"Well," he said, donning his hat, "I'd best let you see to the li'l fella." He was halfway out the door when he turned to add, "I'm not at liberty to say much, but I can tell you this...."

Callie held her breath, hoping he wouldn't tell her to get ready to say good-bye to Reid.

"There's really no reason for you to be afraid."

When the door clicked shut behind him, Callie raced up the stairs. The instant she stepped into the baby's room, he smiled and held out his arms. "Ma," he said. "Ma-ma!"

Tears sprang to her eyes as she gathered him close. "Oh, sweet boy," she crooned, "I love you every bit as much as if I'd carried you for nine months!"

"Lub."

"Yes, I lub you," she said, blowing a kiss into the crook of his neck.

She remembered the detective's parting words. *Please, God, let that mean what I hope it means.*

Micah dismounted and took his time tying Goldie to the hitching post. He knew he shouldn't be here again so soon, but the lure of Callie's honeyed voice and tender glances had called him back. Fiddling with the clasp of the saddlebag, he retrieved the letters Zack had reluctantly handed him. "Well, you know it ain't proper procedure, givin' mail to a body whose name ain't on it," the postmaster had said, "but I reckon in your case I can keep makin' an exception."

He'd mumbled a clumsy thanks and shuffled outside, the man's parting words failing to register, as Micah had been unable to focus on anything but the sweet, lingering kiss Callie had pressed to his lips. *Are your feelings for her that apparent?* he'd wondered as Goldie had cantered toward Callie's shop. But the closer he'd gotten, the less crucial it had seemed to find an answer. What difference did it make if others could read what she'd written on his heart? He loved her. How could he not, when it took him only a blink to picture her replacing the fever-warmed cloth on his forehead with a cool one, or sitting cross-legged on the floor, soothing him to sleep with Dickens and Stevenson and the Good Book when the sickness wouldn't let him rest?

Yes, he loved her, and he was fixing to admit it to her, too, as soon as he mustered the courage again. Micah stifled a groan. Wasn't it ironic that he'd ridden into the thick of stampedes and faced rustlers, robbers, wildcats, and snakes with barely a flicker of fear, and yet it'd taken him three days to summon the courage to say "I love you" to Callie? The first time he'd said those words to a girl, pigtailed Miranda Campbell had wrinkled her nose and clocked him with her lunch bucket, leaving him with a goose egg on his forehead that lasted a week. The second time, after Peggy Dorset ran off with a one-eyed gunslinger, Micah nursed a bruised ego and vowed never to utter the phrase again.

But he hadn't counted on love crashing into his life in the form of Callie Roberts.

He climbed the porch steps and heard a pot lid clatter back into place. Immediately, the whiff of something beefy met his nostrils. Callie was humming, the way she often did while tucking blankets around Reid. If she hadn't silenced him with that kiss, he wondered as he lifted his arm to rap on the door, would she have said she loved him, too?

"Micah," she said, stepping up to the screen. "I would've thought you'd be home by now."

Even through the dark mesh, he could see her eyes twinkling. Was it because he'd come back, or because she'd spotted the stack of mail in his hand? "Got talking with Birdie and Otis," he said, "and lost track of time." He shrugged. "I thought I might as well stop by the post office." He nodded at the stack of envelopes. "Figured as long as I was there...."

Callie held the door open and stepped aside, and he entered the parlor. "How sweet of you," she said, relieving him of the mail. After tossing it onto the roll-top desk near the door, she hurried into the kitchen.

Like a love-struck pup, he followed. "Something smells mighty good in here."

She laughed softly. "I'm about to take a cobbler out of the oven. And there's coffee, too. May I pour you a cup?"

"How 'bout if I pour *you* a cup?" He grabbed two white mugs from the shelf above the stove.

With her hands clasped under her chin that way, looking at him as if he'd offered to hire a live-in maid to wait on her hand and foot, Callie reminded him more of a fresh-faced little girl than a full-grown woman.

"I'll run upstairs and get Reid," she said, smiling. "I know he'd love to see you."

"Isn't that the truth," Jonah said as she raced up the stairs.

"Good to see you, man," Micah said, shaking his hand.

"It's still so good to see you dressed in your regular clothes," Jonah replied with a grin. "I hope I never have to slip another nightshirt over your head!"

"Don't know how I'll ever repay you for everything you and your sister did while I was ailing."

"Better not let Callie hear you talking like that. She's liable to fetch her broom."

Chuckling, Micah nodded. "Yeah, it'd be just like her to try to sweep away all that kindness and caring under the rug, wouldn't it?"

"Whup your backside with it, y'mean."

"What's all the laughing about?" a male voice demanded.

Micah's gaze whipped to the door, where Gus Applegate stood, grinning through the screen.

"Been lookin' high and low for you, Neville," he said. "Kept tellin' myself a man your size oughtn't be so difficult to locate."

"Mr. Applegate," Callie said when she reentered the room, with Reid on one hip. "Good to see you again so soon. Please, come in."

"Thank you kindly, ma'am." He stepped inside, whipped off his hat, and hung it on the rack beside the door.

"Have you met my brother, Jonah?"

"Nope, can't say I have." He thrust out a big hand. "Pleased to meet you, boy."

"Likewise," Jonah said, nodding. "And, just so you know, I'm as deaf as a box of rocks, but I can read lips."

Gus's eyebrows rose slightly, and then he smiled. "Well then," he said, "I'll be sure to face you head-on when I talk." Winking, he added, "Unless I say something that ain't fittin' for a young man's tender ears, that is."

Jonah smiled as Callie shifted Reid to her other hip. "Would you like some coffee, Mr. Applegate?"

"Please, call me Gus. Always find myself lookin' over my shoulder when somebody says Mr. Applegate, half expectin' to see my pa."

Above the man's hearty laughter, Reid giggled and reached for Micah.

"Seems that young'un is right fond of you, Neville."

"The feeling's mutual," he said, taking the boy. "How long have you been in town, Gus?" The latter part of his sentence came out strangely, because Reid's chubby fingers had pressed Micah's mouth into a fish-like pout.

"Just got in on the mornin' train. Ain't even checked in at the hotel yet. Thought about wirin' you the information, but I wanted to deliver this report in person." He patted his shirt pocket, and a crinkling noise indicated some paper tucked inside.

Micah held Reid a little closer. "It's good news, I hope."

Gus's smile dimmed as he glanced at Callie and Jonah; then, he aimed a steely, all-business glare in Micah's direction. "I'll leave it to you, Neville; you want to discuss this in private?"

Good news or bad, Callie had earned the right to hear it by dint of her steadfast support of him and her equally steadfast devotion to the child. He met her eyes. "Callie and Jonah have been wrapped up in this from the start," he said as Reid stuck a finger into his ear. Grinning slightly, he ruffled the boy's hair and popped a quick kiss to his temple. "Seems only fitting they hear whatever you have to say."

She clasped her hands at her waist, then looked from Micah to Jonah and, finally, to Gus. "How about if we all sit down and enjoy a nice supper together, and then, after I've tucked Reid in for the night, we can listen to what Mr. Applega—to what Gus has to say."

"Da!" Reid said. Micah loved this boy, and he knew without a doubt that if the woman who'd written that letter wanted him back, he'd spend the rest of his days missing him. The sheen of fear in Callie's eyes told him she felt the same way.

For a moment, the room remained silent as an invisible thread connected her gaze to his, and his heart to hers. Another man might have focused on her long-lashed eyes, which couldn't decide if they were blue, green, or golden. On her hair, which shimmered as if sprinkled by starlight. On her milky-white skin, which glowed pink every time she looked at him. On her slender body, which somehow concealed a heart so big, it put the Texas prairie to shame.

Oh, he noticed these things, to be sure, but, mostly, Micah thought about how he knew for certain that he wanted to spend the rest of his life with this woman.

"Now, then," she said, ending the enchanting moment with a single clap of her hands, "why don't you boys retire to the parlor while I get dinner ready?"

As they moved to fulfill her request, Gus asked to hold Reid. Micah begrudgingly handed him off to the Pinkerton, who carried him to Callie's rocking chair, sat down, and bounced the boy on his knee while singing an off-key rendition of "Yankee Doodle." Jonah stoked the fire, and Micah settled onto the divan, praying for a double dose of courage. He'd need it if Applegate's news wasn't good, but he'd need it even more if Callie said no when he asked her to marry him.

Chapter 19

"To hear her tell it," Gus began, picking at a nub in the tablecloth, "the whole mess started when she was used to pay a gamblin' debt and ended up in the clutches of some fella by the name of Jeremiah Turner." He took a swig of coffee. "Mind you, I don't believe a word of it, but I feel duty-bound to tell you everything.

"Anyway, to go back a ways, one of Pauline's dance hall girlfriends got pregnant by an unknown man and had a baby. Pauline an' her friends took turns carin' for the kid." He proceeded to explain how Turner had told Pauline that the Nevilles owned half of West Texas. "Way she told it," he said, chuckling, "y'all used hundred-dollar bills to light the wood in your fireplaces. Anyways, they got him good an' drunk, picked his pockets clean, an' hatched a scheme to see how much a Neville might be willin' to pay to keep an ugly story from spreadin' all over Texas. Pauline drew the shortest straw, so she got stuck writin' the letter an' arrangin' the blackmail."

Micah leaned both forearms on the table. "So, Pauline Devereaux has no legal claim on Reid?"

"None."

"What about his real pa?"

"According to her, the baby's mother didn't know who that might be."

It took every bit of self-control Callie could muster to keep from blurting out exactly what kind of woman she considered this Pauline person to be. "How long did she take care of him between the time her friend died and she pawned Reid off on Micah?"

Gus shrugged. "That she didn't say, but it couldn't have been long, given the boy's age."

"Well, I still don't understand it." She looked at Micah. "I fell in love with him even before we left your mother's house that day."

"Anyone with eyes knows that's true," he said, patting her hand. Then, he looked at Gus again. "So, what does the law say about things like this? I mean, we can't just keep him. Can we?"

Callie held her breath as Gus leaned forward and said, "Nobody knows or cares a whit about that boy, save the people right here in this room." He drummed a forefinger on the table to emphasize his point. "He's too young to remember meeting Pauline or having a ma, for that matter."

"But...but what if that horrible woman comes back someday, demanding more money from Micah?"

Gus pulled an envelope from his pocket, then softened his tone to reply. "Miss Roberts, I doubt she's given Reid a moment's thought since she signed her name to this." He slid an envelope across the table.

Micah opened it and took out a piece of paper. "It appears this recounts everything you've just told us."

Gus nodded. "It does."

Micah frowned and handed the document to Callie. "Is it legally binding?"

"It's also signed by the sheriff and the judge, who served as witnesses. It should hold up, were anyone to question it."

"But what if Callie's right? What if she runs out of money and decides to come back and try to squeeze another egg from what she perceives to be the golden goose?"

"Then, you show her that." Gus pointed at the page fluttering in Callie's trembling hands. "I took the liberty of discussing the entire matter with a friend of mine who wields a lot of clout in Austin—stopping off there is the reason I got here later than anticipated—and his off-the-record advice is...y'all can raise the boy as your own."

Elated, Callie managed to refold the paper and return it to Micah.

"And that's legal?" he asked.

"Well sir," Gus said, "it ain't illegal." He got up to refill his mug of coffee, then returned to his seat. "But, just to be safe," he added, grinning, "y'might wanna marry this purty li'l gal. That way, there'll be no doubt that you're providing a good, stable home for the boy."

Callie's gasp was drowned out by Jonah's robust laughter. "Best idea I've heard all night," he said, slapping the table. He looked at Callie, then at Micah. "You're crazy in love with each other, so don't tell me you haven't both thought about it."

Callie took one look at Micah's shocked expression and got to her feet. How awful for him to be put on the spot this way! The glare she aimed at her brother sent the silent message that she'd deal with him later. "Goodness," she said, stacking dessert plates and gathering spoons, "would you look at the time." She feigned jollity. "Sunup seems to come earlier and earlier every morning, doesn't it? I'm sure you gentlemen need to be on your way."

Gus was the first to stand. "Yes, yes," he said, grabbing his hat. The screen door squealed as he added, "That desk clerk might not think too well of me if I wake him to reserve a room. Thank you kindly for dinner."

Jonah got up, too. "And I left some drawings out back. Better fetch them before the dew settles and fades all the pencil lines."

That left Micah alone at the table, sliding a calloused fingertip around and around the rim of his mug. His left brow rose slightly, and so did one corner of his mouth. "You have two choices, as I see it," he told her.

Choices? She hoped he wasn't referring to marriage. She'd come nowhere close to summoning the courage to tell him about her part in the destruction of the *Maybelline*. Until he'd heard the truth and had time to decide if he could live with the knowledge for the rest of his days, it simply wouldn't be fair to discuss a future together.

She turned toward the counter. "I can wrap up a nice, big bowl of cobbler for you to take home, if you like," she said. "With a little warm milk, it'll make a delicious breakfast in the morn—"

"Callie," he said softly, placing his hands on her shoulders. "I know you're tired, but won't you sit in the parlor with me for just a few minutes?"

She'd been too busy babbling to hear him get up from the table and walk the half dozen steps from his chair to where she stood, cringing. Right above them, Reid slept the peaceful sleep of an innocent child. Would that change once she'd made her confession?

When she turned around, Callie searched the face so near her own. Would the warm light of love beaming from his eyes change, too, when the ugly truth was out?

"Sit down," she whispered, "because I have something to tell you."

And then she prayed that she wasn't about to make the biggest mistake of her life.

As Callie's story unfolded, Micah didn't have the heart to tell her that he'd heard it all before.

Jonah had told him that Callie never talked about that night on the *Maybelline*, so it was easy to promise not to interrupt her. But, even if he hadn't given his word, Micah would have listened in silence, for it moved him deeply that, after carrying the burdensome secret for so long, she'd chosen to bare it to him.

But the woman she described was a complete stranger, a coldhearted, self-centered, hideous creature who, by putting her own needs and wants above others', had started the dominoes toppling— a sequence that had ultimately brought down the steamboat.

After a flurry of words and gestures, she grew still and silent. He watched her shoulders rise and fall with a shuddering sigh. Was that a show of relief that the tale was finally told, or keen-edged fear that he'd judge her as harshly as she judged herself?

Micah had read a dozen or more articles about steamboat explosions, and he couldn't believe that the disaster aboard the *Maybelline* had been the result of overloaded boilers alone. In most cases, shoddy materials and careless welding had been to blame. But Callie didn't need to hear that right now. She'd carried her guilt close to her heart for so long that it might as well have been a part of her body, and it would take more than one night to cleave a bond that strong.

He had nothing but time, and, for this woman, he'd summon the patience required. Micah leaned forward in the overstuffed chair by the hearth and balanced both elbows on his knees. "Well?"

She looked genuinely surprised by his response. "Well, what?"

"Are you finished?"

Callie nodded once and stared at her hands, clasped tightly in her lap.

"Good," he said. "Because now, it's my turn." He made a move to slide an arm across her shoulders, because he wanted to hold her close and tell her exactly how much he disagreed with her outrageous portrayal of herself. But he didn't move fast enough.

Callie was on her feet and standing at her front door in less time than it took him to say, "Where are you going?"

"It's late, and you're tired," she said, her voice now devoid of the music he'd grown to love. Lifting her chin, she opened the door.

See, there? he wanted to shout. *More proof that you're selfless and kind, and not at all like the woman you just told me about!*

"Go home, Micah," she said on a weary sigh, "and get some sleep."

Of all the fool suggestions! How did she expect him to do that when the woman he loved was hurt and afraid? "Callie, I don't need rest," he protested, standing up and going to her. "What I need is—"

"To sleep on things," she finished for him. "Take some time to think about what I just told you." A shaky giggle escaped her lips. "You're too sweet and gentlemanly to tell me to my face what you really think." Until then, she hadn't met his eyes, but she looked straight at him to add, "Give it a few days to sink in. Pray about it. *Then* I'll listen to what you think you need."

"But—"

"Ride safely, dear Micah."

With that, she gave him a gentle nudge onto the porch and closed the door behind him. The quiet click of the lock could just as well have been a bullet piercing armor, the way it echoed in his heart. He stared at the bolted door for what seemed like an hour before shuffling over to the tree where he'd tied his horse. "Well, Goldie," he said, climbing into the saddle, "looks like it's just you and me."

The horse's ears swiveled, and she bobbed her head, as if to say, "And a long, quiet ride home."

It dawned on him then that Beth was scheduled to arrive on the morning train. It didn't make much sense to tire Goldie out by going all the way to the Lazy N only to make the trip back tomorrow. After unsaddling Goldie at the livery, he gave her a good brushing and got her a feedbag of oats. Confident that she'd relax in her clean stall, Micah checked into a room at the hotel and stretched out on top of the bedcovers.

Linking his fingers behind his head, he stared up at the dark ceiling and thought of Callie. He'd been in a pickle or two in his day, but this was by far the sourest: Callie had said she was selfish, when, in truth, she didn't know the meaning of the word. Micah did, though, and his own self-interest solidified his resolve to dig up and deliver the evidence that would disprove every awful thing she'd said about herself. Without proof, she'd never agree to become his wife. Why? Because her bighearted, self-sacrificing nature would fire her decision to hold him at arm's length to protect him from her.

And so, first thing in the morning, he intended to find Gus Applegate, and if the Pinkerton wasn't agreeable to rousting out the truth about the accident, he'd do it himself.

As it turned out, Gus had business in the capitol city, and he agreed to see if his friend the judge could help him uncover the records about the sinking of the *Maybelline*. Micah bought a newspaper and a cup of coffee at the hotel restaurant and then parked himself on the bench across from the station to wait for Beth. But the coffee grew cold and the paper went unread as he sat, wondering how long it would take the Pinkerton to find something to substantiate his belief that Callie hadn't caused the accident.

When he heard the distant whistle of the ten o'clock train, Micah got to his feet. According to his pocket watch, it was only forty minutes late. The gray plumes of smoke chugged closer, and then the train came to a screeching, hissing halt. He stood amid a steamy cloud, surrounded by disembarking passengers and the folks who'd come to greet them. Men grabbed valises, women unfurled parasols; the chatter and laughter of welcomes were everywhere, except here where he stood.

Where was Beth? Had she missed the train? He was about to walk over to the conductor to have a word with him when he heard a familiar voice. "Hey, cowboy. Is your wagon for hire?"

"'Course it is," he said, hugging her. "How was the ride from Oklahoma?"

Beth rolled her eyes. "Bumpy. Long. And one of the windows in my car got stuck in the open position, so it was windy, too." She gave him a playful shove. "You sure don't look like a man who just had a near brush with death." Grinning, she pointed a few feet away. "That's my trunk, right over there."

"I'd almost forgotten that you took half of your room with you when you left. Can't tell you how many times I worried it was because you aimed to stay with your in-laws."

"Can't tell you how many times I thought the same thing." Beth sighed. "But we won't tell Ma, will we?"

He hadn't realized how weakened the strange illness had left him until he tried to heave the massive chest into the back of the wagon. "Good grief," he said, grunting. "We have rocks here in Texas, too, y'know."

Beth's brow crinkled with confusion. "What?"

"How many Oklahoma boulders did you pack to remember the place by?"

"Aren't you just the funniest thing. Just one of a hundred reasons I missed you so much." Giggling, Beth patted the wagon seat. "Come on, now, let's get moving. I can hardly wait to see Ma and Pa and the girls."

"They're excited to see you, too. Though I can't say I don't need to catch up with them, myself. I was at Callie's, down and out with the illness, for more than a week, and most of my time since then has been spent trying to make up the work I've missed. And I've been visiting Callie's whenever I can."

"Busy making eyes at that adorable little baby boy?"

Yeah, and the adorable little gal who's taking care of him.

"How is he, by the way? You never wrote to me, but I guess that's hard to do when you're lying unconscious in bed. It's a good thing Emma and Astrid took the time to write, or I wouldn't have heard any of the gossip from home!"

Micah signaled the team, and, as they started off toward home, he gave her a brief update on what had gone on in her absence. Then, he looked over and studied her for a moment. "You look good, Beth," he said. "I trust that means you've set aside your crazy scheme to join James in paradise?"

"Oh, that was just grief talking," she said, patting his knee. "Not a day goes by that I don't miss him, and my heart aches every time I see a prickly pear or a bluebonnet."

James's heart had never been very strong, so getting into a saddle had always proved difficult for him. Once, when he couldn't quite manage to pull himself up by the horn, the poor man had slid off the horse and landed on his backside in a patch of the thorny cactus. He was nothing if not good-natured, though, and he'd grinned like a buffoon once he'd scrambled to his feet. "I meant to do that," he'd said, handing Beth the scraggly handful of flowers he'd plucked from his spiky nest, "so as not to spoil your surprise."

"How's his mother taking the loss of her boy these days?" Rumor was, Mrs. Hammond had nearly grieved herself into an early grave, mourning her only child.

"Oh, she'll never get over it, I'm afraid." Beth shook her head. "Makes me all the more determined to have lots of children when I marry again."

The comment so stunned him that Micah nearly threw his neck out of joint, turning to face her. "You have somebody in mind?"

"No, no, of course not." She patted his knee again. "But I did realize during this trip that the Lord didn't intend for me to live alone." Nodding confidently, she said, "I started praying last night, as a matter of fact, that He would show me which fellow I'm to spend the rest of my days with."

No one had been better suited than Beth to marry James. Few women had paid attention to the thin, pale, sickly man. Not so his sister! The first time she'd seen him at a church social, she'd plopped down beside Micah and said, "Oh, just look at his big, sad eyes! He seems so *lonesome*."

If he'd known what would come next, Micah would have done everything he could have to talk her out of marrying the poor fellow, for it seemed Beth was the only person who didn't realize he was not long for this world.

Days before James's death, Micah had stopped at their home to say good-bye. He hadn't been there five minutes when James had asked Beth for a glass of cold water, and, when she'd left to fetch it, he'd beckoned Micah nearer. "I realize your family thinks it was selfish of me to marry her, knowing I couldn't give her children or a long life together, and I suppose it was. But she gave meaning to my dreary life, and I'll love her for eternity for that."

Micah understood now better than ever what James had meant, and he made a promise to himself to dote on Callie for the rest of his days—if she'd let him.

"Why so quiet all of a sudden?" Beth wanted to know.

"Oh, just woolgathering, is all."

"Thinking of Callie, are you?"

Chuckling, he said, "Why don't you save us both the trouble of going over old ground and tell me what you know?"

It seemed his sisters had spoken of little else in their letters to Beth than speculation about when Micah would ask Callie to marry him. And, evidently, just about everyone else in Eagle Pass was waiting for them to set a wedding date.

"Looks like I need to set a few records straight," he said, frowning. "Callie and I...our relationship is...she and I aren't—"

Beth giggled. "As amusing as it is to watch you squirm, Mr. Stoic, I feel it only fair to come to your rescue. We are all aware that you aren't the type of man to take advantage of a young woman's infatuation, and, might I add, we're just as certain that Callie isn't the kind of girl who would let you."

"Well, that's comforting to hear. I think." He raised an eyebrow. "But who is 'we,' if you don't mind my asking?"

"Ma and Pa and our dear sisters, of course, along with every aunt, uncle, and cousin at the Lazy N."

Out of the corner of his eye, he saw her lean forward to get a better look at his face. "Who'd you think 'we' were?"

Micah didn't like where this conversation was going, so he searched his mind for a subject that would change its direction. "Say, is that a rattler in the road up ahead?"

Beth gasped and scooted closer to him on the wagon seat. "Goodness, I certainly hope not!" she cried. "Remember what happened the last time a snake spooked the horses?"

"How could I forget the mishap that nearly cost me a toe?"

"Oh, just listen to you," she huffed. "How like you to laugh at something that frightened me nearly to death. Men! You're all such puzzles."

"You'd be wise to keep that in mind when you decide it's time to go shopping for a husband," Micah teased.

Beth grinned. "Speaking of which, what can you tell me about Callie's brother? I've spoken to him a few times in Callie's shop, when I was being fitted for various dresses, and he seems kindhearted. He's handsome, too."

"Jonah?" Now, there was a match he'd never have thought of. "He's a decent, hardworking man who's devoted to his sister. To Reid, too."

When Beth nodded eagerly, Micah added, "Hold up just a minute, girl. You do know he's deaf, of course?"

"Yes."

"And that he's a full year younger than you?"

"If he's a good, decent man, as you claim, what difference could any of that possibly make?"

He liked Jonah. A lot. But as a husband for his sister? "What do you know about taking care of a man who can't hear?"

She shrugged. "What did I know about taking care of a man with a weak heart?"

Micah shook his head. *All right,* he thought, *time to play devil's advocate.* "So, let's just assume for a moment that this harebrained notion of yours has feet, and you end up married to Jonah Roberts." He paused. "What if your children are deaf, too?"

"My understanding is, Jonah lost his hearing due to a boiler explosion. So, there is no reason whatsoever to suspect that our children—if we married and had any, that is—would inherit their father's deafness."

Micah rubbed his neck with a gloved hand and groaned. "Just listen to you," he said, "saying things that strike fear in a brother's heart. Women! You're all such puzzles."

"You might keep that fact in mind while you're seesawing between asking Callie to marry you and not asking her."

Chapter 20

"$\mathcal{M}$a," came Reid's whimper from down the hall. "Ma-ma-ma-*ma*!"

Callie sat up in bed and rubbed her eyes, then lit the lantern on her bedside table. She must have forgotten to wind the little carriage clock, because surely more than an hour had passed since the last time he'd roused her.

Shrugging into her robe, she trudged down the hall, passing Jonah on the way to the baby's room. "You felt those vibrations, too, did you?"

He uttered something between a yawn and a groan, and pulled his own robe tighter around him. "How many times has he been up tonight?"

She grinned. "I've lost count."

"If I had a white flag, I'd wave it."

"That wouldn't do any good," Callie said, giggling. "He'd just see it as a signal to come and eat."

"You're probably right." Jonah grinned. "Well, it'll be daylight soon. Makes no sense to go back to bed. I think I'll stoke the cookstove fire and get the coffee started."

"And I'll check on Reid." She wrapped Jonah in a grateful hug. "What would I do without you?"

Reid was standing in his crib when she walked into the room, but he didn't flash his usual, happy smile. "Have you worn yourself out, sweet boy?" she asked, then bent to kiss his forehead, as she did every morning. "You poor little thing," she sighed. "Still feverish, despite the cool compresses." The instant she picked him up, he laid his head on her shoulder. "If only new teeth didn't come with such a high price tag, hmm?"

An hour later, after bundling the baby up to protect him from the wind and rain and setting out in the elements, Callie was seated in the straight-backed chair beside Doc Lane's exam table, hands clenched in her lap, as the good doctor examined Reid.

"He does have a low-grade fever, and I agree that cutting teeth caused it."

"Well, that's a blessed relief," she said, sighing. "One of the ladies who came into the shop yesterday said her neighbors are quarantined with—"

"Whooping cough," he said. "Yes, that's even more contagious than the flu-like illness that laid everybody low, weeks ago." His brow furrowed, he pressed his stethoscope to the boy's chest. "He is a mite congested. Might be a good idea to put a steaming kettle in his room. Could be nothing more than the dry air from the fireplace and the cookstove, but it doesn't hurt to be careful."

She nodded.

"How's his appetite?"

She thought of the meals and bottles he'd refused over the past few days. "Not good, and he isn't sleeping well, either, especially with his occasional spurts of coughing."

Doc Lane rummaged around in his medicine cabinet, then handed her a brown bottle. "Try giving him half a dropper of that at bedtime. It'll clear up that congestion, suppress the cough, and help him sleep."

"Thank you," she said, tucking the vial into her jacket pocket.

"Is Jonah showing any symptoms of either what Micah had, or what's bothering Reid?"

She shook her head. "No, his only complaint is lack of sleep."

"Is that so? And what seems to be the reason?"

Callie patted the baby's head. "This little fellow might have a bit of congestion, but it hasn't hindered his ability to holler!" Smiling, she bundled him into the blanket again. "He hasn't slept through the night in days, but I'm sure that between the steamy air and the cough remedy you gave us, he'll sleep more peacefully." Lifting Reid from the exam table, she said, "How much do I owe you?"

The doctor chuckled. "Maybe I'm the one who should be asking that question."

"Oh, my," she said. "It's lucky for me you're an honest man, because with all that's been going on, I completely forgot about that. Soon as I get home, I'll add everything up and—"

"Add everything up? How many garments did that wife of mine order?"

Callie propped Reid on one hip, and he tucked his head into the crook of her neck. "Oh, just a few blouses and skirts." The baby wasn't the least bit interested in looking around the unfamiliar space, as he usually was. This worried Callie, and she wasn't sure how to mask her fear. "And a hat."

Groaning, Doc Lane slapped a hand to the back of his neck. "Goodness. I had no idea she'd taken up so much of your time." He walked with her to the door and then stepped outside, holding it open for her. "Take all the time you need adding up her total," he said, laughing. "And don't you worry about Reid. He's healthy and strong, and, with you watching out for him, he's going to be just fine in no time."

She looked up from the bottom step and tried to smile. "Thank you, doctor."

He probably didn't think she heard him mutter, "First-time mothers worry more than old ladies." Doc Lane was probably right, but that didn't stop the disquieting concern ebbing inside her.

Reid whimpered, and she peeked under the blanket. "We'll be home before you know it," she promised. Somehow, she needed to inform Micah that his boy was ailing.

But he isn't Micah's, she reminded herself. *He isn't Dan's or Pauline's—or yours, for that matter.* Gus Applegate had made that more than clear when he'd told the story of Pauline's friend. But how could a woman like that be trusted? What would Micah do—or sweet little Reid—if she returned with a whole new story, one that prompted the judge in Austin to award her custody of Reid?

Callie held him tighter and picked up her pace, running in part from the storm, in part from the possibility of having to give him up someday, as if that were possible. The very thought brought tears to her eyes and squeezed her heart with an ache like none she'd ever known.

Well, that wasn't true. She'd felt pain like that before, on the day she and Jonah had buried their parents and their brother and said a final good-bye to Seth.

Pull yourself together! It wouldn't do any of them any good, least of all Reid, if she allowed herself to slide down that slope of self-pity again. For better or for worse, she was all he had right now, and she intended to meet his every need for as long as the good Lord allowed her to.

If only she'd known how completely she'd grow to love the little fellow! Would she still have volunteered to take care of him? Yes, of course she would have. Micah never could have done it on his own. But, given the chance to do things over again, would she have the presence of mind to guard her heart after making the offer?

"Oh, what sense does it make to lie to yourself?" She would have loved Reid with all her heart, no matter what decision she'd made that fateful day.

At the sound of her voice, Reid whimpered and tried to peek out of the blanket flap, which protected his face from the misting rain. Smiling, Callie nuzzled his nose. "It's all right, sweet boy," she whispered. "Just a little farther, now, and we'll be home, where you'll be safe from this howling wind."

"Well, now, Callie Roberts, I do declare, it looks as though you've seen a ghost."

The hearty voice startled her so much that she nearly squealed with fright. "Goodness, Mr. Applegate! I didn't see you there," she said as he fell into step beside her.

"Obviously!" he said. "Now, tell me, what's got your pretty face all twisted in a frown?"

As they walked the rest of the way to her shop, Callie told him everything the doctor had said about Reid's condition. "If it is whooping cough, it's very contagious," she cautioned him, "so you ought to keep a safe distance until we know—"

"Aw, now, I'm touched at your concern, but you needn't worry about me. Had the whoopin' cough years back, and the doc said it made me immune. I'd be much obliged for a cup o' your delicious coffee, if it ain't an inconvenience."

The rain fell harder now. Callie raced up her porch steps and flung open the door. As much as she wanted to be neighborly, Reid's needs came first. "Maybe you could stop by tomorrow," she said over her shoulder, "and I'll bake another one of those cobblers—"

"Won't be here tomorrow," he said, following her inside.

"Another assignment?"

"Yes'm, I'm fixin' to retire, this time, for good. I have some money in a bank in Austin, and the train leaves at first light."

Dread hammered in her heart. She knew that he'd talked to an Austin judge on Micah's behalf about custody and adoption. "Has Micah hired you again, to get more information about Reid?"

He wasn't smiling when he said, "Not exactly."

She was about to ask what he meant when Gus touched a forefinger to his hat brim. "Well, I'd best be on my way," he said, then turned up his collar and ran across the road, where he disappeared into the hotel.

Gus felt as if he'd embarked on a wild goose chase, meandering from Eagle Pass toward Abilene and the old Salt Fork of the Brazos River. Why the locals had thought it necessary to change the name from Mobeetie to Sweetwater, he didn't know, especially since Mobeetie was the Kiowa word for sweet water! "You're gettin' old and crotchety, Applegate," he mumbled, trudging toward the courthouse. Still, it just didn't seem right to try to erase the history of this country just because some know-it-alls could.

He remembered all too well a time not so long ago when bands of Comanche, Kiowa, Southern Cheyenne, and Arapaho Indians had called this land home—until a conflict had erupted, which had been dubbed the Red River War. If the government thought he and his comrades in the Fourth Cavalry knew nothing of the Medicine Lodge Treaty of 1867, well, they had another think coming, because Gus and his fellow soldiers were well aware that the Indians had been rounded up and moved to reservations, where they were expected to be happy, trading their freedom for useless farmland. Was it any wonder that a stubborn, angry few—like Isa-tai, Mow-way, and Quanah Parker—had led movements to fight for the land of their ancestors?

When the army and the Indian Bureau tired of defending raids on buffalo hunters and settlers, they planned a five-pronged attack and declared full-out war on the "hostiles," then drove five thousand Indians from every southern tribe west and into Panhandle territory.

Disgusted, exhausted, and ashamed, Gus had decided that as long as men like Colonel Ranald Mackenzie, Indian agent James Haworth, and interpreter J. J. Sturms were running things, he wanted no part in the army. When his time was up, he hadn't reenlisted, and nearly a year later, right here in Sweetwater, he had sat, unarmed, on a stool in Henry Fleming's saloon, as Bat Masterson and Sergeant Melvin King had squabbled over cards—and over a dance hall girl by the name of Molly Brennan. In a matter of seconds, their dispute had turned into a gunfight, and the shot King had intended for Masterson went straight through Molly, killing her and giving Bat the limp he would no doubt take to his grave. Other patrons had gotten involved, too, and more than likely it had been one of their bullets that had ended King's life. But when the smoke had cleared, Gus had decided to join up with the Texas Rangers.

And he hadn't been without a sidearm and a badge of some sort since.

Recently, though, Gus had been off his game, and that didn't sit well with him. Not well at all. He felt old, impotent, and stupid, because—hard as he'd tried to get to the bottom of the mess between Pauline Devereaux and Micah Neville—he couldn't shake the feeling that he'd missed something important. During his career as a lawman, he'd rounded up dozens of train robbers and strung up at least that many killers. So, why couldn't he dig up the evidence that would give that big-eyed baby a name.

He identified with the boy, because he'd been five years old when the Apache had raided his grandfather's farm in New Mexico. They'd brought him back to their village, where a barren old squaw had claimed him as her own, saving his scrawny neck. Inayat—which meant "kindness"—lived up to her name by taking him into her humble wigwam. She taught him to sing, pray, and gamble. Taught him that bugs and birds and coyotes had once been Indian, and that it was important to decide by which definition of the word "Apache" he would live: the Zuni definition, "enemy," or the Yuma term, "fighting men."

Sadly, Inayat had died before she could see which he chose.

He was twelve when her sister had walked him into the foothills, ignoring Inayat's dying wish, and left him there with nothing but a skin of water and a sack of beef chips. As night fell, he'd wished the name Inayat sounded more like Miller or Smith, so that he could honor her by attaching it to his first name. As it was, he'd told no one—not even his late wife—about his years with the Apache, or how he'd come by the name Applegate. The shame of his cowardice would burn in his soul until he drew his last breath.

Maybe, before that happened, he'd tell someone, so that Inayat's name would not be buried along with him. Callie seemed the likely choice, because she knew what it was like to carry a secret.

Gus slumped onto a bench in the depot and ran a shaky hand through his hair. What a comfort it would be to lay his head down and fall asleep at the hotel tonight and wake up in the past, where he could meet up with Inayat again. He sighed. Enough reminiscing. He needed to bring this last bit of information back to Eagle Pass. "Seems only fittin' the girl should have some peace of mind...."

"Excuse me?"

He looked up into the wide-eyed face of a woman barely older than Callie. "Don't pay me no mind," he said, grinning. "Seems the older I get, the more I talk to myself."

She giggled. "I suppose that's one way to be sure someone is paying attention."

"Ain't that the truth," he said, and as she walked away, he noticed the tiny apples printed on the fabric of her pretty dress.

Applegate.

The first house he'd come to after leaving Inayat's had a board fence all the way around it, and an apple tree that shaded the front gate.

Chuckling softly, Gus muttered, "If that ain't poetry, I don't know what is!"

Chapter 21

I think it's wonderful the way you help Callie with everything," Micah heard Beth say to Jonah at the mid-December church social.

Jonah grinned and nodded. "She helps me a lot, too, you know."

Beth's cheeks glowed bright red. "Of course. I never meant to imply...." She narrowed her eyes and propped a fist on her hip. "Are you teasing me, Jonah Roberts?"

He shrugged one shoulder. "Well, if I am, it's your own fault."

"My fault!"

"For making it so much fun."

She gave him a playful shove, which made him stumble into Micah's path.

Now, it was Jonah's turn to blush. "Sorry," he said. "I was just—"

"It was my fault," Beth insisted. "Sometimes," she said, giggling, "I just don't know my own strength."

Micah wasn't sure how to feel about the budding romance between his sister and Callie's brother. On the one hand, he'd never seen Beth happier, not even when she'd been married to James. On the other hand, he wasn't at all sure it was fair to Jonah; what if the novelty of being with someone "different" wore off, and she broke his heart? Maybe later, he'd have a little talk with her to find out where things stood between her and Callie's brother.

A cheerful squeal from Reid broke into his thoughts. Relief that the child's sickness had passed even more quickly than his own had put Micah on his knees to give thanks to God a dozen times. He studied the now rosy, chubby-cheeked face, then followed the baby's gaze to the other side of the room, where Callie stood with half a dozen other ladies of the church, dishing up pie. "Are you thinking what I'm thinking?" he asked, lifting the boy from his baby buggy.

"Ma?" The boy looked from Micah to Callie and back again.

"Yep. She's the prettiest girl in the room, all right."

This time when he looked at her, both chubby arms flapped. "Ma!" he hollered, pointing. "Ma-*ma*!"

"If he keeps that up," Gus said, "he might just take flight, like a fat little bird." He extended a hand.

Micah gave it a hearty shake. "Didn't know you were back."

"Got in yesterday, but the trip plumb tuckered me out. Laid down for a nap, thinking to come find you in an hour or two, and didn't wake up till the sun come up this mornin'." Laughing, he added, "Guess that's just part o' gettin' old."

"Old, my foot," Micah said. But, in truth, Gus did look a little rough around the edges. Maybe all he needed was to spend a few days in one place, without the demands of detective work to worry him. "You here to stay?"

"Yessir, I do believe I am." Gus nodded. "Got my eye on that old house over on Leona Street. She needs some work, but I've decided to hang up my badge and gun, so I'll have plenty o' time to sand and paint and—"

"What's this," Callie interrupted, taking Reid from Micah's arms, "the rough 'n' tough Ranger-turned-Pinkerton was serious when he talked about retiring?"

Smiling, Gus gripped the fringed lapels of his leather vest. "Yep, and some would say it's high time, too."

"Well, whatever you do, if you do buy that house, don't waste your money on curtains for the windows or doilies for your tables and sofas. I have shelves and shelves of them, and I'd love to see them put to good use."

"Curtains and doilies?" Gus's laughter echoed through the church basement. "What's a grumpy ol' bachelor need with frills like that?"

"If I ever meet a grumpy old bachelor," she said, "I'll be sure to ask him."

Gus grinned at Micah and shook his head, and Micah read the expression to mean, "If you let this one get away, you're plumb loco." If they hadn't been standing amid a crowd of parishioners—with Callie beside them—he would have confessed how he planned to remedy his own bachelor status just as soon as the *Maybelline* mystery was solved.

"I'd better get up there and take a turn serving," Beth said.

Callie tidied Reid's shirt. "I'm sure they won't turn you away, but really, there are more hands and elbows at that table than desserts and people to eat them. If I were you, I'd stay right here and keep my handsome brother company." She winked at Jonah. "Unless, of course, you've grown tired of talking to Beth...."

Jonah faced Micah's sister. "Impossible."

"Sorry," Beth said, "I was staring at this adorable little boy, and thanking the good Lord that his cough is completely gone." She looked up into Jonah's face. "Now then, what's impossible?"

"Me, growing tired of talking to you."

Micah thought her blush could probably light up a room, and it didn't surprise him to see that Jonah wore the more masculine version of the same expression. Too late for that little talk, obviously. Nothing left to do now but pray the union was in God's plan for their lives.

Gus gave a jerk of his head, and Micah read it as his cue to follow the man outside. No doubt, he planned to fill him in on whatever he'd learned about the steamboat explosion. "We'll be out back," the Pinkerton said, "catchin' a little fresh air."

"Save us a slice of that chocolate cake, will you?" Micah asked.

In a blink, Callie's expression transformed from fearful and suspicious to accepting. She raised one eyebrow and sent the silent message, "Fresh air, indeed." Then, smiling sweetly, she said, "I'll try, but if I were you, I wouldn't be gone too long."

"So," Micah said once they stepped outside, "what's the story?"

Gus lowered himself onto the top porch step and pulled the makings of a cigarette from his pocket. He rolled it as Micah sat down beside him, then, slowly, he let the story unfold. "They built those steamers out of the cheapest materials money could buy, and the *Maybelline* was worse than most. I got a gander at the permits and plans Callie's pa had to file before he got permission to float that old tub."

For starters, Gus explained, each of the three cylinder-shaped boilers was constructed from copper, which looked mighty pretty when all shined up but didn't provide nearly the strength required to endure so many pounds per square inch of steam pressure. To make matters worse, the architect had sketched out hundreds of rivets to hold the big smokestacks in place, but the bill of lading listed only half as many. "Worst of all," Gus concluded, "the workers who were hired to fix the problems never installed the pressure gauge or the relief valve."

"So, what you're saying is, it wouldn't have mattered who loaded the boiler."

"Nope. And it wouldn't have mattered if they'd used coal instead o' wood. Truth is, that steamer was an accident just waitin' to happen. The only real question is why she didn't blow years earlier."

"A miracle," Micah whispered, nodding.

"Yep. I'm inclined to agree."

Micah could hardly wait to tell Callie the good news and watch the relief wash over her lovely face. Hopefully, he'd have the patience to give her time to digest the information before he got down on one knee.

In the ensuing silence, Gus chuckled. "What was it Jefferson said?"

Micah grinned. "'Great minds think alike'?"

"There's no arguin' with that, but...." He scratched his head. "...but I don't recall hearing that one attributed to ol' Thomas. I was thinking more along the lines of—"

"'Why put off until tomorrow what you can do today'?" the men said in unison.

The moment of friendly laughter was disrupted by a fierce rumble that shook the town hard enough to knock a pot of posies from the windowsill behind them.

For the second time in as many seconds, Gus and Micah spoke simultaneously: "The mine!"

The crew standing topside blamed a "windy shot" for the explosion, and their face boss, Conrad, agreed, grumbling that if that last charge had been properly tamped, it wouldn't have sent sparks down the shaft. The way they were going at it told Micah they'd argue for months—years, even—about whether those sparks had ignited coal dust or methane gas. Everyone was like-minded about one thing: a blast like that could travel miles below the surface and set off additional explosions in any of a dozen different tunnels.

"How many miners are down there?" Micah asked.

The miner nearest him wiped his eyes with a greasy neckerchief. "Twenty, twenty-five, I reckon. Thank God a bunch came up when the lunch whistle blew, to fill their water buckets."

"And to get fresh mesh for their lanterns," added another grubby-looking fellow.

Micah had read newspaper articles about explosions in Kentucky, Pennsylvania, and West Virginia where Davy lamps had been responsible for the devastation. According to those reports, the heat dispensed by the lanterns, coupled with poor ventilation in the mines, proved a dangerous and, too often, deadly combination.

A red-faced woman raced up and grabbed the face boss. "I don't see my man up here!" she shrieked.

"What's his name?" the safety inspector asked, snatching a clipboard from the seat of a nearby wagon.

"Peter. Peter McCall."

Micah had gone to school with Pete, who'd signed on as a drover on a number of Lazy N roundups and cattle drives. He was as reliable as any man Micah had had the pleasure of working with, and he'd earned the respect and admiration of his uncles and cousins, as well. It hadn't been his decision to freeze wages during the drought of '84, but Micah understood why they'd needed to. He also understood that with four hungry young'uns to feed, Pete hadn't had much choice but to go to work in the mine, which would allow him to be with his family for longer stretches of time, as well as to bring home more regular pay.

As the inspector read the names on his list, Micah felt the urge to join the rescue team. By the time the man looked up with a grim expression to face the dusty, gritty group that had vacated the mine, he'd decided to go along.

"Any of you seen McCall?" the face boss asked.

"He was loading a car last I saw him," one man said.

Micah figured that meant Pete was among the miners still down there.

His wife must have come to the same frightening conclusion. "Well, what are you waiting for?" she demanded. "Get down there!" Sobbing hysterically and trembling from forehead to feet, she pounded on the inspector's chest. "Get down there now and find him!"

The mayor, who'd arrived shortly after Micah and Gus, stepped up and took hold of her shoulders. "Easy, Mildred," he said. "Easy."

But she jerked free of his grasp. "Let go of me, you pompous old fool! You know as well as anyone here that if they wait too long, the gas will set off more explosions." She clutched at his starched lapels. "You're in cahoots with Olmos Coal, Coke, and Oil, aren't you?"

"Of course not!" he said, trying to dislodge her grip.

"Don't give me that! You're a swollen-headed politician, more worried about the votes these greedy owners can buy you than the men whose backbreaking work is what made them rich in the first place!"

"Now, see here, Mildred, I realize you're upset, but—"

"Upset?" Hysterical laughter bubbled from her, and then she snarled, "I'd like to see how you'd behave if your wife was down there!"

The man only shook his head, at which Mildred slapped him hard enough to knock the spectacles from his nose. Then, she stood there, open-mouthed, staring at her hands as if they belonged to a stranger. "Oh, Lord," she cried, burying her face in her hands. "I didn't mean to do that. I'm sorry...."

When she came out of hiding, Mildred wiped away the tears coursing down her cheeks and faced the small crowd that had gathered. "Help me," she said, pointing at the face boss and the mayor. "Help me convince them to stop wasting time, or we're all going to watch the Black Maria grinding down the streets of our town."

Gasps and "oohs" filtered through the group, but no one said a word, nor did anyone meet her eyes. She had voiced their own fears of seeing the black, horse-drawn paddy wagon that served as an ambulance—or a hearse—roll down the road, carrying the miners who'd been recovered from the shaft.

"Soon as we assemble all the right tools, we'll move in, and not a moment earlier," the inspector said. "Last thing we need is to cause a second—"

"Come now, Mildred," the mayor interrupted. He shot the man a glare, then led the woman away gently. "You'll be more help to Pete back in town."

A temporary clinic would be set up as close to the entrance as possible, Micah knew, to tend to the miners' injuries. That meant every available woman would be called into service to roll bandages, boil water, and sterilize knives and needles for performing surgery and sewing up the incisions.

The solemn silence ended with the harsh, high-pitched whistle, alerting the townsfolk that a tragedy had occurred at the mine. Soon, the site would fill with those whose husbands, fathers, brothers, and sons worked in the tunnels, and they'd keep their quiet vigil until, one by one, the men were brought into the light of day by the rescue team. Some would rejoice, others would mourn, and a few would leave this place knowing that their loved ones had already found their final resting place.

Callie stood among the group of those already gathered, clutching Reid tight to her. He glanced at her and read concern, trepidation, and indecision on her lovely face. She wanted to help, he could tell, but how could she, with Reid to look after? On her right, Beth and Jonah linked hands; to her left, Birdie and Otis stared at the wood-framed mine entrance. How dour-faced they all looked, Micah thought, and with good reason. Did his own expression reflect the same glum defeatism?

"You'll need more mules," Otis said, nodding toward the soot-covered animals that blinked and snorted coal dust from their nostrils. "Just look at those critters. Why, they're done for the day."

Unlike other mining companies, Olmos, founded in '85 by F. H. Hartz, had started out using horses to haul excavated material from the tunnels. But it hadn't taken long for the management to find out that horses liked to cool off in the river and, once there, were often reluctant to come out again. Mules, on the other hand, didn't much like water. They might not look as formidable as their taller, sleeker cousins, but they were smart enough to know better than to work themselves to death. When a mule got tired, it stopped, which was probably why they'd earned a reputation for being stubborn. If a driver tried too hard to convince them otherwise, they could be downright cantankerous, too—nothing that couldn't be cured, Micah had learned, with fair treatment and their favorite treats: apples, carrots, or, better still, pinches of tobacco. Whether it had been old man Hartz who'd decided to substitute these sturdy four-legged haulers for their prettier predecessors, Micah didn't know, but he was sure that they'd prove themselves today, just as they did every day in the mine.

Had the present owners been just as smart when they'd purchased the timbers that supported the tunnels? From a business standpoint, it didn't make sense to fork over thousands of dollars for steel rails and iron-wheeled carts, then cut corners by installing beams that hadn't been properly seasoned.

Micah would have the answers to his questions just as soon as the face boss gave the go-ahead to enter the tunnel, because he aimed to join the search party.

Chapter 22

*H*e'd barely spelled out his plans to Callie when her eyes filled with tears. "But why do *you* have to go in?" she wanted to know. "It hasn't been that long since you were too sick to stand. Besides, there are plenty of men here who've been in there before."

How like her to put it in a way that wouldn't hurt his feelings or his pride. But her meaning was clear, all the same: What did he know about the inner workings of a mine?

"I'll be careful," he said. "You have my word."

Gus tweaked Reid's cheek, then said, "Don't you fret, young lady. This cowboy might not know his ear from a coal cart, but I do." He briefly related how he'd once been part of a rescue operation that had saved the lives of nearly fifty miners, and he concluded his story with a wink and a grin. "I'll see to it he comes back to you, safe 'n' sound."

"I'm going, too," Jonah said, stepping into the small circle. "I can wield a pickax or a shovel as well as any man here."

"I'm sure that's true," Gus said, planting a beefy hand on the boy's shoulder. "But, son, how would you hear a warnin' to duck? How would you know to step aside at the sound of a crackin' support beam?" He shook his head. "No, you'll be more use to everybody topside. They'll need water for the clinic, and for the mules."

And the face boss agreed.

Micah hadn't needed a lifelong association with Callie's brother to read the disappointment and humiliation burning on his face. If there had been time, he might have followed when Jonah stomped off, head down and hands in his pockets, muttering under his breath. But the men who'd been chosen to make the initial penetration of the mine had already begun to assemble at the opening, and Micah wanted to join them.

He pressed a kiss to Reid's cheek, then gave in to the urge to kiss Callie, too. "You're cold as ice," he said, stepping back. "You should go home. Put Jonah in charge of Reid to give him something to focus on besides his wounded pride. Then, you can help comfort the wives and young'uns who have menfolk down there." As an afterthought, he tacked on. "And don't worry, I'll be fine."

Walking away from her and the little boy was the hardest thing he'd done to date, but he did it—for Pete and Mildred and their children, and to ensure that Callie didn't see him as a man who could be talked into taking the easy way out.

And, God willing, he'd have the rest of his life to make up for the fear his decision had etched on her pretty face.

By all appearances, it was an ordinary afternoon. Callie stirred a pot on the cookstove, Reid happily banged a wooden spoon on the tray of his high chair, and the scent of fresh-brewed coffee mingled with the aromatic steam billowing up from the stew.

Yet it was anything but ordinary. By now, Micah and the others had entered the gloom of the mine, lanterns and shovels in hand, to dig their way through the debris in hopes of finding Pete and his fellow miners alive and well. She prayed for them all—those trapped and the ones willing to risk their lives to save them. She prayed for herself, too, because if anything happened to Micah down there....

A chill snaked up her spine at the very thought of him buried forever amid black coal and dusty timbers. *Stop dwelling on the worst that could happen!* she scolded herself. There was absolutely no reason to believe he wouldn't come back to her, whole and healthy. He'd lived a good life, after all, and trusted in the Almighty, who would surely watch over him!

Soft voices filtered in from the parlor, breaking into her thoughts. Beth was in there, talking with Jonah; hopefully, Micah's pretty sister would raise his spirits. Callie certainly hadn't been successful when she'd tried!

Though Jonah tried his best to hide it, Callie knew how disappointed and frustrated he'd been, hearing Gus and the safety inspector imply that his deafness would put him and others at risk. Beth must have realized it, too, as evidenced by her sweet smiles and sideways hugs as they'd walked back from the mine, hand in hand. It was easy to see that she cared deeply for Jonah—a surprising turn of events, considering how recently she'd become a widow.

On the shelf above Callie's dresser stood a seldom-read copy of *The Art of good behavior; and letter writer on love, courtship, and marriage: a complete guide for ladies and gentlemen.* If Callie had a mind to, she could fetch it right now and find among its pages a whole chapter of rules on the subject of mourning. But if she turned to any book for advice right now, it would be the Bible, for surely God had a better idea than C. P. Huestis Publishers on how long a young widow should grieve.

Did Beth truly care for Jonah, Callie wondered, or was she simply extending the hand of friendship? The former, she hoped, because Beth's reputation for taking on "needy men" wouldn't apply in this instance; except for his hearing loss, Jonah was a hale and hearty man who'd live a long life. A happy life, too, if heartache didn't get in the way. Before the steamboat explosion, he hadn't been interested in girls and romance, and, afterward, the handful of girls who'd deigned to share a few minutes of their time with him had quickly made it clear they wanted no part of life with a man who would never hear their voices.

Speaking of voices, why had it suddenly grown so quiet in the next room? Callie couldn't very well just barge into the parlor. Jonah had a right to privacy, after all.

Soon, though, curiosity got the better of her. She prepared a tray of two teacups and a teapot—her best china—sugar, cream, a plate of shortbread cookies, two embroidered napkins, and an early-blooming orange lantana blossom in a cut-glass bud vase. As she rounded the corner to deliver it, Callie understood why the two of them were silent. Jonah stood, eyes closed, wearing an expression of contentment she'd never seen on him before, and rested his chin on Beth's shoulder, amid her golden curls. Meanwhile, Beth gazed at the head so near her own through eyes that overflowed with unadulterated affection. If that wasn't love in its purest, sweetest form, Callie didn't know what was.

"Oh, look, Jonah," Beth said. "Callie has brought us tea."

"Guess it's true what they say."

Beth traced the contour of his jaw and let her fingertip linger on his chin. "What do they say, darling?"

"That time flies when you're having fun."

Callie set the tray on the wheeled cart beside the hearth, which she then rolled close to the divan. "I don't know about you, Beth," she said, "but I haven't the foggiest idea what this brother of mine is talking about."

The young woman laughed, then settled herself on the sofa. "I think he means, 'Is it four o'clock already?'"

Chuckling, Jonah sat down beside her and kissed the tip of her nose. "Exactly!"

Hands on her hips, Callie pretended to frown. "I hate to be obtuse, but I still don't get it."

Jonah lifted his teacup, which looked tiny and fragile in his hand. Why hadn't she noticed before how big and manly her little brother had grown?

He raised an eyebrow. "Don't they serve tea at precisely four o'clock in London?"

Giggling, Callie walked back toward the arched doorway, then turned around. "Goodness," she teased, "if that's your idea of a joke, I hope you never decide to become a comedian."

It was his turn to look confused.

"Because you'll go hungry, for sure!"

"Oh my," Beth said solemnly. "We can't have that. What would my father say if you took a job that couldn't support his eldest daughter?"

Callie froze in the doorway. What did that mean?

"Bring another cup," Jonah said. "And bring Reid, too, so we can celebrate."

Celebrate?

"I just asked Beth to go courting, and she said yes."

Chapter 23

*T*he memory of the preacher's prayer echoed in Micah's head as he followed the narrow beam of Conrad's helmet light. It lit the passageway dimly, barely exposing rough-hewn beams and the glittering coal embedded in the walls. Bent over at the waist, the men took small, careful steps over the damp, spongy ground beneath their feet, each movement a test to ensure the tunnel below wouldn't swallow them up.

The sheen of the tracks helped guide the way, and they shuffled along, deeper and deeper into the gloomy bowels. Suddenly, Conrad raised his arm. "Hold up."

No one moved, except to suck in shallow breaths of gritty air.

"Smell that?"

"I don't smell nothin'," said Bill.

"Me, either," Harry confirmed.

Frowning, Conrad grunted. "Can't be too careful," he said, then continued the slow plod into the belly of the cave.

"Nobody can smell that gas, right?" Gus said. "Ain't that why they use canaries?"

Conrad chuckled. "Canaries. Pfff!" They walked in silence a few more steps before he added, "Those sissies over in England use singin' birds to sniff out the gas, but I never heard-tell of such nonsense here in Texas."

"Dime novel fodder," Bill put in.

"And that's about it," said Harry. "Why, I'll wager that—"

"Shh!"

Instantly, every man obeyed Conrad, who craned his neck left and right. "You hear that?"

"I don't hear nothin'," said Bill.

"Me, either," Harry confirmed.

"Can't be too careful," their leader said again.

Gus chuckled. "This sounds familiar," he whispered.

But Micah couldn't bring himself even to grin. If death had a smell, this was it. The place swirled with dust, and the particles danced on the orange and yellow glint that flickered from Conrad's lamp.

"What if the boss makes a turn?" Gus wanted to know, squinting into the gloom.

"Then, you're on your own, Applegate."

Micah didn't know which of the men had barked out the warning.

"Y'don't have to tell me twice," the big man said.

"Good. 'Cause I'd hate to have to haul a man your size outta here, feet first."

The crevices and creases that made up the walls and ceiling bulged and rolled, and Micah nearly tripped on the track, looking for signs of weakness. Ten minutes in this never-ending, sideways pit, and already he'd developed a strong appreciation for the men who stayed down here for days on end. He'd also mustered more determination than ever to find those who were trapped up ahead, because even if a few of them were bound for hell, it seemed unfair to let them travel there by way of this nightmarish route.

It felt to him as though the walls pulsed with some strange, unfamiliar form of life. In the places where they swelled out, it looked as if they were trying to grow arms and grab hold of the men who skittered past like fire ants hurrying back to their nest. Yet, some of the hollows seemed tall and broad enough to fool a man into thinking they were entrances or, better still, exits.

As the tunnel continued onward, down deeper into the earth, it dawned on him that if the mine collapsed and buried this dirty little band of rescuers, no one topside would hear their calls for help. Did that explain why they couldn't find the men still trapped down here? For all he knew, they could be up ahead, in some deeper, darker channel, running out of air as they called for help. *If the ceiling collapses, don't waste your breath*, he said to himself. Because something told him that even the most ghastly shriek of agony would be swallowed up by the noxious invisible gas.

He heard it then—a plaintive wail that seemed right around the next bend, but also as far away as the other side of the earth. The others must have picked up on it, too, for all the men stopped marching and stood, silent, with frowns on their faces.

"It's comin' from over here," Conrad announced. He picked up the pace, the glow of his lamp flickering off the walls like a minuscule dancing sun.

Micah couldn't tell if the voice was coming from the right or the left, from above or below, but he followed. What choice did he have but to put his faith in the man who, as they'd entered this tomb, had claimed to have been born in a coal mine?

"Lord," he whispered, "let us find them all, and find them alive." Yet again, he recalled the reverend's words, uttered in somber syllables as the five volunteers had traded in their Stetsons and Winchesters for wool caps and axes: "Heavenly Father, You called Abraham out of Ur and kept him safe as he wandered, for it is Your will to protect Your children. Watch over these men as they enter the shadows in search of their brothers. Defend them against the cold and the darkness, and protect them from fatigue and uneven paths. Above all, almighty God, bring them safely back to us, carrying their lost brothers, now found. Amen."

Then, as if in response to his prayer, Micah spotted a rugged boot sticking out of a pile of rubble. Nearby, he saw a lunch pail and a short-handled shovel, and, beyond those, a hand.

The others saw them, too, and rushed forward to dig the fellow out.

"Whoa," Conrad said to Bill. "You'll pluck out an eye with that pickax!"

It took all of ten minutes to expose the man's forehead. His eyes and nose appeared, followed by a mustached mouth, which spewed grit and dust. It was Pete, bloody and dirty but alive.

"You boys sure know how to build suspense," he choked out with a grin.

"Who was with you when it happened?" Conrad demanded.

Pete wiggled his fingers, as if testing to make sure they still worked, then used them to count. "Norton, Scott, Flynn," he said, wincing at the last one. "Bishop and Hood, Gardiner...."

A coughing fit interrupted his recitation. When he caught his breath, Micah held a flask of water to his lips. "Slow and easy, now."

Pete took some water, then nodded and continued. "Hicks, Turkel, Stevens, and Rowan." He tried to sit up, wincing as he did, and Gus and Micah helped him. "They were behind me, all in a cluster," he went on, "so they'd be...." Pete tried to turn; failing, he merely thrust a thumb over his shoulder. "Right about there."

"You're sure some of 'em didn't wander off?" Conrad asked. "Maybe move into another tunnel, or—"

"I'm sure. I was kiddin' 'em for hoverin', sayin' if they didn't quit breathin' down my back, I might sit on 'em. Scott piped up and called me Mother Hen, and I was about to tell 'im that hatchlings should be seen and not heard, when the ceilin' caved in."

Nodding, Conrad said, "Bill, give Applegate and Neville, here, that stretcher. They're the greenhorns, so we'll let the pair of 'em hoof it outta here with Pete."

When Gus opened his mouth to protest, the face boss silenced him with an upheld hand. "Bring water when you come for the next man. And bandages, and plenty of 'em." He stared at the sparkling stack of stone behind Pete. "No tellin' what we're gonna find next."

"How're we supposed to find our way out and back in again?" Gus asked.

Ignoring the question, Harry handed Micah his lantern. "See to it you bring that back in the same shape it's in now, you hear?"

Micah took one look at it and grinned. "That shouldn't be hard; I don't think there's a place on it that isn't dented or scratched."

Harry grinned right back. "Well, be that as it may, that hunk o' junk saved my skin a time or two, so I'm right fond of it."

Micah squeezed the man's shoulder. "Thanks for the loan of it." Then, he handed the lantern to Pete. "Now, if something happens to it, it's on your shoulders," he said, lifting his end of the stretcher.

And with that, he and Gus made their way toward the sunshine, where Doc Lane was waiting with most everyone in town. Otis and Meb carried Pete to the makeshift tent the men had constructed of poles and canvas. Then, Otis pointed to another stretcher. "You're lookin' a mite flushed there, Applegate. You want one of us to relieve you, so's you can catch your breath?"

"I'm fine," Gus growled, mopping his face with a black-streaked handkerchief.

Micah traded Harry's lamp for a hat with a torch, while the doctor asked him how many men were down there.

"Ten, by Pete's count." He stuffed his pockets with gauze and bandages. One of the women who'd come to help tend the injured tossed a few more rolls onto the litter, while another added water flasks. "They hadn't dug any more out yet when we left with Pete," Micah added, "so there's no tellin' what shape they'll be in."

"Well, let's pray the injuries are superficial," Doc Lane said as they returned to the mine entrance.

Four hours later, as the sun set, all eleven men lay on cots in the temporary hospital. Bloodied bandages and splinted limbs might have led the casual observer to conclude that not one of them would survive, but, thankfully, the overall prognosis was good. And, by the time the moon lit Eagle Pass with a swath of silvery light, every last man had been delivered into the loving arms of his family.

Gus slapped the pharmacist on the back. "You'll make a small fortune, rentin' crutches and wheelchairs and the like," he said.

The men laughed at the joke, then went their separate ways. When Micah knocked on Callie's door, she flung it open and threw herself into his arms. "Micah," she said, pressing her cheek to his chest.

He held her at arm's length. "I'm filthy and sweaty," he said, chuckling.

"If you think I care about that, you don't know me at all." She hugged him again. "Do you have any idea what a relief it is to see you?"

He opened his mouth to say that he'd missed her, too. That she'd been at the front of his mind as he and Gus had carried each bedraggled miner out of the tunnels. That he'd promised himself, as the last man was delivered into the doctor's capable hands, that he wouldn't waste another day mulling things over. Tonight, he aimed to ask her to marry him.

But Callie never gave him the chance. Tugging his hand, she pulled him into her parlor, where his sister and her brother sat cuddling on her divan.

Beth leaped up and all but threw herself into his arms. "Oh, Micah! I'm so glad you're all right!"

"Yes," Jonah agreed, pumping his arm as if he expected to find water. "It's good to see you're fine. Did everyone else make it out?"

"To the last man," he answered. "Some are a little banged up; nothing serious."

"The answer to our prayers," Callie said, joining the little huddle. "And we have some happy news of our own to celebrate."

"Celebrate?"

"I've asked to court Beth," Jonah said.

"And I said yes," Beth said, beaming.

Amid a flurry of handshakes and hugs, Micah smiled and hoped for the life of him that it looked sincere, for Beth's sake as well as Jonah's.

Chapter 24

"Gus, don't stand out there on the porch," Callie called. "Come in and have some coffee!"

"Don't mind if I do," he said, stepping through the doorway and hanging his hat on a wall hook. "Where's that young'un?"

"Upstairs, napping. I needed a break!" She grinned. "Have you had breakfast?"

"Nope. Wanted to tell you what I found out while I was out of town."

He was smiling, so Callie had no reason to fear what he'd say next. Still....

"Please, have a seat. I'll fix you a plate of eggs while you tell me all about it." Fortunately, listening while she cooked would allow her to put her back to him. "How do you like your bacon, crispy or floppy?"

"Just this side of burnt," he said, chuckling. Then, he pulled out a chair, sat down, and proceeded to tell her everything, from the shoddy materials used in the construction of the *Maybelline* to the lack of attention to the architect's design.

It was all she could do to focus. She nearly burned the bread and almost forgot to turn the bacon slices. She missed the edge of the skillet when cracking an egg, and the yolk almost fell onto the cookstove instead of into the skillet.

"Like Micah said when I told him," he said when she delivered his plate, "it's a miracle that tragedy didn't happen sooner."

She sat down across from him. "How long has he known?"

"Told him when I got back." He shrugged and dipped his toast into the egg. "But there's been a lot of hubbub around here these past few days. I was beginnin' to think maybe the good folks of Eagle Pass had grown tired of bein' just another quiet little town on the Rio Grande."

Callie had heard stories about all about the outlaws, bandits, Indian raids, and gunfights that had once brought the Cavalry to town and caused Eagle Pass to earn a reputation as a rough, dangerous place to live. "I trust all this recent activity hasn't changed your mind about settling down here, because I, for one, would miss you!"

"As a matter o' fact, I'm goin' straight from here to the bank, where I aim to buy me that house I was telling you about."

She passed him the butter. "That's wonderful, and my offer to make it a little more presentable still stands." She winked. "Who knows? If the place looks inviting enough, you might just attract a wife!"

Gus grunted. "The last thing I need at this stage of my life is a woman, naggin' me to oil the hinges and sandpaper the handrails." He narrowed both eyes. "You're not doing a very good job of pretendin'."

"What?"

"You haven't said a word about what I told you."

What did he expect her to say? That it was a blessed relief to learn that after years of blaming herself for the explosion, it hadn't been her fault, after all? How could she feel good about news that turned her father into the culprit, instead?

"I hope you don't think I was trying to sully your pa's good name, pointin' out how many shortcuts were taken by the men he hired to build that steamer."

"No, of course I don't." And yet, that's exactly what Gus had done, however unintentionally. "Everyone who knew my father understood his tendency to scrimp and save." But, until now, Callie had considered that a positive trait that had helped him provide for his family.

"It's a lot to wrap your mind around. I reckon it'll take a while to shift the blame to where it belongs."

Oh, how right he was! "How can you be sure that what you learned is the truth?"

"Darlin', give a tired old man some credit, will you?" He smiled. "Let's just say I know what I know, and leave it at that."

Come to think of it, Gus did look tired. For a moment, she focused on that instead of her own shock. "You should pay a visit to Doc Lane's office. I'm sure he can give you a tonic to—"

"A tonic? Now, what would I need with something like that?"

"Because you haven't stayed in one place long enough to get any proper rest in ages, for starters."

"Well, that's true enough," he said, rotating his left shoulder. "But now that I'm retired, I'll have plenty of time to rest up."

"Pulled a muscle, did you, carrying all those burly miners to safety?"

"Guess so." He stood and pushed in his chair. "Well, I'd best get over to the bank before Buckner comes up with some harebrained scheme to double the price on that old eyesore he advertised as a house." He grabbed his hat and put it on. "Thanks for breakfast."

"No," she said, hugging him, "thank *you*. I don't mean to seem ungrateful for all you've done...for Micah and Reid, and now for me, as well. I really do appreciate it, more than you'll ever know. You're a good friend, Gus Applegate."

He planted a fatherly kiss on her forehead. "Does my hard old heart good to hear that, but it's Neville you should thank, not me. He financed your peace o' mind, after all."

"True enough. But you're the one who endured all the hardships to give me this gift."

He waved the compliment away. "Say, I don't suppose I could sit a spell and wait for that young'un to wake up from his nap...?"

Callie hoped it was her imagination that he seemed short of breath. "Stay as long as you like. Why, it'll be lovely, having someone to keep me company while I clear up the breakfast—"

He sat down, then rolled the shoulder again. "There's something I'd like to tell you. Something nobody on this earth knows but me."

The dishes could wait, she decided, and so could the soup she'd planned to make for dinner. She forced a smile. "Seems only fitting that I know one of your secrets, since you've been privy to mine for months, now."

He reached across the table and gave her hand a light pat. "Let me tell you how I came to be called Gus Applegate...."

For the next hour, he held her spellbound with the story of his youth. When he stopped talking, there were tears in his eyes. "I didn't want to go to my grave without knowin' somebody would remember Inayat and all she did for a poor white orphan boy."

"I'm sure you did as much for her as she did for you."

He laughed. "How d'you figure that?"

"Taking care of Reid all these months has shown me that a woman doesn't need to give birth to a child to love him as her own. Inayat understood that; I'm sure of it."

He sat quietly for a moment before saying, "Well, I'll be." Then, he smiled broadly. "When you get it in your mind to make a good point, you don't fool around, do you?"

They heard a big thump overhead. "Mouse?" Gus asked.

"If it is, it's the biggest one either of us will ever see!" Standing, Callie pushed in her chair. "Reid's taken to tossing all the toys from his crib when he wakes up." She glanced at the ceiling. "Something tells me there's one less picture on the wall next to his bed."

He nodded, then said, "Now I see what you mean."

"About...?"

"That look on your face. It explains everything. How a motherless boy and the woman who loves him are good for each other."

"He's about the best thing that ever happened to me. And what do you bet Inayat says the same thing to God and His angels every day in paradise?"

Gus stood, too. "You don't have to worry about giving him back," he said, one hand on the back of his chair. "I have a friend in Austin who's a judge, and he says the law's on your side. Well, more accurately, on Neville's side. Since there's nobody to claim Reid as their own...." He let his shrug lead her to her own conclusions.

"You're convinced Pauline won't come back?"

"I am."

She took a deep breath.

"Now, fetch that boy so I can bounce him on my knee before I head on over to the bank."

For the next half hour, while Callie cleaned up the kitchen, Gus cooed and crooned as Reid devoured a whole biscuit and half an egg.

"All right, this time I'm bound for the bank," he finally said. "The way I'm procrastinatin', a body would think I don't want to buy that dilapidated old shack."

"Why not stop at Doc Lane's office and see about that tonic? If not for yourself, then for me."

"All right," he said, grinning, "if it'll put an end to your infernal nagging."

"After you've made the house yours officially, come back and we'll celebrate."

"I'll do that. And just as soon as I buy a table and chairs and a stewpan, you'll have to share a meal at my place. It'll be easy to find. Just look for the house at the edge of town with frilly curtains in the windows and doilies on the porch swing."

Callie hugged him again. "I love you, Gus Applegate!"

"Love you, too, li'l darlin'." Then, he lumbered out the door and down the porch steps.

"Don't forget that visit to Doc's," she called after him.

Gus raised one hand in a backward salute before collapsing in the dusty street.

The cousins stood side by side on the lawn as people filed out of the church after the funeral service for Gus Applegate. "He sure made an impression in the short while he was in town," Dan said.

"That he did."

"He left a letter for me...."

Micah looked at his cousin. "A letter? Why?"

"Because he thought I ought to know what you were willin' to sacrifice for me."

Frowning, Micah shook his head. "I thought there were rules binding investigators to protect the privacy of the folks who hire them."

"Leave it to Gus to write his own." Dan paused. "Why didn't you tell me?"

Micah shrugged. "Didn't know if you could handle it."

"I suppose I have no one but myself to blame for that, living the life I lived for so many years. But you were an idiot, carryin' that around alone all this time."

Micah returned his teasing grin. "I didn't. I had Callie to help."

"Yeah, you got lucky on that score. So, what will you do with Reid?"

"I'll keep him, of course."

"How?"

Micah met Dan's eyes. "Remember the time I hung you by your belt from the barn loft?"

Dan grinned. "When I busted your guitar?" He chuckled. "Ain't likely I'll forget flappin' like a holiday banner, and for hours, no less." He shook his head. "But what's that got to do with anything?"

"You tell anybody what I'm about to say, I'll do it again."

Dan held up his right hand, as if taking an oath.

"It'll have to wait, because Callie's pretty broken up over losing Gus, but I'm gonna ask her to marry me."

"That's cold."

"Cold?"

"Takin' a wife so you'll have somebody to take care of the boy?" Dan shook his head. "Cold."

When he laughed, Micah forced a stern frown. "Show a little respect, will you? We're at a funeral, for the luvva Pete."

"All right," Dan groused. "But only if you'll show me a little respect in the future."

"What's that supposed to mean?"

"Next time you have a mind to protect me from something, don't. I've been clean and sober for a while now. Don't get me wrong, it ain't that I don't appreciate what you tried to do. It's just that—"

"I figured I owed it to you for all the times you came to my rescue when we were boys."

"Then, let's call it even, okay?"

"Okay."

Dan held out a hand. "Thanks, Micah."

He shook it. "What for? The score's even, remember?"

Epilogue

February 1, 1890

*H*ow strange it was to be seated in the same church pew she'd occupied at Gus's funeral, less than two months later, for a festive occasion. After a whirlwind courtship, Jonah and Beth had gotten engaged, and they were minutes away from saying their vows. *Thank You, Lord, for bringing Beth into Jonah's life,* Callie prayed. *Please bless their marriage with health, happiness, and prosperity.*

Reid squirmed in Callie's arms, so she handed him his teething rattle. "Now, mind your manners, young man," she whispered. "It isn't every day your uncle Jonah gets married, you know."

Almost as if he'd understood, the baby quieted and settled back in her lap.

"He looks almost as content as I feel," said a deep voice.

She looked up at the speaker. "Dan! It's so good to see you."

"Just wait till you see Beth," Levee said, stepping up beside her husband. "That dress you made her? It's dazzling, Callie."

"Thank you for your kind words." Her gaze went immediately to Levee's slightly rounded belly. "How long before your big day?"

"Seven months. It feels like an eternity!" Giggling, Levee added, "I can hardly wait to meet the little angel!"

"Me, too," said Micah, coming up behind Dan and Levee and slinging his arms over their shoulders.

Callie still wondered if Dan had any idea what it had cost Micah to protect him and Levee—not in the dollars he'd spent to track down Pauline or keep Reid dressed and fed, but in worry and heartache and fear. A man who could love like that...well, he was just the sort of husband she'd always dreamed of having.

Dan and Levee joined the rest of the Nevilles, and Micah leaned down to kiss Reid's temple. "Are you saving this seat for anyone?"

"As a matter of fact, I am." When his face showed a hurt expression, Callie giggled and scooted over. "We're saving it for you, of course!"

Just then, the organ music started up, and he slid into the pew beside her.

Jonah looked so handsome in his black suit. She couldn't believe he was about to become somebody's husband. Yet she knew he would take good care of Beth. Thanks in large part to Jonah, their business was still thriving, so he would be able to support her, financially as well as emotionally.

Reverend Peterson took his place at the center of the altar as the doors at the back of the church opened. All heads turned as Mrs. Peterson pounded out a rousing rendition of Wagner's "Bridal Chorus" on the organ. Callie said a silent prayer of thanks that Princess Victoria had selected the beautiful processional when she'd married Prince Frederick William of Prussia.

Reid squirmed and grabbed Callie's hair, so she quickly made a move to re-cover her scar.

Before she could, though, Micah grabbed her wrist. "Don't."

She blinked up at him as the heat of a blush rose to her cheeks.

"If you think that makes a bit of difference to me—or to anyone else—you're out of your ever-loving mind."

"But Micah—"

"But nothing. You're by far the most beautiful woman I've ever set eyes on."

She tried to free her wrist, but it was no use.

"I'll let you go on one condition: that you promise to stop hiding behind your hair."

The organ music stopped, and the pastor said, "Dearly beloved, we are gathered here today to join this man and woman in holy matrimony...."

"I'm not kidding."

Callie rolled her eyes. "All right, you win," she mouthed.

She'd worn her hair across one eye for so long that she didn't know if she could stand to wear it any other way. She tried reaching up to put her bangs back where they belonged, but Micah shook his head, reminding her that she shouldn't allow something so relatively unimportant to distract her from her brother's wedding. Sitting up straighter, she

282 ~ LOREE LOUGH

concentrated on the ceremony, and before she knew it, Reverend Peterson was saying, "Do you, Jonah Everett Roberts, take this woman to be your lawfully wedded wife?"

Tears filled her eyes when Jonah said, "I do."

"Do you, Elizabeth Ann Neville Hammond, take this man to be your lawfully wedded husband?"

And Beth said, "I do."

Callie bit her lip to still its trembling. Later today, the newlyweds would leave on their honeymoon, and in two short weeks, they'd move into the house Gus had planned to buy.

"I now pronounce you man and wife."

They'd be just down the street, and she'd probably see them every day. So, how was it that she missed her big brother already?

"You may kiss your bride."

With that kiss, it was official. Beaming from ear to ear, Jonah and Beth faced the congregation and proceeded up the center aisle.

As they neared Callie's pew, Micah leaned in again and whispered, "Will you marry me, Callie?"

For an instant, her eyes met Jonah's. He must have read Micah's lips, because he winked and nodded as he led his bride past them.

When Callie looked into Micah's eyes again, she saw the love and acceptance that had been there all along, despite her painful past and the physical reminder of it in the scar on her face. Finally, she was ready to accept the love that she'd felt she didn't deserve.

"Did you hear me?" Micah asked. "I said, will you marry me?"

Jonah turned around, so she made sure to exaggerate the movement of her mouth when she whispered, "Yes."

About the Author

*L*ong before becoming a writer, best-selling author Loree Lough literally sang for her supper. She enjoyed receiving rave reviews and applause and touring the country but sensed it wasn't what the Lord had in mind for her. She tried everything from shrink-wrapping torque wrenches to spinning pizza dough to working as a chef in a nursing home kitchen, to name just a few of the jobs she took, without finding one job that fit her. Then, while visiting her parents in Baltimore, Loree worked for an insurance corporation, where she met the man she would marry.

Loree began writing when her husband, Larry, had a job change that moved the family to Richmond, Virginia. She started out writing a neighborhood column and soon began getting assignments from the publication's editor—as well as the editors of other publications. But it wasn't until she penned her first novel, the award-winning *Pocketful of Love*, that Loree finally understood what the Lord had in mind for her. Seventy-five books (and counting) later, she's still touching the hearts of readers worldwide.

Unbridled Hope concludes her Lone Star Legends series, which also includes *Beautiful Bandit* and *Maverick Heart*.

In addition to her books, Loree has sixty-three short stories and 2,500 articles in print. Her stories have earned dozens of industry and Reader's Choice awards. Loree is a frequent guest speaker for writers' organizations, book clubs, private and government institutions, corporations, college and high school writing programs, and more, where she encourages aspiring writers with her comedic approach to learned-the-hard-way lessons about the craft and industry.

An avid wolf enthusiast, Loree is involved with the Wolf Sanctuary of Pennsylvania. She and Larry, along with a formerly abused, now spoiled pointer named Cash, split their time between a remote cabin in the Allegheny Mountains and a humble house in the Baltimore suburbs.

Loree loves hearing from her readers, so feel free to write to her at loree@loreelough.com. To learn more about Loree and her books, visit her Web site at www.loreelough.com.